The Dormant State

THE DORMANT STATE

DIBYA SATPATHY

PARTRIDGE
A Penguin Random House Company

To order additional copies of this book, contact
Partridge India
000 800 10062 62
orders.india@partridgepublishing.com

www.partridgepublishing.com/india

CONTENTS

Dedicated to my grandfather (aja) Dr L N Kar......for instilling in me, the love for writing.

ACKNOWLEDGEMENT

It isn't natural for a soldier to sit and write a story. A set of equally crazy and hysteric people are responsible for driving me to this extreme. I cannot let this piece of work see the day of light without acknowledging their contribution.

My lovely parents, Durga and Minati Satpathy, who allowed me to grow the way I always wanted to.

To, Sthita, a brother who stands like a rock forever.

Nimitta, the sis-in-law, who beautifully compliments the family. The rest of the flock that cannot be named here, as they would consume many pages.

To a bunch of school friends that have sparkled the memory with a million worthy moments. Special thanks to Sidhanta Patnaik and his friend Manoj Narayan from Wisden India for helping me with the editing work.

To a school that has always encouraged a free mind, and where creativity is nurtured naturally.

To my organisation, the Indian Army.

To my lovely wife, Minoo. I couldn't have completed it but for your constant kicks and pep talks.

Lastly, but in no ways the least, to the '*dormant state*', my state and my people.

"There is no air that freshens up the breath as your air,
There is no sky that soothes the mind as your sky,
There is no water that quenches the thirst as your water,
There is no touch that heals as your touch,
For, you my mother, are my origin, my destiny and you shall be my end."

If Darwin was to live today, this great country of ours could have given him eternal pleasure. There could be no other place in the whole world that would justify the theories of survival. The fascinating madhouse that we have created for ourselves to live in, get irritated and yet feel patriotic about is a mystery. We protested peacefully, fought non-violently and got our freedom from the British Monarchy. We then formed our own version of a "cocktail democracy", wherein each ingredient fights for its identity without realising that the real kick comes only if the drink is stirred up well.

History has bequeathed adequate honours to some fascinating personalities that have evolved in our great land. It is not very difficult to be famous in a land that has so many shades of confusing characteristics. Nobody is a hero or a villain here, it is circumstances and social equations that make or break your character here.

So when a leader feels the urge to splurge millions of dollars for a nuclear bomb while thousands of people die of poverty, she is still honoured for her courageous stand. So when a man peacefully fights out the British by uniting a jigsaw puzzle to a country, he can still be blamed for the partition. So when a leader spends millions of dollars in building symbols of social equilibrium while the lower caste still suffers from acute poverty and lack of amenities, she is revered as a messiah.

To put it simply, emotions take over decisions and personalities take over ideologies in our great nation. The most engrossing of the national activities which engages almost 1/4th of the population either directly or indirectly is "politics". People in India, love talking, arguing, criticising or just being in politics. Nothing symbolises India as much as the land's politics. The diversity it displays, the equality it offers and the opportunity it creates are all what modern India is built from.

This implausible epitome of a democracy is endowed with a political setup that was messy right from its inception. However, it is also the most empowering tool of the democratic set up that binds this mystery of a land together.

The book's story revolves around characters and incidents that could evolve our setup. It is a story about few young men who enter this wilderness and shun their true characters gradually, before becoming masters of the same system they once despised. It captures a series of events that shape the ambitions of a young man who sets out with noble dreams and revolutionary ideas of changing the system.

Does he succeed? Or, does the system overwhelm him? Or even better, does he learn the trick to balance his act?

CHAPTER 1

Aniruddh Mishra was born in the mid 1980s – a period when India was this giant elephant growing at the infamous Hindu Rate of growth. A promising country with a million challenges and a billion people. He grew up to the haunting tunes of Doordarshan and the social barricades set by the daily soaps like 'Hum Log'. Television in India was only as old as him. Telephone was a luxury few could afford, and a four-wheeler was the ultimate status symbol. It was an India just recovering out of the image of a country of *'snake charmers'*.

Education was strictly ghettoised between the public school kids and the kids attending government schools. Aniruddh was fortunate enough to have been attending a public school. The topic of discussion in most social circles in those days had shifted from the regular political trash to what's-your-kid-doing-after-college. It was an era when literature was publicly shunned in the academic sphere and people embraced science. The study of language and its intricacies were considered a waste of one's time as the computer languages quite unceremoniously replaced the Shakespearean vocabulary. It was an era when social evenings and sports were superseded by tuitions and computer classes. A host of computer institutes mushroomed all around the urban areas and almost created a social apartheid against those who dared to stay unaware of this new technical wonder. Parents would wish that their kid was born with a mainframe cord instead of an umbilical cord. They decided that something as important as choosing one's career should not be left to the naïve wisdom of the child and that the decision has to be taken by them.

Aniruddh also grew up in the same social strata with unsophisticated middle class expectations of his parents. He grew up in an academic environment that was slowly turning hostile even to kids who would score above 80%. The 100% mark was the in-thing.

An environment where parents encouraged their kids to give up everything in pursuit of those middle class expectations that in simple words meant – score more marks. Indulgence in sports, cultural or any other professional activity would bring in doom. "Everybody cannot become a Sachin Tendulkar or an Amitabh Bachchan, so stop dreaming about one and be practical in life," would be the most heard about dialogue for a generation that grew up then.

Professions like law or journalism would be shunned for their lack of earning abilities, music would be condemned in the worst form and painting was considered a poor man's activity. Business would be left for the Ambani's and the Tata's for it was beyond the reach of the middle class. Everything that involved any amount of struggle or risk would seem unachievable to a generation that lived throughout an era of austerity in aspirations. A generation that struggled for the basics could never really imagine anything ambitious for its children.

The safer choice was always preferred and that made medicine and engineering, the most popular career options for the middle class. The Information Technology wave that got along with it the scope of a guaranteed job would make Engineering the most craved for option. The new mantra of success was a 90% score in the board exams, followed by an entry into a good junior college, followed by a comfortable rank in the competitive exams, followed by an entry into a prestigious engineering or medical college to get a degree and take the first flight to USA.

Education in India was never about learning and trying to improve one's knowledge. It was never about satisfying a curious mind filled with questions and certainly never about giving someone the right to question the theories and break the stereotype. Education here has always been confined to being a medium for social acceptance and a gateway to earn a livelihood. It has never encouraged anyone here to develop a sense of curiosity that could lead to an invention or a discovery. People here are not too serious about the knowledge they would gain, the more important thing would always be the question of what you would gain out of this knowledge.

Then came the days of 8% growth rate and this sleeping giant was slowly waking up from its slumber. The effect of the second phase of globalization and the economic reforms had begun to reflect. After an almost undisturbed rule of 44 years the country finally decided to bid farewell to the Congress government as the lotus bloomed out. The country voted for a man called Atal Bihari Vajpayee as the Prime Minister. The people of this great nation were slowly waking up to a change that would for the first time affect everyone irrespective of their class, creed, sex or religion. India was marketed to the world like never before. A country that could give a bloody nose to its adversaries when it came to misadventures and could display its nuclear capabilities even under immense international opposition. From individuals who dominated the Silicon Valley to doctors that earned global respect for themselves. From a handful of local billionaires registering their names in the catalogue of the rich and powerful to a couple of them winning the Nobel Prize. Suddenly India and Indians were finding a space for themselves in the talking towers of the international community. The success story of this South-Asian marvel soon attracted a host of investors as the country would now welcome them with open arms.

The socio-economic makeover of India was also quite visible from the change in the living standards of the people. The birth of cable network and DTH revolutionised the idea of broadcasting in the country. A horde of channels kicked the haunting intro tune of the Doordarshan, and they gave way to sassy daily soaps. The Maharaja of the Air India was pecked by Kingfisher and a host of other private players in the business. The fore walls of the Indian household had no space for the Gandhi's and the Nehru's as new age role model like Sachin Tendulkar and Shahrukh Khan had made their way in. The 100 million mobile subscribers ripped apart the socio—economic partitions the BSNL had carved in for the upper class. The Indian society was slowly getting divided into two distinct classes—the haves and the have-nots.

The Indian success story opened up new avenues of employment for the youth. The IT sector was seen as the single largest employer as it needed lakhs of Engineering graduates to satisfy its rapidly growing appetite for cheap technical labour. Engineers were the new B.A.'s, and Engineering and Medical colleges mushroomed all around the country. These colleges got along with them a weed called 'Tutorials'. As developing India offered professions that were hitherto unknown, parents became more and more liberal in offering choices to their kids. They were now open to all sorts of professional studies that their kids were interested in, provided it was legally accepted. The jinx on a certain professional choice was certainly eroding fast. The Indian father realised that even his son could be a Sachin or a Sourav Ganguly. Parents got more enthusiastic in making their kid a sportsman as they walked their five-year-old kid into a cricket or tennis academy. The dance reality shows on television made the whole country look like a dance academy, as parents became desperate to see their kids in those shows. The middle class Indian was suddenly finding himself making ways to the primetime. It seemed as if a generation was desperate to see their kids live their unfulfilled dreams. Melodramatic emotional outbursts on camera and near infant kids pushed to perform on the stage was the new high of the Indian middle class. It seemed as if the middle class was suddenly trying to break the shackles of the mediocrity that they were tied to for a long time. Certainly both India and Indians were changing. Although it was difficult to say who was living whose dreams?

Meanwhile, this social rage gave birth to a few misfits. One of them was Aniruddh Mishra.

One fine afternoon, like most of his other colleagues who had their kids appearing for the Board exams, Shri Damodar Mishra had also taken a month's leave from his department. The PI department was never a busy entity, so a month's leave was not a problem for the '*badababu*'(UDC – upper division clerk). The leave was to ensure that Aniruddh would be serious with his studies and that he could sit next to him to keep a vigil on him. It clearly reflected the typical mindset in most Indian households.

It was noon and the city was bearing the worst of the summer brunt. Mishra Sr had rolled over his dhoti so as to let the free underpass of cool air from his newly acquired Godrej air conditioner. It was lunch time and the Mishra family was on the dinning table. Aniruddh was sitting right across him and glaring onto some news channel on the 29-inch Samsung TV. The General elections were just over and the new government had taken office. The people of India were politically drained out by the extensive coverage from the various news channels. But the poor channels! They had to make news for 24 hours of the day. So every unusual thing became news and that was the phase that changed the definition of reporting in India. A bespectacled journalist with his highly flavored Bihari accent was proudly blaring his achievement of having done the presumably impossible thing of having caught an A grade bollywood star with a female in a restaurant. The jubilation in the eyes of the journalist could easily be compared to any Nobel Laureate at the award ceremony.

"What nonsense is this?" exclaimed an annoyed Aniruddh.

"These media guys can clearly make a mountain out of a mole. The 24x7 news channels have made a mockery of sensible journalism," said Aniruddh, cherishing the roasted brinjal.

"He he…poor guy, now they will make his life hell, these guys will now park right outside his house with their OB vans and crew," chuckled Aniruddh's baby sister Deepti, sitting next to him. Deepti was five years younger to his brother and was in the same school as him.

"So Ani baba, have you decide anything as yet?" questioned Mr Mishra. A son is often addressed as 'baba' either out of extreme affection or when he is being trapped into a conversation.

"You must concentrate on your board exams as of now, but do keep in mind the entrance exams that would follow," added Mr Mishra carefully separating the bones out of the *hilsa* fish.

"Beta, this is the most crucial time of your life, be very serious now. You saw how Pradeep got through IIT last year. The kid used to study for 18 hours. That is the amount of effort required to get through any college now," now it was Mrs Mishra who spoke, in an unusually soft voice as she was on a fast and had to survive only on half a dozen bananas, four apples and glass full of mango shake.

"Look beta, I do not want to sound enforcing, but I am really interested in knowing about your decision," added Mishra Sr struggling to pull out every single edible part out of the Rs 250 per kilogram *hilsa*. Yes, it is a fact, Odias and Bongs can be outlandishly lavish when it comes to fish.

"So, what' s running in your mind, son? You know we are not that kind of parents who would force their decision on their kids," repeated Mrs Mishra.

"Papa, I don't want to sit for the engineering entrance exams," replied Aniruddh firmly and almost abruptly. May be he was planning to break this shocking news for quite some time now.

"That's okay, Ani, if you don't want to be an engineer, nobody will force you. Medicine is also an equally lucrative career provided you can crack the entrance," jumped in Mrs Mishra, with a concerned look as distinct folds appeared on her forehead.

"No, ma, not even the medical. Why do you guys get stuck with medical and engineering? There are so many other interesting things out there," said the frustrated teenager. These are moments any teenager would hate to go through, especially when he has to justify his wish to do something different than what others have been doing. Firstly, the poor guy convinces himself and then he has to go around convincing the whole world.

"Okay, so what's running in your mind? You need to be frank with us, maybe we can advice you better. Beta, we shall encourage you in any endeavour," said Mr Mishra trying to win over the confidence of his young son.

"Papa, I want to do a graduation in Arts, with Political Science as my honours subject, and then do a Post Graduation in Public Administration or Masters in Social Work before finally getting into active politics," replied

Aniruddh as his parents looked at him, as though he had revealed the plans of getting into the organised crime sector. Mr Mishra's face turned sour and his wife took some time to gather strength out of her already fasting-affected weak body.

Damodar babu always knew that his son wanted to do something different, but never had he imagined that the definition of 'different' was so rebellious in his son's dictionary. It was rather unassuming for an 18-year-old guy brought up in a typical middle class upbringing to reveal his interest in politics so blatantly. It was indeed blasphemous for a teenager in those days to aspire to become a politician in India.

Mrs Mishra was visibly furious with the ideas of her son and immediately rebutted him in the most aggressive tone.

"Are you out of your mind, kid? Listen, this is not the time to joke around with life. If you joke around now then life will joke with you throughout. Don't think that life is a bed of roses as it has been till now..."

It would always remain a mystery as to how mothers get these classy dialogues about life and its nuances. Maybe it was the effect of the daily soaps that they cherished every evening.

"Calm down Vimla. Look Ani, I appreciate your frankness and respect your attitude of service to the nation. But I would suggest, you do something more professional, earn a name for yourself and then enter public life," said Mr Mishra to his son.

"Papa, as you know I have been involved in a lot of social activities since my early school days. I want to continue doing the same, but at a level where I can bring in a certain difference to the society. Moreover, I shall complete my education and thereafter join in. I want to learn the nuances of politics and public administration through proper education and then take a dip in it." The conviction in the young guy was certainly admirable.

"Son, we are middle class people, neither do we have the power nor an established platform to enter into public foray. Moreover, you are old enough to know the filth that surrounds politics. Don't you?" added his mother.

"Ma, I shall make my own platform, one doesn't need power to serve people and make changes. One needs the conviction to do so and the support of the people automatically comes once they know your intentions," said the boy, not one to give up easily. This was no teenage infatuation or illusion; the intentions were rigid to the extent of being called an obsession. Dama babu knew his son well, he knew that this was the result of a genetic behavior which percolated down from a freedom fighter grandfather.

CHAPTER 2

◆≫≪◆

Yes, India was certainly a different country now. This sleeping elephant was now being pitched as one of the fastest growing economies. It was no more the land of Corbett's adventures or the spiritual mecca of the world. We were unfortunate enough to have slept through a larger part of the Renaissance and the 18th century Industrial revolution, but we were catching up fast for sure though. The IT revolution brought India once again into the much-needed international spotlight. A host of IT companies spurred out of the success stories of individuals. A number of rags-to-riches stories were broadcasted and people were ecstatic. Cities like Banglore, Hyderabad and Pune became IT hubs and investors were more than generous with these cities. Banglore became the topic of discussion in the Silicon Valley circles. It seemed as if India saw Industrial Revolution a good two centuries late.

As people migrated for jobs, the social parameters changed with the modern requirements of the neo-urban family. The spending power of the average middle class family grew meteorically. Nuclear families, call centres, dot coms and six figure packages were the new buzzwords. Young India was now more vibrant and flamboyant than ever before. The generation was living a dream that their predecessors hadn't even dreamt of. The instinct to achieve and the attitude to take risks was the definitive trait of this new India. The Indian woman also came out of her shell with equal vigour, and made space for herself behind the wheels of a taxi to the cockpit of a commercial aircraft. Indian women discovered their capabilities beyond confines of their kitchen or living room.

Slowly, the social pyramid of India was up for a welcome change. Although internal bigotry and division prevailed in some parts, the class barriers with respect to one's caliber were soon diluting. It was a clean market, if you can sell yourself, you shall be up for a price. Nobody really bothered about something as frivolous as caste or religion as long as you

7

were up for some stake. Social nuances in the form of caste and religion still existed in some or the other way though.

Everyone was busy earning money and leading a Technicolor life. Everyone was an achiever in his own sense. It was not only the 30% population in the urban areas that was affected by this wave but the Indian hinterland also felt the ripples. Technology percolated down to the remotest corner of the country. Mobile phones, Dish TVs, SUVs were now the buzzwords in Indian villages.

India was so engrossed in its material achievement that it almost forgot of its own darker side. Everybody was so inebriated with the economic advent callously neglected our social side. We remained deliberately oblivious to basic issues pertaining to governance and the distribution of power in the society. We mercilessly dissociated ourselves to the lacunas of our system and preferred to remain a silent critic of it. Corruption, communalism, vandalism and intolerance would educe out of this collective indifference in the society.

The executive was supposed to be accountable. They never were. The legislature was supposed to be answerable, but they never did. We all chose the path of convenience, the path of remaining silent, as long as we are not affected. India was divided into two distinct social and moral categories. One that was morally correct would not stand against the immoral and chose to suffer under the ruler. The other was the blatantly immoral ruler that ruled over a distinctly indifferent subject. The declining socio-political environment gave rise to a new dimension of dissent in the form of Naxalism. The increasing margin between the rich and poor created an economic compartmentalisation of the society.

There was no doubt that the living standard of an average Indian had increased manifolds, but the number of people who came in the category of average was declining exponentially. India was growing but with it also grew the population and the plethora of problems associated with it. The consumer market had an upward curve while the basic infrastructure and grass root governance plunged miserably. Important factors like public health, education and agriculture were grossly neglected.

If statistics were to be believed, in rural India an average of 62-65 households per 1000 were in the income bracket of Rs 690 to Rs 1100. Primary health services were at a dismal state as even after 65 years of independence only 27% of birth cases got medical assistance. No wonder that out of every 1000 children born in this country, 60 never live to see the next day. The crippled judiciary complimented with an archaic police made law and order a laughing stock in majority of the states. The alarming state of police public ratio and the infestation of corruption in almost all departments dealing with law worsened the situation. Almost 30% of the population lived below poverty line as intellectual's debated over the actual definition of 'poor'. The list of our failures clearly overtook the list of our achievements. While a part of India was shining, a large part of it was actually whining.

Inequality and lack of infrastructure is not a result of poor growth but direct fallout of poor governance. The Gandhian ideology of service by politics had largely frozen into the past and politics truly became the final destination of scoundrels. We conveniently put our future in the hands of people who were least concerned about it. There was a permanent stigma that got associated with the idea of politics and politicians. History sheeters and criminals made their way into the parliament and legislative councils that once housed people of impeccable conviction and morality. Roudism and hooliganism became the new form of expressing dissent in a country that introduced non-violence to the world. More than a symbol of democracy, elections became symbolic to personal strength, money and manipulation. The queen of justice stood blindfolded as the law breakers became the new law makers. The country was now aggressively divided into caste, creed, sex, religion and sect by the evils of vote bank politics. The united India had a divided mandate.

Amidst all this, young India was basking in the glory of its newly acclaimed modernisation, conveniently ignoring the dark realities of its own country. We were a country of a billion let loose without a leader. Yes, modern day India was suffering from a leadership deficit. As the intellectual and educated distanced themselves from the nuances of politics, the vindictive and incapable made inroads into this profession.

While at one end a majority of the Indian youth was largely indifferent to this growing moth, a section of the youth realised the agony of the hour. Aniruddh was just one of them.

-----x-----

"So, finally, the school days are getting over," said Vikas with a hint of nostalgia in his tone.

"Yeah! Last few days, I still can't believe a life wherein we don't have to get up early, adorn the uniform and come to school. I mean, since the last

14 years we have been unfailingly doing this," added Deepak, expressing his feelings on the thought of saying goodbye to school life.

"Two months from now, we all would be busy with our lives, trying to shape our future," muttered Ramakant, the brightest in the group. These boys had been together since they first stepped into the school 14 years back. Their definition of friendship could be the purest in all forms as these feelings were nurtured in the most innocent stages of life.

"Everything will change so suddenly, new place, new people, new worries and new priorities," said Aniruddh.

"New challenges as well, entrance, career, job, family …," Anupam was cut short as he was about to flow with his emotions.

"Oye, hello, hold on bhai, control yourself before you become a father and get your daughter married," said Deepak as the group burst into laughter.

"Hey, anybody's got a Centre Fresh or something?" asked Vikas taking the final and the largest puff out of the Charms he was smoking.

"Arey, wait for an hour, we get it when we go out," remarked Deepak.

"Arey, I need it now, c'mon try to understand, I cant go like this in front of Nitisha, she will slit my throat if she smells it," said Vikas sheepishly.

"Hey, look, who's coming?" remarked Deepak as they saw a girl approaching them.

"Sheetal Verma. What's wrong with her? Why that anger on her face all the time? Especially, each time I say 'Hi!' to her," muttered Anupam.

"Guys, can you believe this female scored 98 in English in the pre-boards?" said Vikas.

"Arey, the three of us could have cleared with those many marks, heheh…" remarked Anupam as the group laughed hysterically.

"Excuse me, Aniruddh, can I talk to you for a second," said Sheetal, the school prefect, maintaining the irritatingly elegant voice and the attractive lividity that she was famous for.

"Watch out Aniruddh, those words are like the sharp edge of a knife, you won't even know when you start bleeding," said Deepak, in the most lecherous of tones. The others smirked while Aniruddh gave him a dirty look and approached Sheetal who seemed visibly irritated.

"Hi. Finally, I was successful in locating you. You know, you are the most difficult person to trace," said Sheetal.

"Why? I am always with these guys?" justified Aniruddh.

"Precisely, that is why you guys are always huddled up in some corner of the school. Aniruddh, its deeply saddening to see someone as decent and sensible as you roaming around with these buffoons."

"They have been my friends for the last 14 years. Can we expect some amount of dignity when we talk about them, at least in my presence, please?" Aniruddh was firm yet polite in expressing his discomfort over Sheetal's remarks.

"Anyways, I am least bothered about you and your friends. I just wanted to inform you that you have been nominated to deliver the farewell speech on behalf of the course at the farewell meet."

"Are you okay with it?" queried Sheetal.

"Yeah, sure, no problems," replied Aniruddh. He was certainly the most obvious choice for the speech, thanks to his remarkable oratory skills and popularity amongst the teachers. He had this unique ability to instantly connect with his audience.

It was the farewell day and there were mixed emotions in the milieu. Some were sad to leave the school and friends, while some were excited of being free of bondage and discipline. Although all of them were aware that very soon they were to be exposed to the cruel and competitive world outside that would not spare the weak. They would no more be confined to the secure four walls of the school under the watchful and caring eye of their teachers. They would no more be in the circle of people they knew as 'friends' since the day they understood the meaning of this word.

After, the usual niceties and formalities came the time for the farewell speech. Aniruddh walked on to the stage as the school Prefect introduced him to the crowd. The popular guy was ushered amidst huge applauds and cheering as he started his speech.

"Respected teachers and my dear friends, I am thankful to my batch for having nominated me to speak on their behalf on this important occasion. As I stand here to speak on the last day I remember an incident which would define my experience in this institution. We were in the fourth standard and I was detailed by the class teacher to speak in the morning assembly. I was asked to speak on 'My favourite game', for 2 minutes. I remember, as I started speaking, I could continue only till the first four lines before the butterflies within me took the better of my confidence. I stood still as the whole school stared at me with an unforgiving look. I was about to break down when something happened that rebooted my confidence in me. My class teacher Mrs Jha started clapping and shouted 'Well done, Ani, keep it up, c'mon' and the whole school followed her. The school applauded a failure standing in front of them. Friends, since then I have never lost my confidence in myself. Since then I have never felt intimidated when confronting a huge crowd. While I speak about myself, I am sure that I am also conveying the feelings of all 122 of us who are about to leave the portals of this fine institution. I believe that this institution shall continue to instill the same amount of confidence in every scared child as it did in me. Friends, this is not a place to develop mutual enmity over marks; this is a place to feel good over the achievements of your friends. Let this remain a place to learn and have fun, rather than compete and curse. I once again pay my sincere gratitude to the entire staff of the school on behalf of my course. Thank you," he ended with these words as the silence broke with a hysterical applause for Aniruddh and the school, which he so simplistically glorified.

-----xx-----

CHAPTER 3

———◆———

The good old days of schooling are over, thought Ani as he sweated profusely in the queue in front of the college's Forms Counter. Aniruddh had thought about his future, and the SD College for Arts and Sciences was certainly the city's most prestigious government college. The beeline outside the college on the first day of the sale of forms was certainly a proof of that. Most of the aspirants were accompanied either by one or both the parents. Hundreds of people were lining up outside the yet to open counter, trying to save themselves from the wrath of the merciless summer heat under whatever little shade was available. The queue had not moved an inch in the last two hours, and expectedly there was utter chaos with a group of young guys hurling abuses at a languorous office clerk sitting there. There, however, were some, who entered the 'No Entry' office amidst the chaos and came out with the colorful prospectus-cum-form.

In India there are two ways of getting a job done. First, the official way and then, the way of the offices. Nothing here moves without a push in cash or kind. Similarly, there are two kinds of people. Those who acknowledge both ways and get their job done, and the second that do not comprehend the ways and silently suffer. Indians were almost immune to suffering silently. We somehow seemed to be in love with the idea of being deprived of what was right fully ours.

"Excuse me, can you show me the way to the Registrar's office," asked Aniruddh to a girl who was moving up the stairs right next to the crowded Forms Counter.

"Yes, follow me, I shall lead you to his office," said the girl as she guided Aniruddh and Vikas to the Registrar's office. Outside the office was hung a wooden plank supported to a nail with 'Registrar' inscribed on it.

"May I come in, sir?" said Aniruddh peeping into the room.

"Yes, come in please," came the reply, and Aniruddh entered the room. A man in his late 50's with a heavy built and a smirk of vermilion on his forehead was sitting on a swivel chair with a noisy air-conditioner popping out of the window behind him. The nameplate kept on the table read, Shri MM Rao. The man looked through his black-framed lenses with a question in his eyes.

"Sir, can you kindly come down with us to the Forms Counter and resolve the confusion out there? We have been standing out there since the last two hours and the office clerk hasn't yet started distributing the forms," Aniruddh's request had a tone of exasperation that the Registrar acknowledged and decided to act instantly.

Mr Rao barged into the office authoritatively and sought for a reason behind the ongoing bedlam outside the counter. The two young complainants also followed the Registrar with equal vigour. The office resembled an abandoned storehouse. Rusty iron shelves stocked up with papers and files of British vintage made up for the ambience. It looked more like a mismanaged library or a museum.

"Yes, Majhi, what's the confusion all about?"queried Mr Rao.

"Sir, there is a small issue that has come up. We had declared 18th and 19th as the dates for the sale of forms, but that Gauri Shankar, the owner of the printing press mistook it for the next month. We are yet to receive the forms from the press, although he had promised me that he is working overnight to meet our requirements. I have already said this to those standing outside, but they are just not ready to listen," replied the Clerk

"That is not our fault. We have come according to the dates released by the college, and how come a few manage to get the forms while most others are given this silly excuse?" fought back Aniruddh.

"Those were a few forms that we had received in the first lot," rebutted the clerk immediately trying to save himself from the embarrassment.

"So, why can't you start selling those forms that you have, at least some of us will be benefitted," suggested Aniruddh.

"Look, you don't have to tell us about our job, we know how to do it," came the reply from a defenseless clerk.

Mr Rao, a quiet audience till then, finally broke his silence as he found logic in Aniruddh's suggestion. He advised Majhi to immediately open the counter and start distributing the available forms.

As the counter opened and the sale of forms started, the Registrar made his way back to his office.

"Excuse me sir, I have another small request," he stopped as the young man addressed him.

"Yes?"

"Sir, I feel the college should make some more arrangements outside the Forms Counter. Considering this is an annual affair and a lot of elderly people come here, it is inhuman to make them stand for such a long duration in this heat. The college should have at least catered for an overhead shelter and drinking water," said Aniruddh looking at the old man.

"I couldn't agree more with you, young man. I assure you that we shall look into these aspects seriously," said Mr Rao as he climbed up the stairs.

-----x-----

The Science stream looked at the Humanities as its unworthy cousin. The lack of respect amongst the Science stream guys is more because of the false sense of academic ascendency they seem to possess by virtue of their marks in the board exams. The story was no different at SD College.

This Victorian era institution was established as the Sir Dunston's College of Arts and Sciences in 1915 under Lord Macaulay's ambitious programme to popularise British culture and values in India and break its inherent social fabric. It was rechristened as the Sarala Devi College in 1999, in an attempt to do away with the colonial fervour attached to the name. This institution, by virtue of its excellence had earned a special place in the heart of the people of the state. It was considered as a symbol of academic excellence where the youth of the state aspired for higher education. But off late, the institution was struggling to keep up with its name and reputation. Thanks to the callous management and an indifferent state administration the college was losing its sheen. Student union politics, vandalism, poor faculty and the advent of drugs had led to the withering standards.

The first day in college was an experience in itself. As Aniruddh and Vikas entered the college premises they experienced a strange smell of freedom in the air. There were no uniforms, no closed gates and no strict riders on behaviourism. There was a sense of awkwardness in the unrestricted freedom. College by no means is simply an extension of formal education post school life. It is a place where a teenager gets the first feeling of being a youth. Where a young mind gets dissipated with the illusions that surround him, and a place where every individual yearns for his identity.

As they headed towards the Department of Arts, Aniruddh noticed the newly built fabricated shelter ahead of the Forms Counter with hundreds of chairs arranged underneath it.

"Hey, Ani, look at that," said an excited Vikas, pointing at the shelter.

"Yeah, I guess we fingered the right man."

The freshers walked through the corridor encountering a host of hungry seniors awaiting the arrival of the new guys for a healthy session of ragging. Ragging was officially banned after a boy had committed suicide in one of the colleges in the city. Anti-ragging squads conducted surprise checks in colleges and strict action was initiated against any individual found harassing the juniors. Yet, the juniors weren't spared of regular embarrassment and humiliation in the initial few days.

The first few days have its own blues, but the high school kids get over it and soon become a part of the justifying insanity called college life. Youth is a wonderful seduction. You get a kick each time you break the ethical and moral barriers set by the society. You just go about embracing the maddening sense of freedom and euphoria that you experience for the first time. You are like a fish from a pond that had been let out to venture in the sea. There are no embankments, no barriers to your exploits. Sometimes you blindly follow a horde of other seemingly more colourful fish. The murkier the water, the more excited you get in exploring it. Until one day, when you are trapped and realise the difference between adventure and foolhardiness. Some of us understand this difference while others prefer this illusion till it takes them too far in their exploits, making it impossible to return.

The darker alleys of the college were filled up with such elements. Drugs, violence and a false sense of pride had made them oblivious to the reality of life. The infamous names of student leaders had spoiled the once popular election culture of the college. Rich kids spent unimaginable amount of money in college elections that had become a platform to showcase their strength. The college elections were marred with violence and illegal practices. The involvement of petty leaders of major political outfits made things worse.

CHAPTER 4

"This is certainly the most purified version of malt. The way it slides down the throat pacifying every thirsty cell en route is heavenly. The froth at the top and the desperate bubbles rising up to ooze out like the capped emotions of a deprived lover," said Deepak, lusciously staring at the beer bottle.

"There goes the sin of Shakespeare. Everybody here knows that you are a student of literature. Stop advertising yourself at the behest of the beer," taunted Vikas.

Once together in school, they were all in different colleges of the city. Despite the separate institutes they went to, the long time friends made it a point to meet on Saturdays. They enjoyed this newly acquired sense of freedom in beer with a mixed sense of guilt and satisfaction. What age and maturity fail to do, a sip of beer does that so easily. It was the sip of the beer that freed them from the shackles of social restrictions as they could now endorse themselves as adults.

College is a place always bustling with some or the other activity. The college elections were approaching and they were no less than the assembly poll in grandeur and feel. The whole campus was abuzz with groups campaigning for their respective candidates. Walls were filled with graffiti as the 'Stick No Bills' statutory message got buried under the huge banners. The enthusiasm sometimes led to bitter rivalry and resulted in violence. The 'good' boys and girls avoided the elections like the country's intellectual elite, and chose to conveniently distance themselves.

Shirley and Aditya soon joined the trio of Aniruddh, Deepak and Vikas. Shirley was the cool catholic girl who had done her schooling from a famous boarding school in Ooty. She was the daughter of a famous criminal lawyer of the state, Mr Rounak D'Souza. Aditya was son of a businessman and the heir apparent to his father's multi-crore empire.

"Hey, guys how about catching up with a movie tonight?" proposed Aditya.

"Yeah, the new one starring Aamir Khan," said an excited Shirley.

"I heard it's directed by some new guy called Farhan Akhtar," commented Vikas.

"Yeah, Javed Akhtar's son," clarified Shirley.

-----x-----

The Inter-College youth fest was being organised by one of the colleges of Delhi University. As usual, SD had to send its team for various events ranging from debate to dance. Aniruddh Mishra had already won his first major debate competition for the college and was selected for the fest.

"I know you will do well, but remember, the only way you can fight them is by contesting their oratory with your substance. They may be far better than you in speaking but when it comes to the judges there, they look for sense in those words," advised the college principal before sending them to Delhi.

They were put up at the South Campus along with teams from other eastern states. It was the first major exposure for a young Aniruddh outside his state. He was appalled by the confidence in the youth from the metros. There was an event on the first day wherein respective students had to introduce their state's culture and the audience would ask them their relevant queries.

Students appeared on the stage alphabetically promoting their state's culture and achievements. When it was Odisha's turn, the richness of the Odissi dance, the temples, the pristine sea and the undisturbed wilderness were highlighted. During the questioning session, Aniruddh was shocked by the sheer ignorance of the students about a state in the country.

"Why is it that we never hear anything about Odisha, other than its astute poverty and suffering?"

"Why is it that people have to die of hunger there when the entire country has a surplus production of food grains?"

These young representatives stood on the stage helplessly trying to answer questions about their state that they themselves have been asking for long now. The terrible confrontation with reality made them uncomfortable, but more than that it made them feel accountable. Aniruddh was sitting next to a group, and he overheard them say, "Honestly, I haven't heard of Odisha in the news for any reason other than natural calamities and drought."

Aniruddh tried to explain to them the geographical vulnerability of their state, but he soon realised his effort was going in vain when they asked him the name of his state capital.

A larger question roved around in the young mind. He knew that these questions were actually not as irrelevant as they sounded. These questions were not only a naïve reaction of a class of young *'metroites'* who also were unaware of the seven north-eastern states. These questions were a reflection of all that his state had ever been highlighted for in the last few years. So, it wasn't after all as uncouth as it sounded when these people from the rather sunny parts of the country questioned about the failures of his state.

Aniruddh went on to win the debate competition on "The relevance of history in India's unification". But, he went back from the fest with a heavy heart and a struggling mind desperately looking for the answers to those uncomfortable questions.

-----x-----

The rains were expected because of the low pressure in Bay of Bengal. This part of the country is infamous for its sudden depressions and unexpected rain accompanied with storms. Aniruddh and his friends were loitering outside the tuition classes after it got over an hour ago. It was almost a routine to spend an hour after the tuition classes before proceeding home. The unexpected showers brought their *'khati'* (daily meet/adda) to an early end as they headed home amidst heavy rain and gust.

"My god, mama, its bhai," howled out Deepti as she noticed her elder brother opening the gate and moving in with his bike.

"Thank God you are back in time, we were all worried," said Deepti handing over the towel to her drenched brother.

"Why? It's not the first time it's raining while I am out of the house," commented Ani sarcastically.

"Arey, haven't you heard the news," exclaimed Deepti.

"No, but why, baba, why are you all glued to the TV? Some breaking news, some actor bitten by a dog, or this time it's the other way round," joked Aniruddh as he threw the wet towel on his sister.

The news channel flashed the satellite image of the country's eastern coast and kept highlighting on a white whirlwind that indicated the depression that had turned into a severe cyclonic storm and was heading towards Odisha.

"The met department has forecasted a severe cyclonic storm rushing towards the state," said Mr Mishra, still glued to the television.

"Oh, so what's new, they keep giving such warnings every other day. We are a state doomed to bear the brunt of the Bay of Bengal," said Aniruddh.

"No, this time it seems to be worse. By the kind of warnings that are being issued by the met department and the government it doesn't look good," expressed Mr Mishra.

Geography has a major role in determining the fate of a nation state. The role geography has had on the future discourse of countries can never be undermined. India is a classic example of a country that has largely been a victim of the geography. Surrounded by the mighty Himalayas on one side and the Indian Ocean on the other, the country has always been at the mercy of the capricious weather gods. The same can be said about the states of this huge conglomeration. While the coastal states have enjoyed the privileges of the sea they have also been subjected to its merciless mood swings from time to time. Odisha was one such peculiar state largely surviving on the mercy of the meteorological department. Every season, precious lives were lost either by flood, drought or cyclonic storm. This cursed coastal state would at times be subjected to more than one calamity a year.

This time it was the infamous cyclonic storm of the Bay of Bengal, known for its fierce nature and the ability to blow at speeds crossing 200 km/hr. The forecast was not only threatening but fierce on ground as well. Fishermen were advised not to venture out in the sea. Announcements were made, warning people in the city to stay indoors. The wind was getting fiercer by the minute. The cemented structures were put to test as few old buildings gave up in their fight. The non-cemented structures and mud houses were no contest to the gruesome assault by Mother Nature. Stronger trees were uprooted from ground below as the weaker one's swayed madly before giving up. The onslaught continued for good 48 hours before the infuriating wind retreated back to the sea.

The 48 hours were the worst ordeal the state had ever witnessed. Odisha was cut off from the rest of the world. An emergency was declared in the state as the centre acknowledged the national calamity. The power supply to the affected areas was out as people pondered over the plight of those living in the coastal areas. As expected, the coastal districts of Paradeep, Jagatsinghpur and Ersama were the worst hit by the cyclone, with the latter two districts completely wiped off the map. Aerial sorties were unable to trace out the actual geographical location of these places. The very thought of the plight of mankind in those areas was terrifying.

The state administrative machinery, clearly not prepared for this type of a catastrophe, had broken down beyond repair, and the Chief Minister looked helpless. The Army was called in for the rescue operations and help poured in from neighbouring states. As the first columns of Army made inroads into the affected districts, they were witness to devastating sites of death and destruction. The deluge of human bodies and animal corpses left behind by the acrimonious nature was horrible.

The wind got milder on the third day as the body count began to surface. When the seawater receded, all that was left behind was death and destruction. The deluge left more than half a lakh people dead and almost a million livelihoods were lost. Although, the official figures still say that only 20,000 died, the missing people were never accounted for. As dead bodies and carcasses lay scattered all around, the fear of an epidemic loomed large over the state.

The fear and agony among the people was the breeding ground of a large number of scathing rumours. Without proper access to official information, the rumours of another cyclone hitting the state created panic. As people tried to desperately stock up the essentials in the light of an impending disaster, black marketers and hoarders had a gala time. People had no other choice but to succumb to these excesses made by some notorious 'kirana' store owners.

"That rascal store keeper is selling a pair of batteries for Rs 60. These people have no morality, they can think of loot even in these difficult times," Aniruddh overheard two elderly men talking about the local grocery store owner.

All along his way back home after his own ordeal at the grocery store, Aniruddh kept on hearing all sort of people who had turned experts in their own right. We Indians have a reporter hidden inside each of us. We are obsessive about 'breaking news', however irrelevant or misinformed it might be. We love to be the earliest bird when it comes to sharing news pieces. When the flow of information is not monitored or whenever there is a blockage in the flow of information, these street talks become the source of information. It is this information that spells doom on the routine public discourse at many times, post any such incident that demands human fortitude. There is a huge army of such misinformed and callous people that are ready with their exaggerated experiences and concocted information. You will easily find them at prominent public spaces like a store, a diary outlet or a tea stall. As far as an audience is concerned, this part of the country is famous for the only luxury people could afford here – 'time'.

CHAPTER 5

—◦◦◦—

"**D**o not forget the water camper, there must be a shortage of clean drinking water in those areas," howled Mr Mishra as he waited in the Maruti Omni for his son to join him. A week after the catastrophe, as the Army opened the roads, Mr Mishra and Aniruddh planned to go to their village, which lay in one of the worst affected areas. It was Mr Mishra's eccentric love for his village that prompted them to take this step. The communication lines were out and hence no information was available about the well being of his near and dear ones there.

The capital city, otherwise festooned with the greenery around, depicted a ruined kingdom now. The 'Daya' river furiously jettisoned the banks, quite unlike its name. As the father-son duo moved closer to the sea, the signs of destruction became more visible. Ransacked villages, uprooted tress, water logged fields and dead carcasses all around offended the naive beauty of the countryside. It seemed as if even the almighty had abandoned this place. The calamity reflected the true side of the society. While people helped each other to fight back at many places, there were number of reported instances of robbery, loot and extortion. The most visible signs of these were on the main roads leading to the coast. Villagers gathered around tress that blocked the road and collected money from the commuters. Morality is an illusion that is often shredded out of the human discourse when reality hits out with the toughest of challenges. Few can uphold the morality in them under tough circumstances, and fewer still can demonstrate that. It takes just one heavy blow of wind for a man to shred the facade of moral values and display the inner devil residing in him.

After a five-hour long journey that on any normal day took nothing more than a couple of hours, the Mishras finally reached their village. The doomed parish, a mere two kilometers from the sea, faced the fury at its peak. The site of his devastated native shook the otherwise composed Dama babu. As he set his foot out of the car, he was quick enough to put his shades on. Aniruddh knew the motive behind his father covering his eye with dark glasses on a cloudy day.

The village temple which symbolised the divine blessings of '*shiv shankar*', stood witness to the row of dead bodies lined ahead of it.

"Sixty people are dead only from our village, the numbers are more or less same from all the nearby villages," said Ratikanta Mishra, Dama babu's cousin.

The pain was evident in every body's eye, but what was more disturbing was the loss of hope. One can never rate sorrow; it doesn't necessarily have a benchmark. From a father who has lost his son, to a farmer who has lost his livestock, a loss is a loss.

Being a Brahmin dominated village, they always had a separate cremation ground. The Brahmin funeral ground across the road was waterlogged and it could not accommodate the sheer number of dead bodies, so the relief officials, who were also overlooking the cremation of dead bodies, directed them to go to the community cremation ground. Nature did not discriminate in its onslaught and man had no choice. There weren't enough wet wood available for a mass cremation of this size. Corpses and carcasses were piled up after the usual ritual and burnt with the help of kerosene and whatever wood available.

"We have been hearing of the relief vehicles since the last three days, nothing has reached us yet," said the helpless Block Development Officer.

"Only the Air force people have dropped some useful items, that would soon be exhausted and then we shall again be left to the mercy of god," he added.

"The real fear is of the disease that has been spreading so rapidly, diarrhea, cholera and other water-borne diseases have started spreading," said a worried Ratibhaina(brother).

The problems were endless and the solutions none. The father-son duo left back for the city, with the aim to reach back before dark. On their way back, neither spoke a word to the other. All along the way, they passed by helpless, homeless people. People who had such meager expectations out of life, people who were so used to living under negligence and people who only had faith in their nature. Sadly, this time, even their nature betrayed them.

The sites he saw throughout the day moved Aniruddh. He cursed his helplessness every time he thought of the pain of those men who suffered the brunt of the cyclone.

Why wasn't the government prepared?

Why wasn't help reaching the affected areas even after five days?

Where were the elected representatives of those places at this time of grief? Why is human life so insignificant in this country?

These were the questions that lingered around in the young mind and didn't let him sleep.

Fifteen days had passed after the cyclone. The city was back to its regular chores, but the situation in the coastal belt was still precarious. Relief was yet to reach those parts, as the pace of the relief work was lethargic. As more and more dead bodies were being recovered with each passing day, the inefficient administration was conveniently absent.

"20,000 dead and the count is still on," said Vikas, as Aniruddh and his group sat at the famous tea stall outside SD college. For decades, the students of this college vouched for the Sahoo Tea Stall, located right across the college premises. It was a favorite hangout spot for the students. Sahoo bhaina, as they would call him affectionately, was the no nonsense owner of this joint. His age and vintage earned him unprecedented respect from the young and the old. His shop stood witness to a lot of events with the same interiors since the days of Gulzari Lal Nanda's musical chair with 7 Race Course Road.

"The state machinery has crippled beyond repair. It's the Army or the team from Andhra that is working now," said Aditya, the class representative.

"How can a state with the worst record of natural calamities function without a Disaster Management Plan, bloody total lack of perspective," he added.

"The relief trucks have been lined up outside the Kalinga stadium for eight days, and god knows why they aren't moving," commented Shirley.

"The government has made itself and the state a laughing stock. People sayhe should quit office immediately," said Vikas.

"Nobody is bothered, nobody is concerned. Neither the state, nor the centre," added Aditya.

"What on earth are we doing? Sitting over here, sipping in hot tea and criticising everyone from top to bottom," Aniruddh, silent till then, said out loud, attracting the attention of the others in the tea stall.

"We are equally culpable of all that we are blaming them of being. Why can't we step in and contribute in whatever little way we could," added Ani.

"What can we possibly do, Ani," queried Shirley.

"We can form a small group or a committee, a Student's Relief Group, request the people of the city to donate whatever little they wish to and send that to the affected areas," suggested Aniruddh.

"We can always encourage more people from the college to join in, help us in this small endeavour of ours."

"But, Ani, how much do you think we can collect and how do we send the stuff, we simply don't have the wherewithal," argued Vikas as Deepak also joined in, who was now studying in a nearby college.

As Deepak was told of Anirudh's plan, he also felt a sense of involvement in it. He knew well that Aniruddh was pretty infectious and it was about time that he convinced a whole lot of people to volunteer for his idea. As Aniruddh's proposal got instant acceptance and support in the college, the manifestation of his ideas began.

Pamphlets were distributed all around the college campus, and it galvanised support beyond Aniruddh's expectations. Students volunteered to go for collection of relief materials donated from various residential colonies of the city. The faculty was rather supportive of the whole idea as they promised leniency in attendance on account of this project. The first rally was a success, although only 35 students finally turned out for the collection. The city donated magnanimously making Aniruddh confident of the success of his idea.

Aniruddh became popular in the college as the mastermind behind the 'Relief Rallies.' Everyone knew that some guy from the first year BA was behind this noble idea. The word soon spread to other colleges as inquisitiveness grew over the rallies. Aniruddh realised that the idea would soon flop, if all the other colleges started off with their own modules of relief collection and by no means could he stop them if at all they wanted to do so. He found out a wilier way to get over with this problem.

Bhuban Baral -popularly addressed as Bulu Bhai was the college Student Union President. He was a third year science student who was in his fifth year in the college. With the support of the youth wing leader, Bhuban had become a known figure in the locality as well as in the student leader circle. His hold over the state's youth politics had grown by leaps and bounds after his role in the protest against the proposed changes in admission policy. It was a known fact that Bhuban was not too happy with the Relief rallies Aniruddh had done without his patronise. The popularity of the rallies prevented him to come out openly against the move. Aniruddh knew this and wanted to use this movement for resolving his issues with Bhuban as well as get his work done.

"Hey, Bulu bhai, how are you?" addressed Aniruddh, his tone casted with multiple layers of cosmetic deference.

"Arey, Ani, come, come, so how is the rally going on?" queried Bhuban reciprocating in the same manner.

"By the way, I must tell you, you are doing wonderful work, our total support is with you, let me know if I can help you in anything," added Bhuban.

This came as a surprise to Aniruddh, who was rejected just two days ago by the general secretary when he had approached for funds.

"Bulu bhai, I just need your advice. Considering that you have a vast experience of such social work, can you suggest to me one thing?" That much of obsequiousness was enough to make someone like Bhuban slip into his pocket.

"Bulu bhai, I was thinking of adding other colleges into this project and increase the amount of collection and make this a huge event," he added.

"Bhai, every soul in this college knows that it's your dynamic leadership and PR that can get the top colleges into the foray. The event will be managed and controlled by us, so SD still takes the praises for it," Aniruddh spelt his plan as the student leader calculated his stakes in the whole affair.

"Aniruddh, don't worry, I am with you in this. Kalinga college, Dayanand college and Gopabandhu college will join in from tomorrow, though I am not very sure about Vidyadhar and National college. The union leaders are political opponents, you see, but don't worry, we shall get them also," assured Bhuban as he tapped Aniruddh's back and hugged him.

"Thank you, Bulu bhai. I always knew you shall be of great help in this noble cause," said Ani.

"Arey, no thanks and all that, don't worry of the administrative things, they will be looked after now. You are like a younger brother to me," Bhuban was now being more than kind.

Vikas was present with Aniruddh all this while during his interaction with Bhuban. He was astonished to see how this crafty young lad turned a possible confrontation into a plausible advantage to him.

"You got him, you slimy rascal," said an excited Vikas as Ani smiled back in affirmation.

The movement spread across the city as more mainstream colleges got involved in it. Various NGOs and the Rotary Club also supported the drive wholeheartedly. Thirty truck load worth of relief material was collected in just a week's time. The media highlighted the issue showering praise over the student leaders and mocked the government to take a cue from the youth. Aniruddh Mishra's name would prop up occasionally as the mastermind of the event.

Aniruddh persuaded Bhuban to use his influences to convince the president of The State Truck Owner's Association to donate around 30 lorries for transportation of the relief material. Shri Sudipta Majhi, the association's head, grabbed the offer to reinforce his popularity for the upcoming municipality corporation elections. In India, people can do anything for a 15-minute fame on primetime television. The trucks were lined up carrying huge posters of the Truck Owner's Association and Student's Relief Team before their departure. Aniruddh and his teammates left for the affected villages amidst huge media coverage from both the print and electronic forums. Majhi got his share of limelight as he was seen affirming his support for this noble cause on a news channel.

As relief trucks arrived in their locations, distribution started of peacefully with the support of the Army and the local administration. The team got huge support and applause from all the villages they covered on the first day. The sense of hope in the people gave the team the energy they needed to continue till late in the evening. After an arduous day of distribution and covering almost 15 villages, the team went to a local Circuit House allotted to them by the District Collector.

The circuit house had two huge rooms where the boys and the girls had to pitch in for the night. The day's hard work had taken a toll on all of them. The hungry bunch immediately settled for dinner. The in-charge had the dinner laid out in the backyard, as the dining hall was too petite for a crowd of that size. As Aniruddh savored his lentil dal and chapatti, he noticed a girl with a red Fila jumper sitting on the stairs that led to the backyard. The girl was persistently struggling with her untied hair that kept disturbing her vision. It seemed to be disturbing her, but she wasn't too bothered with it, as she made no attempt to tie it back. She had the face of a schoolgirl but was elegant in her etiquettes and conversation. It wasn't very difficult for her to attract eyeballs amidst a group of young students.

"Who's that girl?" queried Aniruddh, looking at Deepak who had joined him for the relief, although his college wasn't a part of it.

"Which one? Anyways, I don't know anyone here, except for you and Vikas," replied Deepak, concentrating on his dinner.

"Arey, the one in the red jumper," pointed out Aniruddh, looking at the girl.

"Radhika Pattnaik, granddaughter of Mayadhar Samanta, the owner of the media house Chakyu. Her mother is Mrinalini Samanta, the famous danseuse. Her parents are divorced, father is a huge mining magnate, Dhiren Pattnaik," Vikas revealed.

"What made you interested in her, Mishra babu," queried Vikas trying to tease him.

"Nothing, she just looked pretty different, you know, as in…," he was cut short by Deepak.

"Different, hmm… She has to be, she is the heir of a million dollar property, she has to be different," said Deepak, licking through his fingers while cherishing the simple yet tasty rice *kheer*.

Aniruddh kept wondering as to what really brought this 'million dollar baby' here on this onerous journey, even as Radhika scrunched her face and closed her eyes each time she licked through the tangy lemon pickle.

The team started off early the next day as they had to head back after their distribution. The devastation in the form of nature's fury was scary. People had taken shelter in government school buildings or Block offices as their houses were swept apart by the wind. Government help was yet to reach these parts, which truly bore the brunt of the cyclonic wind. They were bitten by nature and betrayed by the system. The young volunteers witnessed the apathy and were in a quandary that left them wandering of the system, the government, the democracy that they were so proudly flaunting around in the comfort of their intellectually sound cluster. It all seemed so baseless and ruined to them as they saw the expectations of an impoverished population being neglected by the one they had chosen with faith.

The programme on day two of the relief rally met with some difficulties when a group of local politicians tried to stop the distribution in a village. Their quest for cheap popularity even at the time of this national disaster was unmatched in its tawdriness.

"So, which party has sent all this?" queried a middle-aged man as Aniruddh looked at him with pity.

"We don't represent any political party, we are students from various colleges of the capital city and are here on a goodwill gesture to help these people," replied a composed Ani.

"We don't need this donation, we are not beggars looking for your collected stuff, take your vehicles and leave this village, "ordered the man in a white kurta.

The man was Kanhei Das. He belonged to the opposition and had a stronghold in the village. He brainwashed the villagers that it was the government's stunt to prevent them from getting the actual stuff. It was sad that even the people took for this cheap popularity and distanced themselves from the primary school building where the team was distributing the relief material.

Whoever says India is a victim of cheap politics must admit that it is also a country prejudiced with the excesses of a minority mob. It is a country where a handful of loud voices speak for a majority of silent sufferers. Many in the village wanted these essential items but were suppressed under the nonsensical rhapsody of a few shoddy minds.

It is indeed true that misery brings out the true reflection of a man. With the waning of good times the illusion of goodness also fades away and man unmasks his true character beneath the wrapping of his false skin.

In the two days of reckoning, Aniruddh and his team came to know a lot about the true character of men amidst pain and agony. They saw the naked truth behind the failure of their state as the period of dormancy continued.

As the group headed back for their home, there were mixed feelings of satisfaction and anger, enthusiasm and sorrow, helplessness and emancipation. They came with gesture of goodwill and were going back with a mind full of questions. The silence in the van was pregnant with uneasy minds and unanswered queries.

As Aniruddh looked out of the window, he noticed the liberated strands of hair fluttering out ecstatically a couple of seats ahead of him. The same red jumper that had hijacked his attention last night was now making him inquisitive.

As the team returned back after their largely successful endeavour, the newspapers and the electronic media went overboard with praise. The government was highly criticised as some newspapers carried a rather tacitly sarcastic headline: "Student's show government the way to act".

The comments had an element of truth in them for the stoically passive government. The matter heated up as the governor also went on records, praising the students and criticising the government for inaction. Amidst the massive upsurge of criticism and public anger, the ruling party was forced to change the Chief Minister. The step was more of a face-saver for the party that had lost the support of the people of the state. The new CM acted upon a few issues and hastened the release of the huge amount of relief material that was rotting at the Kalinga Stadium.

In the meanwhile, the popularity of one young man was rising meteorically.

"Who is this guy?"queried a man in white kurta to his associate sitting in front of a television set in his office at the Democratic Congress Party, Youth Wing.

"Oh, that is Bhuban Baral, our guy from the student wing," replied back the associate.

"Not him. I was asking about the guy standing behind him. When the second fiddle scores more than the lead actor, its time to shift the focus. This boy has managed to earn more spotlight than Bhuban in a very short span of time," said the son of two-time Chief Minister and an influential youth leader of his party.

"Oh, he is some Mishra," said the associate.

CHAPTER 6

———◆———

A sudden downpour is not a new thing in this part of the world. The people here always welcome the pre-winter showers.

"See you in the evening," shouted Aniruddh as he kicked his Pulsar to a start.

As the bike rushed out of the college gate and picked up speed, a thin arm with pink bangles and a shiny bracelet forced him to stop. A girl was requesting for a ride back home on a coarse-weathered day. Chivalrous as he was, he had to stop. He couldn't make out the face clearly as the girl was trying to prevent the raindrops from falling on her with the help of her books. He did, however, notice the untied hair falling across the face and he sensed a fair amount of proclivity over his thoughts. It seemed as if he wanted his guess to be correct on this one. Much to his excitement, those alluring strands of hair, made it rightly so.

"Can you drop me at the Forest Park?" asked a mellifluous voice trying hard to overcome the noise of the lashing raindrops.

"Sure," was the obvious reply that Aniruddh could have offered. But the familiar face avoided him of the pain, as she elegantly became his pillion, even before he could answer back in obligation.

For the first time, he noticed her through the rear view mirror of his bike. Those liberated strands of hair were now ecstatic as they fluttered in the wind sprinkled over by the inconsiderate lashes of rain. They resembled the spring harvest that celebrated the summer rains in a similar fashion.

God bless the creator of the rear view mirror he said to himself. This was probably the first time; he had found it of any use since his father forced him to put it. Just when he was busy exploring the view in his rear, a quadruped, quite apathetic to her surrounding, thought it wise to cross over the road. The sudden intrusion forced Aniruddh to apply his brakes in a desperate attempt to prevent a collision. He was expecting an embarrassing skid unknown of the fact that Bajaj was too reliable a brand to have ditched him at such a moment. The brakes held on firm enough, but they did push the pillion a few uncomfortable inches ahead of her seat. Aniruddh felt the sharp dig of her fingernails on his shoulders as she tried her best to beat the inertia.

"Careful!" was certainly not the choicest of words she would have preferred for initiating a conversation with him, but the impulse forced an utterance from her.

"You have been doing a great job, the campus is abuzz with your praises. The campaign was a huge success. Congrats on that," said the girl, preferring to break the ice.

"Thank you, thank you for joining us on the Relief Rally, thanks for the support," replied Aniruddh making sure that he doesn't look back again.

"Both you and your campaign have become one of the coolest things in the recent times," now she had to speak at the top of her voice that would get silhouetted by the raindrops and the noise of the two-wheeler.

"Which one?" asked Aniruddh.

"I mean both the things, your campaign for the relief distribution, as well as you as an…," she was cut short by Aniruddh who slowed down the bike ahead of a turn.

"I meant which turn, which one?"

"Oh, the next one, to the right," said the girl trying to hide her embarrassment.

"Yeah, this one," said the girl as Aniruddh slowed down the bike in front of a huge metal carved gate. The guard at the gate rushed out with an umbrella and handed it over to the already drenched girl.

"Ideally a car should have been waiting outside the college gate to pick you up, isn't it?" asked Aniruddh.

"Yes, but it would have ruined the fun of a bike ride on a rainy day, right?" replied the girl with a deceptive smile on her face.

"The car was in any case following us," she said pointing at the car that entered the lane.

"And yes, your brakes are good," added the girl with a giggle.

"What?" Ani queried, unable to comprehend the sarcasm.

"Yeah, you were testing your brakes with me sitting behind, so I thought I might as well give my opinion on them."

"Anyways, I am Radhika, first year, Science," said the girl as she offered her hand for a handshake.

Aniruddh, still smiling over her remarks on the brakes shook her hand and then tightened the grip on his accelerator giving it some race.

"Bye," said Aniruddh as he rode past the rain looking back for a last time through the rear view mirror, which read "Images on the mirror appear to be closer than they actually are." The remark brought a smile to his face as he zoomed past the lashes of raindrops.

-----0-----

As the state went through a spell of political lethargy, Aniruddh and his group capitulated on the momentum that they built from their post cyclone relief campaign and raised their voices on a number of other issues. Their campaign against child labour and abandoned street children garnered huge support. A prominent NGO helped them in opening a Special Home to rehabilitate these kids. Their education and grooming was looked upon by the NGO. Aniruddh and his friends gathered kids from the railway station, bus stands and busy market places and got them admitted in the Special Home. Most of these kids were already exposed to drug abuse or sexual exploitation.

"Almost 80 percent of these kids are into drugs or petty crime," said Aniruddh to the Secretary for Women and Child Welfare. He was there to approach for government help in the form of funds for the NGO and their project.

"Most of them have either lost their parents or are forced by their parents themselves to indulge in such activities. One mother of two kids made a rather horrific revelation when she said that she deliberately drugged her kids so that they don't cry of hunger. Madam, we are doing our best to get them to the rehab, but sadly the infrastructure won't be able to cater for such a huge number," explained Aniruddh even as he disclosed that the number of homeless in the city has doubled post the cyclone.

As usual Aniruddh walked out of the office with loads of assurances and false hopes. He knew the government had no such plans. He understood the helplessness and swallowed his frustration.

Every day intellectuals talk and debate over the future of India in swanky newsrooms, but its astonishing to see how they conveniently ignore the future generation of the country.

The college exams had just got over and the summer heat was at its merciless peak. The cyclone had damaged the environment beyond repair and thus, there was no relief from the sun this time around. The winds had taken their revenge, and now it was the sun.

Amidst the anguish of the weather there were other issues that grappled the state with almost equal alacrity. Poverty, unemployment and lack of governance pulled the state back instead of pushing it ahead in the race of development. The huge tribal population of the state that remained largely impervious of even the little development that had happened were now getting impatient. The rage in them remained camouflaged by the government's gross indifference towards them. The tribal belt was waiting to erupt anytime. The phenomenon was not restricted to Odisha but to all other parts of the country that never really understood this section of the demography. They erupted as the biggest internal security threat to the country in the form of Naxalism.

A movement that started in the late 1960's with the peasant's revolt would soon become the symbol of struggle for the oppressed class. Although the government crushed the movement each time, it resurfaced in the 70's and the 80's in various forms. This time around it wasn't easy. With access to sophisticated weapons and technology, the naxals were a force that soon grew beyond the capability of the state's police force.

Odisha was witnessing a gradual rise in the naxal activities. The bordering states of Andhra and the newly formed Jharkand were also subjected to similar brutality. The government once again repeated the mistake of taking a microscopic look at the whole movement and identifying it as a law and order problem. In reality, the whole movement was an outcome of the persistent government apathy towards a section of its own people.

A law and order problem can be resolved by stricter implementation of rules and vigil by the law enforcing agencies, but a socio-economic problem needs a deeper introspection into the anomalies that have created it. Where the approach should have begun with reaching out to them, the authorities worsened the situation by segregating them further and coining them as outlaws.

The first instances of Naxal violence were reported from the Northern Odisha district of Sundergarh. The Naxalites raided a fully armed police station and emptied the armoury. The police on being asked about giving a fight candidly said that they had never fired their weapons post their probation training days. The state of preparedness of the police was alarmingly derisory, but the government chose to stay in denial mode.

Sundergarh district housed the only steel plant in the iron-ore rich state. The SAIL Steel plant in Rourkela was a promising industrial venture that soon got engulfed in the malice of mismanagement and corruption.

Lacklustre production, dwindling steel prices and the challenge from China made matters worse at the turn of the century. The plant supported a whole lot of subsidiary industries that were also affected by the performance of the steel plant. The state government could never create an ideal environment for the growth of industries in the state, and this remains the bitter truth in Odisha. Development was restricted to the coastal belt as a large portion of the state remained unaffected by the government's policies. This void in the governance gave rise to the malice of left-wing extremism. Expectedly, Western and Southern Odisha – among the poorest parts of the country – witnessed rapid rise in Naxal activities. The only solution was to get them into the mainstream and increase their representation. The state headed for the new millennium with a whole set of new challenges and shortcomings, but sadly with the same mindset.

CHAPTER 7

———◈———

It was the last election of the millennium. As usual, the state went to the assembly polls along with the Lok Sabha elections. The elections were particularly special as the people were desperate for an alternative to the age-old rule of The Democratic Congress Party. The party had been ruling the state since independence, barring a few years when the vibrant Rabi Pattnaik took over the reins. He was undoubtedly the most dynamic Chief Minister of the state. Rabi babu, as he was affectionately referred to, provided the much-needed influential representation at the centre. He was adamant over his policies, and ruled the state with an iron fist and a velvet heart. His uncanny knack of connecting with the people made him the leader of the masses. His rule was short but memorable. But that was soon followed by an age of puny leadership and indecisive governance. The truth, however, was that there was no Rabi babu now. The people were frustrated with the incumbent government, and the state was once again plagued with the perennial disease of leadership deficit. There was no viable alternative available to the people. All that was left was a cyclone-hit state, lurching towards the 21st century with poverty and malnutrition.

The desperation for an alternative to the incumbent leadership gave rise to the birth of a new party and a new face. The son of one of Odisha's favourite leaders – that was the introduction of the political alternative to the people of the state. The man was a tad bit more educated and polished for a politician, someone who had spent most of his life in the comforts of London, amongst well-known social figures. His transformation into a kurta-clad politician of this state wasn't natural. However, with deep political bankruptcy prevalent, and a desperate need for a leader, the people accepted this alien candidate.

Odisha was always a feudal state, and the acceptance of this foreign-educated, polished man did not come as much of a surprise. While Rabi babu's biggest strength was the connect he had with the people, his son's was his disconnect with them. People loved the idea of being ruled by someone whom they considered socially and politically superior to them. His biggest lacunae, of not knowing the language of the state, in fact, became an advantage for him. Moreover, the new guy did not carry any baggage with him, and was proclaimed honest and incorruptible. His delineated personality bore absolutely no resemblance to the raucous mess that Odisha was.

It was hard to think back to any leader in recent political history who would have enjoyed such unprecedented support from the people even before his debut into electoral politics. He was truly a beneficiary of low expectations. The elections proved the prophets of doom wrong – the Kalinga Janata Dal became the single largest party, winning the maximum number of seats. Furthermore, achieving these figures when the 'Atal wave' was at its zenith was commendable. The KJD went on to form the government, making an alliance with the Swayam Sevak Party.

"The man doesn't even know the language of the state," said a frustrated Aniruddh.

"Does that make a difference? Look, when we can accept a leader of opposition who doesn't know the language of the nation, then what's wrong with this man?" Mr. Mishra countered, making an obvious reference to the leader of opposition at the centre.

"The man is young and is educated. He can take the state to new heights if he is strong-willed," he added. "Moreover, he is unknown to the political filth."

Damodar Mishra was echoing the feelings of a million hearts of the coastal state. A ray of hope flickered around the region that was devastated by both natural and man-made calamities. The government seemed to be headed in the right direction when they prioritised the rehabilitation of millions of people affected by the cyclone. The grants for house-building and the allocation of funds were expedited. The infrastructure development got impetus as well, with hundreds of healthcare units coming up along with nearly thousand kilometres of road that needed rebuilding. Agro service centres, lift irrigation facilities, schools and other facilities saw rapid improvement in the formative stages of the government.

The state government took the most sensible decision in improving its disaster mitigating system. The creation of the State Disaster Mitigation Authority and the Disaster Rapid Action Force were the steps that hinted at the government's sincerity in this crucial aspect. The mood in the state was quite upbeat, as people saw tangible work in progress at ground level, and they believed that their gamble in the elections had paid off. Furthermore, the alliance with the party ruling at the center made things easier for the state government.

Meanwhile, the university elections also saw an unusual trend as the candidate of the opposition won over the candidate supported by the ruling party. This was unusual because traditionally, it was the ruling party candidate that won the elections.

The candidate supported by the opposition was Vishnu Pradhan, the son of an ex-legislator Suramani Pradhan. The 'Pradhans' were a household name in the coastal belt. They had an absolute monopoly on the fishing industry of the state. Their clout in the industry went unchallenged as they had adopted a number of unconventional, and sometimes illegal, ways to acquire licenses and dominate the coast. They were now rapidly spreading their businesses, with investments in education, hospitality and construction. Suramani's loyalty to the previous government had earned him quite a few enemies in the present one.

The university elections were almost a one-sided affair as the money and muscle-power of Vishnu was unmatched. His opponent, Dhananjaya Patra, was meek. Although Dhananjaya enjoyed the support of the NSU, the students were largely in favour of Vishnu. Moreover, Vishnu had the liberty of spending money, whereas Patra belonged to a humble family. Vishnu, however, was in no way the stereotypical spoilt brat from a rich family. He was polite and sensible. He knew the value of his family's reputation. And his role in pacifying the ongoing tussle within the university was appreciated by many. The university was witness to violence almost regularly in those days. Political rivalry would spark clashes between the two factions, and the wrangle would often result in violent outbursts, forcing the management to call the police. All major rifts would begin at the hostels – the hub of university politics – where the dorms were stocked with adequate arsenal. Vishnu's role in getting the two factions to the talking tables was a significant one, and it made him very popular. His plan of a 'Student Welfare Fund', to provide interest free loans to the economically backward students was also an instant hit.

Vishnu Pradhan's popularity had reached its peak during his days at the university.

-----x-----

Spring was a luxury the calamity struck state could ill afford. The end of the placid winters would usually be followed seamlessly by unforgiving summers. So, the people satisfied themselves by anointing February as the 'spring month'.

The otherwise unadorned month of February had become popular for a very strange reason. The 14th of the month was more or less alien to a country that celebrated almost every major festival known to mankind. In fact, till a decade ago, not many would have been familiar with the concept of Valentine's Day. However, the festival has been celebrated with more enthusiasm since then. At times even more than the festivals native to this society. And anybody not knowing of Valentine's Day today would be type casted as a social pariah.

Thus, almost 70 percent of the population that celebrated this day would do so without having any idea of the reason behind it. Who would really be bothered with finding out who St. Valentines was, as long as he gave a reason to an otherwise conservative society to openly express love? We, as Indians, easily embrace any occasion for celebration. If we could celebrate Brazil's win in the football World Cup and Bill Clinton's re-election as president after his office adventures, then why not commemorate the death of a Saint whom the world says had spread the message of love? Basically, we don't need a reason to celebrate. We need an excuse for an occasion.

"This place is so beautifully done up, "said Shirley, as the group entered a newly-launched coffee shop in the city.

"Yeah, this place is truly amazing. The city was in desperate need of a cool place to hang out," Aditya added. Those were the days when the Class B cities were judged by their coffee shops and internet cafes.

"Radhika, we all must thank your uncle for this," said Deepak. Radhika was the newest member of the group, courtesy her growing acquaintance with Aniruddh. The coffee-chain franchise in the city was bought by her uncle.

It was a perfect Saturday evening. The air around was festive, and the youth cherished every moment of this new-found freedom. The coffee shop was filled with couples sharing their moments with cards and flowers. But the happiest men on the day were the owners of the Archies and Hallmark stores, and the innumerable gift shops that had mushroomed all over the city. It was unusual for a city that hardly had couples roaming about in the street to see young boys and girls moving with bouquets and cards for each other.

As Aniruddh and his group chatted at the cafe, a van came to a screeching halt outside the joint. It was followed by another SUV, and from the vehicles emerged men with wooden staffs and iron rods. They had vermilion smirked on their foreheads, and wore saffron imprint scarves around their necks. They marched aggressively towards the cafe howling out slogans – "Jai Shri Ram!","Jai Hanuman!"

As the group closed in, one of them smashed the glass door at the entrance to smithereens. The hooligans then entered the café and vandalised the counter before reaching the terrified people seated beyond. While half of hooligans ransacked the outlet, the others put on a violent show of strength with the customers. They ruined the beautifully-decorated coffee shop in moments. People sitting inside exited in panic as one of the men caught hold of a young girl and slapped her, while another hit her friend who collapsed to the ground.

"We won't let you blemish our religion or dent the Hindu image and our year-old traditions," said a man, probably their leader.

"Go home kids, and stop aping the west blindly. Our culture and religion has no space for this moral decadence," shouted another as he caught Deepak by his collar.

"Who the hell are you to tell us what to do, you bastards?" Shirley shouted, the disgust in her voice coming through loud and clear.

The hooligans were stoic for a moment. They seemed particularly surprised by this unexpected confrontation and that too from a girl. The bearded leader then walked up to her and noticed the cross hanging on her neck.

His blood-shot eyes grew larger as he came closer to her, and said: "It's because of you people that our identity is lost in our own land."

He then yanked the cross out, and pushed her aside. Shirley fell and banged her head on the edge of the wooden table. Radhika screamed with horror and rushed to pick her up. Aniruddh struggled to free himself off the clutches of two men. Deepak tried countering one of them, but was hit by another with a wooden staff on his leg.

The hoodlums rushed out of the cafe as soon as they heard the blaring police sirens. As they moved out, one of them stamped over a saffron scarf that they had around their necks, much like the way they crushed the very ideologies of the religion they represented. A religion that prophesied anything, but violence.

The whole place, which just a while ago was jubilant and celebrated love, became an unfortunate witness of concocted moral values and misplaced religious identities. The incident left the group in a state of shock. Aniruddh stood speechless, as Deepak lay on the floor crying in pain and despair. Radhika sat next to an unconscious Shirley, drenched in blood. It took a while for Aniruddh to get back to his senses, and he rushed out to call for help with tears in his eye.

The young girl lay motionless on her bed in the ICU as Aniruddh peeped through the glass window. He was unable to collect his emotions that were filled with anger, sorrow and a sense of fear. He realised he could not recollect a single moment of that horrible incident.

Who were these people and what was their trepidation? Why did they resort to such violent means? Who misguided them to believe that their age-old civilisation could come under threat? Or was all this nothing but a cheap political gimmick, orchestrated to gain limelight?

Radhika and Aditya waited fretfully outside the ICU. Deepak had sustained a serious contusion on his right knee and thigh, but luckily had no fracture. Shirley was undergoing an operation after a severe head injury. Her parents arrived as soon as they heard of the incident. Mr D'souza, a prominent lawyer himself, was visibly disturbed, especially as the doctors had not yet confirmed the status of her daughter. His wife was in a deep state of shock, but she remarkably concealed her emotions, albeit with a moist eye and a heavy heart. The terrified parents got a sigh of relief when the doctors emerged out of the OT and assured that their daughter was out of danger, but they had to keep her under observation for 24 hours.

Rounak D'souza was an eminent lawyer and a respectable man in the judicial circles. An accident that almost took his daughter's life was something that he had least expected. Now that the doctors had assured him of his daughter's well being, he vowed to deal with the perpetrators.

"What happened out there, Ani?" asked Mr D'souza, taking Aniruddh out to the corridor.

Aniruddh narrated the entire incident to him in detail, and revealed that Aditya could even recognise one of the hoodlums.

"We have to nail them down uncle, we won't spare them," said Aniruddh.

"Hmm…I hope Deepak is doing fine and nobody else is injured?" enquired the worried man.

"There have been two more incidents, orchestrated by the same group. They call themselves the 'Hindu Raksha Abhiyan,'" Mr.D'souza added.

It was already 11 in the night and Radhika's car had come to fetch her home. Mr.D'souza asked the kids to go home and expressed his gratitude.

"I have to get my bike, left it at the coffee shop," said Aniruddh.

"C'mon, we can get it tomorrow. It's too late now, I shall drop you home," said Radhika, and pulled Aniruddh into the car.

It was a tough night for Aniruddh. Lying in bed, he held the cross that was pulled out of Shirley's neck and kept staring at it. Jesus looked helpless, not because he was crucified, but because his message never reached a few ears. God was crucified then, because people disagreed with him, and he was suffering now because a few agreed with him almost obsessively.

Next morning, the tabloids were filled with similar incidents across the nation. Intolerance and bigotry eclipsed the message of love, which some saint had wished to spread across the world. The moral police brigade of the Hindu religion took on the onerous task of safeguarding their faith that they believed was on the verge of annihilation. It was rather amusing to see people fight for the supremacy of a religion that had always preached that it was not the only true religion around. The words Hindu and fanatics sounded like an oxymoron when used together.

Deepak and Aditya had launched an FIR in the nearest police station where the incident occurred. The manager of the cafe deferred and was too scared to give a statement. There were a few more reports that were filed in other stations as well. The police was blatantly evading the issue. A request for an identification parade of the accused was denied by them. They said that it was a mob that attacked these places, and that it was difficult to pinpoint anyone in the mob. One police officer even went on the record, advising youngsters to maintain the social decorum and avoid upsetting the cultural trends of the society. The officer expressed no visible signs of ignominy while making the statement. He just represented the mindset of a group of ethnocentric maniacs who prophesied their very own version of religious precincts.

However, the police weren't expected to react any differently given the fact that the Hindu Raksha Abhiyan was a splinter group of the coalition partner of the government. Any punitive action against the group would draw severe resistance from the coalition member. Although the political outfit had delinked itself from the violent attacks, their support to the group wasn't a secret. The group was an assemblage of a group of imprudent young men who would go to any extent to make headlines. They took to these cheap stunts in order to appease a section of their vote bank and stay in the news.

Three days had passed since the gory incident. Shirley's condition was improving but at a slow pace. She was now out of the ICU, and Deepak was discharged from the hospital. A sense of desperation crept up Aniruddh's mind owing to the helpless state that he was left in. The police did nothing even after Aditya gave them the name of one of the culprits.

"I feel crippled. Why can't we do anything?" said Deepak, anguished about their helplessness.

"What can we do, when Shirley's father, being such a big lawyer, is unable to do anything himself?" replied Aditya.

"He is concerned about the safety of his daughter and his family. One never knows to what level these hoodlums can stoop down to," justified Radhika.

"I just can't digest the fact that while our friend is battling for her life, those responsible for that are still at large and publicly making statements," added Deepak, his anger rising. "Maybe you people can sleep peacefully over this. Not me. I am going to reply back to those bastards."

"What are you going to do?" Aditya asked.

"Give them a taste of their own medicine, thrash them inside their own home."

"Are you mad?" Aditya countered. "You know the kind of people they are. You think they will leave it at that? They will look for you like hounds and then…I think you should get these ideas out of your head."

"Yes, and sit helplessly like all of you," Deepak shouted.

"Come with me," Aniruddh suddenly said.

He led the group to the computer lab and started typing out something on Microsoft Word. After fifteen minutes or so, what shaped out seemed like a declaration or a handbill. The handbill declared the unflinching resolve of a group of students to punish the perpetrators of the February 14 incident. It also appealed others to join the group and pledge their support. Aniruddh requested the students to express themselves on the white banner they were going to put at the college entrance, and invited them to join in for an assembly at the college auditorium after classes the next day.

Copies of the pamphlet were made and distributed all around the college. A white banner and a black marker were at the entrance to the blocks. The next day, the whole college spoke of the pamphlets. Aniruddh was not an unknown figure and hence a move initiated by him garnered huge amount of curiosity. Plus, the coffee shop incident was known to all. By noon, the banner was full of slogans and solidarity for Shirley. It was a healthy sign as it indicated that their move had already attracted a lot of supporters.

However, by half-past three, only five people had gathered in the auditorium. Almost an hour and half had passed by since the classes. It was quite evident that the support of the students was restricted to expressing themselves via graffiti, and that no one really bothered to spend any extra time for the cause. The empty chairs and the void in the auditorium were symbolic of a society that was taught to stay away from the troubles of others. People were shamelessly habituated to accept this 'social euthanasia' rather than scour for preventive measures. They were the pedigree of a generation that preferred to remain apathetic to anything that did not affect their immediate social envelope.

"It's disheartening to see such apathy from our own friends. I feel pathetic being a part of this morbid society," said Aditya, visibly depressed.

"It's not their fault, Aditya. They are doing exactly what they were always expected to do. We have been told since our childhood not to put our hands into the spokes of a cycle wheel. This apathy and indifference has been systematically ingrained in us. So it doesn't come as a surprise when our own friends turn their backs at us," said Aniruddh, dejected.

"You need not feel so miserable about it, guys, At least you people took the pain to raise this issue. Most people ignored it," said Radhika, in a bid to counsel them.

Aniruddh felt betrayed by his own generation who seemed so indifferent to something that affected them in one way or the other. Was it fear or was it simply a lack of concern? The young man went home with a heavy heart, but certainly with a stronger resolve than ever before. He knew he had to plan something bigger now.

As Aniruddh finished his dinner and headed for his room, his mother called him back.

"Ani, you have a call," shouted Mrs Mishra.

"This boy gets more calls than the Prime Minister of the country," she muttered as he picked up the phone.

"Hello?"

"Hey, is that Aniruddh?" a soft voice asked over the phone.

"Yeah, this is Aniruddh Mishra, may I know who is speaking?" asked Aniruddh.

"I am Vishnu. Vishnu Pradhan. The Student Union president at Utkal University," replied the caller.

"Oh, yes, hi. How can I help you, bhai?" Aniruddh asked, utterly surprised to hear from the union president himself.

"Aniruddh, I got a copy of your pamphlet and I think it is quite brave of you to have stood up against those who lampoon our society. Until we start strongly reacting to these gimmicks, they aren't going to stop. I just wanted to let you know that I support your move and am ready to help you in your crusade to punish the perpetrators," Vishnu replied, and invited Aniruddh for a discussion on future actions before hanging up.

It took some time for Aniruddh to comprehend what had just happened. Vishnu Pradhan was a huge name in student politics, and getting his support for the cause meant a lot. It virtually meant that the entire university was with him now. But then, a question kept bothering him all night: What made Vishnu Pradhan call him up and pledge his support, as Aniruddh meant nothing to him?

'Pradhan's', read the huge granite inscription outside the huge iron gates and the thatched compound wall. A fleet of the latest cars were parked outside, and a couple of them under the porch. The mansion was an architectural marvel and was located at one of the posh localities of the city. The downy lawn and the sophisticated lighting were very much like the price tags exhibiting the worth of the people living inside. Deepak parked his bike as Aniruddh approached the gate, and interacted with the guard.

A hand waved from the second floor balcony, indicating them to come inside. They were guided through the stairs by one of the guards, and as the duo moved in, Aniruddh noticed a few members of the Pradhan family on the first floor. It is not very difficult to distinguish people who are wealthy but not rich. The Pradhans were in no way a truly urbane family. Their humble roots were very much displayed in their attires and their mannerisms. Money can get you to a new world but it can never deracinate your base. They possessed unique rustiness in their richness, and they were honest about it.

"Hey, welcome. I am Vishnu," a slim guy sporting, a four-day old stubble, introduced himself.

"Aniruddh. And this is my friend Deepak," said Aniruddh, and they shook hands.

Vishnu was dressed in a golf t-shirt and a pair of linen trousers. This clearly reflected that he was the most contemporary member of the Pradhan family, with his upbringing mostly in the city.

"Look, I came to know what happened with you and I express my deepest concerns for your friend," said Vishnu. "I am anguished by the fact that we have become so helpless against these hoodlums who can do anything in the name of social reforms."

"We have identified them and even lodged a complaint with the police, but the police just won't act," said Aniruddh.

"The police won't act because these people have got powerful political names to back them," Vishnu replied.

"Arey bhai, it's a powerful equation out there. Bhumi Mishra, the founder of the Hindu Raksha Abhiyan is the man Friday of Rudra Tripathy, the Home Minister. The police won't dare touch Bhumi's men, they don't need a spank from the Home Minister," chipped in a man sitting next to Vishnu.

He was introduced as Jogi Maharana, a student of law.

"So we cannot expect any help from the administration," added Vishnu.

"That means we are left with no other option but to wait for the police to complete their botched up enquiry, and submit a farce report that would ultimately acquit all of them," said a frustrated Deepak.

"No, we have the greatest strength with us, the strength of the students," replied Vishnu. "We have the numbers and the support of the students. We shall take on the government from the streets, we shall protest from the roads and force the police to succumb."

It seemed as if he had already chalked out the future course of action.

"Do you think, the students will join us?" queried Aniruddh.

"Do you doubt Vishnu bhai's support in the university?" asked Jogi.

"No, I doubt the attitude of our generation."

"Don't worry, Aniruddh. I shall get the numbers for you," said Vishnu. "We shall hold a youth conglomeration at the exhibition ground. We shall make a pledge to fight against such communal elements hidden in any religion. We shall redeem the Hindu pride by spreading its core values and principles. The fight shall begin by bringing the perpetrators of the February 14 incident behind bars. Bhumi Mishra and his associate Pavitra Ransingh should be behind the bars."

Vishnu said all this as though he was reading out a prepared script. He also convinced Aniruddh to deliver a keynote speech at the conglomeration as he wanted him to be the face of the agitation.

"He seems to be a nice guy. At least his intentions are good," shouted Deepak, trying to reach out to Aniruddh over the blaring noise of traffic.

"Hmm… can't say yet. Why do you say that?" Ani replied.

"His support for a cause that doesn't benefit him in any way proves his commitment towards social cause," justified Deepak.

"Have you heard of Pavitra Ransingh?" asked Aniruddh, with a smile on his face.

"Name sounds familiar," said Deepak.

"He is the Student Union leader of the other big university of the city, the Agriculture University. Pavitra is a BCP guy, Bharatiya Bidyarthi Parishad. He has grown quite popular after his protest against the mismanagement in the university administration. In the present political configuration he is the only big challenge to Vishnu Pradhan as far as youth leaders are concerned," explained Aniruddh, maintaining the smile on his face.

Aniruddh slowed the bike at Deepak's house and as he dismounted, Aniruddh said: "There are no free lunches, my friend."

It was a gloomy Sunday. An overcast sky made the environment uncomfortably humid. The miniscule response at the exhibition ground did not surprise Aniruddh, who reached the venue a good two hours before the start time.

"Hmm ... all we people can ever dream of doing on a Sunday afternoon is hit the sack after an overdose of rice," said Aditya, frustrated.

They went behind the makeshift stage that was prepared by Vishnu and his accomplices. As they awaited the arrival of other members, Aniruddh went through his speech one last time. He could hear the noise levels increasing in the ground all the while.

"Have you seen the crowd?" asked an excited Vishnu as he arrived.

"No, have people come?" asked Ani, his eyebrows raised.

"The ground is full and they are still pouring in. This is the moment. If we can strike a chord now, the whole game can be ours," said an enthused Vishnu.

Aniruddh knew he had a huge task at hand. Vishnu had kept his promise by getting the numbers, now it was up to him to win them over. He was no greenhorn in public speaking, but this was different. He had to motivate them to fight for his cause. He had to be the catalyst and light up the fire in them. This was no elocution or debate. This was his first real test as a leader.

It was half past four and the crowd was getting impatient. Almost three thousand young people of the city had sacrificed their Sundays for this cause.

"Friends, we are extremely thankful to all of you for coming here today," said Vishnu, beginning the proceedings. "We know that the incident on February 14 is a matter of concern for us all. It not only challenges our freedom but also intimidates the very foundation of our country that is based on universal acceptance and tolerance. A few hoodlums with cynical ambitions and malafide political intentions have tried to malign the peaceful image of our city. They have to be punished, shouldn't they?"

The crowd responded with a loud "Yes!"

"Today, we have with us a victim of the incident who has pledged to bring the perpetrators to task and put them behind bars. I request him to come up and share his thoughts with all for us."

Vishnu had set the stage for Aniruddh.

Aniruddh was not a completely new face. His endeavours during the cyclone relief rally had made him a popular figure among the youth.

"Friends, it is indeed heartening to see all of you gather here for a cause on a Sunday," started Aniruddh.

"This is not some kind of a vengeance rally or a show of strength trying to intimidate the people responsible for their acts of violence against us. This isn't an agitation to spread a message of mutual coexistence and tolerance because that is so inherent to us that we shall ensure it anyhow."

The crowd cheered to that, as Aniruddh raised his tempo.

"This convention is more of an attempt to come together to save our identity as a civilisation that has harboured the belief of universal acceptance. A civilisation that safeguards the interest of its subjects irrespective of their religious and cultural inclinations. There would be no idea of an India without these fundamental values. Every religion that has survived the idea of India has adjusted itself accordingly. I am a Hindu, a practicing Hindu, and I am proud of that. I believe in the Bhagvad Gita and I respect its teachings. I know the mantras and Vedas that have been taught to me, and I am proud of them. But, in no way am I scared of losing my cultural identity or civilisational inheritance. In no way do I feel the value of my scriptures deluding away. I am convinced that if a 5000-year-old civilisation that blossomed in a land like India withstood the Mughal invasion and the British rule, it cannot be intimidated by its very own people.

"The foundations of my religion have been strengthened by the pillars of tolerance and acceptance for all. I am convinced more so when I see Ahmed uncle of my colony walking up to my house on Diwali with sweets. When I see Emanuel sweating it out while decorating the Ganesh puja pandal of our college with his beautiful paintings. When I see my father sending Eid-Mubarak cards to his friends and when I am the first one to hop on the Christmas cake at Shirley's place.

"My religion is not threatened by respecting and celebrating the values and traditions of other communities. It is, rather, strengthened by that. My religion is free of dogmas and heresy. My religion has no apostasy or chauvinism affiliated to it. As I see it, it is free of compulsions and heretical doctrines. My religion respects the feelings of all and accepts all forms of the almighty. It is free from any form of bigotry or communal prejudice. My Ram is in my purity of thoughts and my Hanuman is in my strength in unity. My religion gives me my freedom of inquisition towards my beliefs and disbeliefs. My religion is that of the modern world, and it aptly describes the secularism of my nation. Secularism in India is not the absence of religion but the coexistence of all religions."

Aniruddh was at his best. His tone reflected the anger and the attitude he represented in the youth of the country.

"Friends, today we need to take a pledge, a pledge to protect our identity as a nation that spreads the message of 'Sarva Dharma Sambhava'. A pledge to crush those who distort the noble messages of our respective religions, and victimise the very strength of this great country. We shall start a peaceful protest tomorrow, to coerce the government to arrest the perpetrators of the February 14 incident and bring them to justice. Thank you all once again for standing by us."

As Aniruddh concluded his speech, the silence in the exhibition was broken by the hysteric applause from the crowd. Aniruddh had just articulately and expertly stroked the emotions of the crowd. The noise of the hooting and clapping reflected the support that Aniruddh had garnered for his cause. He went on to appeal the crowd to continue their support till the courts punish the culprits.

Widespread agitations started the next day. Students joined the protest in thousands. The streets of the capital city all the way from the university to the Secretariat were filled with young people. Students abandoned their classrooms to join in the protest. The protests were largely peaceful, but for a few minor tussles between the police and the students.

The sight of students crowding up the city streets increased the concerns of the government. The state government, under intense media and public scrutiny, was now forced to act against some members of the 'Hindu Raksha Abhiyan'. Bhumi Mishra and Pavitra Ransingh were amongst the ones against whom arrest warrants were issued.

The ruling coalition was divided over the decision. The coalition partner was apprehensive over the government's decision but did not dare speak out against owing to the massive public anger on the issue. The Home Minister was particularly unhappy with the proceedings, but he too had to succumb to the pressure that had built up.

The arrest of Bhumi Mishra triggered off a huge political row. The opposition got an opportunity to tarnish the image of the ruling coalition. Rudra Mohan Tripathy's image and popularity were tarnished as his key associate was charged. Rudra Mohan was a seasoned politician, who had travelled through the petulant by lanes of public life. He proclaimed he was a revolutionary of the JP movement in the 1970's, although very few actually knew that he was arrested for bootlegging and not for taking part in the revolution. Rudra was successful in getting the 'revolutionary' tag along with the other leaders of Utkal Congress. The novice was giving this veteran a tough fight.

CHAPTER 8

I t was half past nine in the evening and the streets were already empty. Aniruddh and Deepak were on their way back from Shirley's house, after checking on her after her return from the hospital. She kept a continuous track of the events, and asked Aniruddh to be more careful now. The city was no more a safe place for him, as the powerful and influential people involved in the incident could try and harm him. Aniruddh pacified her, saying that the thousands of supporters they had garnered ensured his safety.

Aniruddh and Deepak were passing through one of the many dark lanes of the city when they were confronted by a vehicle coming at them. The vehicle came to a sudden stop even as Aniruddh applied his brakes. Four young men hopped out of the Maruti Omni and walked straight at them. One of the guys then pulled out the keys of Aniruddh's bike and asked him to dismount.

"Mishra babu, shouldn't you be concentrating on studies and college rather than being on the streets, trying to become a hero?" said one of the guys in his early twenties, clutching Aniruddh's wrist. The guy was in a velvet shirt and spoke in a petulant tone.

"Who the fuck are you to tell us what to do?" countered Deepak, as someone held him by his collar. The guy smacked him on his face as the other two held him firmly.

Aniruddh realised the wisest thing to do in that situation was to stay quiet.

"I hope you get the message Aniruddh bhai. You know we may come again, if you happen to forget our message at any time," said the man as he pushed Aniruddh. He then pulled out an iron rod from his vehicle and crashed the headlights of Ani's motorbike.

The assault on the streets would have continued had the headlights of a car not interrupted them. The group of klutz then scooted off immediately. As the goons fled, Aniruddh helped Deepak get back on the bike as he drove past the dark lane. Deepak had a sore nose from the blow he had fielded. As he drove back, Aniruddh was consumed by a sense of guilt. He had accepted the fact that once he took on the powerful, such altercations were natural. However, he did not realise his friends, and maybe later his family, could be embroiled in all this.

Serious questions loomed in the mind of this young man. Should he succumb to these petty threats and pull out of the mess? Or should he ignore these threats and keep fighting?

"Are you okay?" asked Aniruddh, examining Deepak's nose.

"Hmm … fine, don't worry. The hit wasn't hard enough to break the bones!" joked Deepak, wiping the blood dripping out of his nose.

"Look, Deepak. I don't want you to get into all this, you are being targeted because you happen to be with me," said Aniruddh as he examined Deepak's injuries.

There was a smile on Deepak's face as he leaned back on the bike. "Do you remember Komal?" asked Deepak.

"Komal Ghosh, AG colony. Yes, your fantasy," answered Aniruddh, quite surprised by the unusual mention here.

"But, why do you ask now?"

"Do you remember the day I followed her behind her bicycle just to find out her house?" asked Deepak.

"Yes, I remember. I also remember having got smacked by her brother and his friends," replied Aniruddh, breaking into a smile.

"Yeah. By mistake we asked her own brother for her address." The two had a hearty laugh, before Deepak asked, "Why did you come with me that day? I had never asked you to."

"C'mon Deepak, that was different. We were kids then. This is a serious issue, these people can actually harm you," said Aniruddh.

"Exactly, Aniruddh. We aren't kids any longer. I know what they can do and what we can do," said Deepak. "Whatever comes we shall face it together. I don't have the brains to plan and do things, but believe me, in all your endeavours henceforth, you shall find me standing next to you."

There was a moment of awkwardness, followed by an emotional embrace that concluded with a pat by Aniruddh. Sometimes, friends convey a million words by a simple pat on the back or a kick on the ass. What's kosher in friendship is the joy that you squeeze out of pain.

"Hey, by the way Komal's bro is in the university now. Want to take revenge?" Aniruddh said drolly.

"Hmmm…leave it, 'to forgive is divine'," said Deepak, and they spilled over in a bout of laughter.

-----x-----

"We should lodge an FIR with the police over the incident," said an anxious Radhika.

"Look, that will be of no help. We all know whose men they were," replied Deepak, soothing his nose with a medical gauge.

"Ani, these are filthy people who fear nothing. The administration is a mere dummy in their hands," said Radhika. "They can harm you anytime they want, why don't you understand, damn it!"

Radhika was a lot more animated this time, her concern for the safety of her friends was evident.

"Look, Radhika. We can't leave it from here," Aniruddh replied. "We are this close from getting justice for our friend and for all those who have bestowed their faith in us. I can't pull out now, it would be cowardice. Moreover, they wouldn't take the chance of hurting me now, knowing the public's support for me. They just want to intimidate me, and test my tensile strength."

"Do you ever listen to anyone except for yourself? Sometimes, you must let people around you matter as well," said Radhika, and stormed out of the college canteen.

Those words left Aniruddh pondering over her reaction.

"I knew they would target you," said Vishnu, walking impatiently in his room. "They are targeting you because they know that you are the face of the agitation, and that you are vulnerable. They will try their best to break you down, Aniruddh."

"So were they Tripathy's men?" queried Deepak.

"No, Rudra Mohan is not so naïve as to involve his own men in this. They are Debu Jena's men, Rudra's old time loyalist," explained Vishnu. "Debu is a trader from Cuttack. He runs the local mafia at the wholesale market. His territory begins from the Capital Haat and extends till the outskirts of Cuttack. Debu was also a councilor from Ward No.7."

Their discussion was interrupted by the sudden entry of a man in his early thirties. The man was dressed in baggie cut jeans and a cheap replica of a DKNY t-shirt. His face was largely dominated by a week-old stubble, and there were dark circles under his eye. The man looked unimpressive but resourceful.

"Juhare, Vishnu bhai," said the man as he wished Vishnu in a subjugate manner.

"Arey, Babula, kana khabar, how is everything going on?" replied Vishnu, offering him a chair, making him feel important.

"Aniruddh, meet Babula. He is our dear friend, and the son of Samal babu, the sarpanch of Jharpada village." Ani got up and shook hands with the stranger.

"Arey, Babula, tell me one thing. Who is Debu Jena banking on? They attacked our friend yesterday evening," asked Vishnu.

"Debu's ... *bhai* they are labourers from the Haat Bazaar. Were they in a Maruti Omni, red colour?" asked Babula.

"Yes," replied Aniruddh.

"Achhaaa! Bulu Bhoi. He runs a fishery in the bazaar, bhai; most of his men are those daily wagers who work for him. They are young boys, hardly 20. Don't worry bhai, I shall talk to them tomorrow," replied Babula with authority.

"No, no, not this time, Vishnu bhai, nothing to be done now. Let's see if they try any other stunt. Then we shall look into it," requested Aniruddh.

"Arey, Ani, they must be sent a message lest they believe it as our weakness," countered Vishnu.

"No, Vishnu bhai. Please, try and understand. Let us give them another chance, if they try something funny, we won't send a message. Then we shall call on the leader himself," said Aniruddh, trying to convince Vishnu.

"Okay, as you wish."

As the day of the trial approached, Aniruddh got a lot of indirect invitations for settlement. The supporters of Pavitra would stage protests against the arrest of their leader. The BBP tried all the tricks in its coterie to secure the release of Pavitra and Bhumi Mishra.

It was seven in the evening, and Aniruddh had just returned from the tutorials. Deepti followed him to his room as he was sifting through his notes.

"Bhai, are you busy with something?" muttered Deepti in a soft tone."Wanted to tell you something."

Her voice lacked the usual enthusiasm. Aniruddh immediately recognised the difference in his baby sister's uncharacteristic request. After all, it's difficult to conceal emotions among siblings.

He pulled his chair to the edge of the bed and asked: "What is it? Is everything okay?"

Tears rolled out of her eye as she started speaking.

"Bhai, today while I was returning from my tuition classes, some boys stopped me on the way," she said.

Aniruddh listened patiently as she described her traumatic experience.

"They abused you and said that I should convince you not to do all this, at least for the sake of our family members," she continued.

It was Aniruddh's worst fear. The tears in the eyes of his sister made him feel more guilty.

"Bhai, these are dangerous people. They can go to any limits and can harm you. I am really scared for you, bhai."

Aniruddh was speechless. He did not know how to pacify his sister. It was because of his actions that his family members were targeted. The concomitant feeling of anger and helplessness engulfed him.

"Don't worry about me, dear. I assure you they won't bother you again," said Aniruddh, trying to comfort her. He held her hand reassuringly.

Deepti left the room leaving her brother entangled in a web of thoughts that questioned his stand. And the following night, something happened that forced Aniruddh to make up his mind and send a strong message across.

Aniruddh's father was surfing through the news channels, as Deepti helped her mother with the dinner. Aniruddh was in his room. A car came to a screeching halt outside their two-bedroom government quarter. Aniruddh crawled over the bed to peep out of the window, and to his horror, saw a group of hooligans barging out of the car. The group then hurled stones at their home, and shouted abuses. The vandalism continued for about ten minutes before they left.

The Mishra household was left dazed. Mrs Mishra was in tears as she held Deepti tightly, and cursed Aniruddh for all this. Mishra babu looked at Aniruddh, expecting an answer from him, but he himself was too stunned to comprehend anything. The incident was loud enough to attract the attention of the ever-critical neighbours. The peeping toms had started their analysis.

People in this part of the country generally represent the milder version of India. They are peace-loving, placid souls who are not used to such sudden activity post sunset. Hence, the whole incident came as a rude shock for the Mishra clan. Mrs Mishra even went to the extent of getting Aniruddh to swear on her name to get out of the mess.

Amidst all this, Aniruddh had his answers. He realised that silence was no longer a weapon that he could rely on, especially in a world that didn't hold any moral limits. He understood that it was the weak and the silent that were intimidated. He understood that the game had to be played with equal rules for both the teams. He was scared but his ego wouldn't permit his conscience to reveal his fears.

The next day Aniruddh called up Vishnu and shared the incident with him. He then called up Babula, and directed him to act as per his instructions.

"Remember, I repeat once again, nobody should be hurt," said Aniruddh, stressing on the word 'repeat'.

"Don't worry Aniruddh bhai, I understand," replied Babula.

The next evening Babula came in a bike along with six other boys. Aniruddh and Deepak joined him at a designated point, and they all headed for Niladri Vihar in Chandrasekharpur area. The group then halted outside a two-storey duplex. Babula hinted to one of his boys, who climbed up the boundary walls of the building and reached out for a wire.

"Yes, cut it," said Babula, and his mate cut the wire with pliers.

The group then headed for the building. As they entered the gate, a thin guy walked out and questioned the purpose of their visit and whom they wished to meet.

"Is Debu bhai there? We wanted to meet him?" Deepak asked.

"He is there, but is busy right now. He won't meet anyone, come tomorrow," the guy said petulantly.

"We want to meet him now," said Babula, and he brushed the guy aside.

Five of them barged inside the house, while the rest waited outside. As the group entered, they saw a short man with strands of grey hair. The man was sitting on an easy chair flavoring a drink. Debu Jena was shocked to see the crowd at his place. He looked at the men inside his house and lost his cool.

"Who are you people, how dare you enter my house?" Debu frowned as he rose from his chair aggressively.

Babula pushed him back from his shoulder with enough vigour to force back on his seat. "Hold on Debu bhai, why are you in such a hurry? Let us talk for a moment," said Babula, pushing him further back on the easy chair.

Aniruddh pulled up a chair and sat next to Debu, as Babula asked one of his associates to shut the door.

"There are six guys waiting outside the hostel where your sister lives in Cuttack. She is expected to move out anytime as we speak," said Aniruddh.

"Bastard, don't you dare," warned Debu.

"Hold on, there is more. One of your trucks laden with goods is in the custody of some of my friends. As we speak, they are taking the truck to the outskirts. They are ready with enough petrol, and are waiting for my orders," Aniruddh continued with a torpid face as tranquil as a winter morning.

"Why are you doing all this?" queried Debu, the fear now clearly visible all over his face.

"Look, you try playing games with me, I can play the same game with a 100 friends of mine. Look outside your window. That is the strength behind me," said Aniruddh, taking a chance and playing with Debu's psyche, hoping he wouldn't actually look.

"See, it is better for both of us to keep our differences as far away as possible from our living rooms," said Aniruddh, maintaining the tranquility in his posture and baritone. He conveyed his message in a subtle manner.

Debu was almost on pins and needles. It was too much for him to digest. Debu was the quintessential muscle behind some of the top politicians, and here was a 21-year-old college kid threatening him in his house. In most cases, he was the bully and wasn't used to such bullying around.

The message via Debu Jena passed quite well through the chain. Even Tripathy and Bhumi realised that things had changed. They were not against one hapless individual, but an entire army of students. Aniruddh's real power was the support behind him.

Finally, after three months, the fast-track court gave its judgment in the infamous Valentine's Day incident. Bhumi Mishra and his key associate Pavitra Ransingh were charged with several cases of vandalism and culpable homicide. He and ten other members of his group were sentenced to three years imprisonment.

The judgment was historic and it certainly was a victory for Aniruddh and his group. Rounak D'Souza walked out of the courtroom and hugged Aniruddh. The man was almost in tears when he congratulated him and expressed his gratitude.

"I see a light of hope in you, my son, may god bless you," he remarked as he walked out of the High Court with his daughter.

Aniruddh and Vishnu were surrounded by the media. Although most of the questions were for Aniruddh, Vishnu was the one who answered them, though the cameras certainly knew whom to focus on.

Bhumi Mishra's conviction shook the entire political community. The issue had tarnished the image of the ruling coalition, and the opposition got something to goad the government on. The 21-year-old boy was now the topic of discussion in the political circles of the city.

CHAPTER 9

Aniruddh passed out of SD College and joined university in the subsequent year. Deepak too joined him for Post Graduation in the Political Science stream. Vishnu Pradhan was now out of the university and had initiated a social organisation called the 'Kalinga Youth Social Forum'. Vishnu got a lot of sponsors owing to his family's business and political connections. Aniruddh too was a member of Vishnu's forum. Over the next year, they were involved in a host of youth-related issues. The issues dealt with political and administrative lacunas of the government especially in connection with youth affairs. The organisation also published a journal in the vernacular highlighting various issues in the society. The KYSF, over a period of time, became the most popular non-political youth forum. Their apolitical stance remained unequivocally firm, but the political parties left no stone unturned in appeasing them. Their clout in subjugating the emotions of the blackheads was now gaining momentum like none other.

After the incident of vandalism of their home, Mrs Mishra had Aniruddh swear by her name to stay away from 'netagiri' and student politics. Thus, Aniruddh stayed away from active politics for most part of his university life. He was the most prominent and popular face of the student union, yet he remained apolitical for personal reasons.

Having been born and brought up in the city, his knowledge on the hinterland was limited and surreal. As he got involved with their issues, he was getting enlightened about his own people. The more his horizons extended, the more inquisitive he became. There were several questions that engulfed his young mind. Why did the state remain oblivious to development for a larger part of the post independence period? Why is a large part of the state still devoid of any form of governance? Why is a large part of this mineral rich region swallowed up by acute poverty and lack of opportunities? What is the compulsion that forces people to leave their land and migrate to other states for a livelihood or as bonded labourers?

The questions were serious and compelling enough for Aniruddh to go deep into the roots to find out the cause. He travelled to the most interior parts of the state and met with a variety of people. He had this uncanny knack of instantly connecting with the people. The rawness in his attitude supplemented with a dusty demeanour radiated a certain familiarity in him, and attracted people to him.

It was official now. Odisha was declared as the poorest state for yet another year. The National Statistics claimed so, and almost all the leading tabloids backed it. With the maximum number of people living below the poverty line, the minimum Human Development Index of the coastal state had become a national nightmare. Lack of basic infrastructural amenities, negligible industrial growth, collapsing agricultural production and an abysmal track record in poverty and malnutrition took this coastal province to the rock bottom of the development story that brand India was developing. Incompetent government machinery derailed by the slightest upheavals in the natural discourse of weather only added to the state's misery.

The intellectuals and the idealists hated this underbelly of India called Odisha. The image of skinny bare men sitting next to their malnourished children shattered their 'India Shining' propaganda. Although the story was more or less comparable in many other perpetually neglected parts of the country, it was certainly more comprehensible here. As the nation bloated in the glory of its growth and giant strides, this state made them realise the darker realities of a non-inclusive growth. A nation was reminded of the fact that the economic reforms and the policies have clearly failed to glide beyond the highways.

The developing India conveniently ignored the realities of a major chunk of its population. The affluent India was responsible for creating an exclusive group of angry, neglected and exploited people that rose as a class in itself. The Naxalites were just an insinuation that this class required for propelling its subdued emotions.

The subject is a very insecure and volatile object. It's in the innate nature of man to prefer being subjected to a rule. It makes him feel protected and secured. In a democracy like ours, the rule here is of the state. But when the state fails, the object remains vulnerable and is thus attracted to an alternate system or body that claims to be equally powerful and just in its dealings. Thus, it has to be understood that a community can never exist without the frame of a system of security around it. In the tribal hinterland this ring of security was now provided by the Maoists, simply because the state had failed.

It was rather a horrible fact to digest, that the state with the richest mineral reserves was the poorest in terms of development. Successive governments have to be duly credited for making the impossible look so innate. Ironically, the state's economic surveys published by the state government itself are an eye-opener. If the All India Mineral Resources estimates are to be believed then Odisha contributes 95% of chromite, 94% of nickel, 54% of bauxite, 32% of iron-ore and 25% to the total national reserve. However, if the percentage distribution of the total factory workers is to be considered then it is just 1.77% of the national share, and the gross output in industry is equally abysmal. This clearly underlines the fact that the state hasn't been able to capitalise on its greatest assets – the mineral resources. Industrial output directly links to the fact that not much of investment has been attracted to the state and thus unemployment looms in like a spectre.

The government's claim that the demography here is more agrarian in nature is outwardly supine and unacceptable. The facts from the socio-economic classification of workers clearly indicate the alarming decline in the number of agricultural labourers and cultivators in the state. In the year 1981, 64% of the total working class was in some way or the other related to agriculture or agricultural production. Thanks to the importunate failures of the successive governments, owing to a lack of foresight, the number has come down to 38% in 2005.

Of course, the percentage of employment has certainly increased in the tertiary sector, but that in no way can be credited to the state government. Reasons being, firstly, most of the development in the tertiary or the services sector is an after effect of the overall development in the nation. The percolation of technology irrespective of the regional roadblocks is a major attributer to this phenomenon. So, when one claims that earlier we had only one STD telephone booth in a far-flung corner, and now mobile towers just zoom out of almost everywhere, the credit goes to the telecom revolution in the country and the advent of technology. The state government's role could only be acknowledged with the figures that give us the number of people who have been empowered to take advantage of this technology by virtue of their financial capabilities.

Secondly, the tertiary sector is mostly independent of the state. Private players have actually changed the face of the services sector in India, and hence, the state has absolutely no role in it. The role of the state could have been acknowledged had it created enough opportunities for these private players to sustain themselves here.

One aspect where the government's failure is most evident is in the field of basic infrastructure. From providing basic amenities like health services and drinking water to connectivity, the condition in the state is appalling. After 65 years of independence, only 55% of the villages in the state are electrified whereas most other developed states of the country are on the brink of a cent percent mark. Lack of resources can certainly not be a reason for this debacle in a state that boosts of huge power generation units, and has captive power plants in all the major industries.

The state of primary health services is equally disturbing. Odisha leads the country in malnourishment and infant mortality rate. Abandoned health centres and shortage of staff has compelled the people in the villages to head city ward even for basic health facilities.

So what is it that is pushing this state to the dark ages when the country is heading forward? What is it that makes the richest state in mineral deposit house the maximum number of poor? Who is to be blamed for this misfortune? Is it the state or the people themselves?

The new government had come to power with lot of hope and expectations. The first five-year tenure of the government exposed a lot of chinks in the armour. A green Chief Minister heavily relied upon his imprudent bureaucrats. The bureaucracy in India has historically maintained its asymmetry with the hopes and aspirations of the Indian mass in general. The story in Odisha was no different. To worsen the issue, a quiescent opposition, which struggled mostly with its internal hobnobbing and betrayal, was literally absent. Despicable politics and poor administration ensured that the state remained phobic for industrial houses. Frustrated companies who had already invested at the dawn of the millennium were now distancing themselves.

The bubble had burst. What seemed to be a new ray of hope at the onset of the millennium was slowly turning out to be an equally bungling example of poor leadership. Elections were held in 2004 and the ruling coalition was back in power. The results weren't surprising, considering the fact that the state has a history of re-electing its government until it is eroded by its own mistakes. The most poignant part was that the people who realised this were least bothered, and those to whom it concerned never actually realised that they were constantly being deluded. They never really expected anything more out of their government. So the ruling coalition was enjoying the "prejudice of low expectations" of the people of Odisha.

Meanwhile, Aniruddh was in the final year of his post graduation in the university. The university elections were approaching and the political heat had increased in the campus. With the involvement of the major political parties through organisations like the BBP and NSU, university polls had become another platform for the leading political outfits. The parties went overboard in order to win over the youth.

With Aniruddh's abstinence from student politics, the competition heated up. Both the BBP and the NSU had fielded their candidates. The NSU had Sneha Barik as their candidate. Sneha was a law student and was the daughter of an ex-MLA from the Democratic Congress Party. The BBP had Avinash Dhala as their candidate. Dhala was the son of a businessman and was the quintessential student leader. He was a local but preferred staying at the hostel. Dhala was the self-declared ombudsman of the university. His dominance over the boarders and fear amongst them had made him a popular figure in the campus.

Dhala was taken into custody last year when he ransacked the office of the HOD and threatened to hit him. He claimed that he was fighting for the rights of the students when he went to agitate against the university's refusal to postpone the exams for the fourth time. Dhala did not have the likings for Aniruddh, because he was intimidated by his popularity. Although, Aniruddh did not support any particular candidate, he felt quite strongly against the antics used by Dhala.

It was a Saturday evening. Aniruddh and Deepak were in the hostel premises along with a friend called Amulya. They were busy discussing the upcoming India-Australia Test series when they heard noises from the adjoining rooms. There were a group of boys who had encircled a student and were hitting and abusing at him. As Aniruddh and Deepak rush to check out the incident, they saw a boy lying on the ground with blood oozing out of his mouth and chin roiled.

"You think you could get away with that!?" said one of the boys as he kicked the student on his stomach.

"You do that again and you are dead," threatened another.

As they started dragging him down the stairs, they were interrupted by a voice.

"Hey, stop it, leave him there," said Aniruddh. "What's the issue, what has he done?"

They were eight of them and looked way over their age to be students in the university. Almost all of them sported a beard and held a hockey stick by them.

"Stay out of it, we don't have a problem with anybody else here," warned one of them.

"You already have a problem with us when you entered our hostel and hit a boarder," replied Amulya.

"Do you also want to join your friend?" asked the man.

"Listen, I am telling you for the last time, stop this and leave him," said Aniruddh firmly.

The oldest looking man in the group walked up to Aniruddh with blood shot eyes, pulled out a local made pistol from under his shirt and pushed Aniruddh against the wall. He pointed the pistol at Ani and said, forcefully, "Do you still have a problem, or what?"

Possession of arms and crude weapons in the hostel premises was not a new thing. But a few outsiders entering the hostel and pointing a gun at one of its most popular student was certainly not going to go down easily with the hostelers.

Deepak was furious to see a gun being pointed at Aniruddh. He immediately rushed out to the corridor and called for the others. Amulya peeped out and asked one of the boys in the ground floor to shut the iron gates in order to prevent the intruders from escaping. Within seconds, the whole of hostel No.2 was out with hockey sticks and iron rods. The group of men immediately realised that the situation had gone out of their hands. The man immediately pulled the pistol back from Aniruddh's forehead.

"Look, we don't have anything to do with anybody here. We were here to give a message to this asshole," said one of them in an obvious underplayed tone.

"What message were you delivering him with hockey sticks and iron rods," queried Aniruddh.

"They want me to step down from the contest, they want me to withdraw my nomination for the elections," the boy lying still on the ground till then, suddenly found the strength to rise and speak.

The crowd was stunned to see this lean and hitherto unknown face clarifying himself. He was N Murali, a student of Economics. He belonged to the lesser known southern district of the state. Murali's popularity could be gauged by the fact that people did not even know that there was a third contestant for the post of the student union president. He had drawn the ire of the NSU while he was making an announcement in the university against the threats that he received from the supporters of Sneha Barik.

"So, you beat up this guy mercilessly just because he spoke against your candidate?" asked a furious Aniruddh. He was quite perturbed to see the plight of an unaided Murali.

"Deepak, call the hostel superintendent and the police," said Aniruddh.

"Why call the police, Aniruddh? Let us beat the shit out of these guys and throw them outside the NSU office," said an agitated Amulya.

"No, we have a message to be sent back through these pigs."

"What is it?"

Aniruddh walked close to the guy leading the gang and, looking straight through his eyes, said, "Once you go back, tell your candidate that N Murali will not only contest the elections but will win it also."

The equations in the university elections had completely changed with Aniruddh's involvement in it. While it was indirect, his support for Murali made him the frontrunner in the race. Dhala was particularly annoyed with Aniruddh for his support for Murali. He publicly criticised him, calling him a coward who fires from the shoulders of other people. Sneha Barik sulked internally as she knew the support Aniruddh could garner for Murali. Suddenly, Murali, the otherwise unheard of name, became the most talked about guy in the university.

Vishnu however was not particularly happy with Aniruddh's move. Sneha was a promising candidate and Vishnu backed her because she was involved with the KJYM on various issues. One evening, Vishnu even raised the issue with Aniruddh only to be left embarrassed with his reply.

"You shouldn't have supported that Murali guy," remarked Vishnu. "He is a novice and has hardly shown any interest. I don't think he will be a good leader."

"Hmm...I know that Vishnu, but neither are the other two candidates," replied back Ani.

"But, Sneha has been involved in a lot of social causes and had also displayed her leadership skills many times," countered Vishnu.

"Let's just say I find her attitude to be dangerous. Moreover, if she is actually a leader, then let her win and prove us wrong," shot back Aniruddh.

Vishnu knew that it was virtually impossible for anyone other than Murali to win the elections. The results were predictable but the elections went on to prove a point. Although Murali won the elections convincingly, it was Aniruddh's power to defeat that was acknowledged by all.

In politics, the power to defeat is significantly more important than the power to win. Anyone who possesses the power to defeat is certainly a dangerous player.

CHAPTER 10

———◆———

"So how's your course going on?" queried Aniruddh over his new Nokia 1100. Mobile phones had by then percolated down to the average youth and came as a relief for most long-distance couples.

"It's going fine, but has been pretty hectic over the last few days," replied Radhika, who was now pursuing law at the Symbiosis Society, Pune.

"I am still confused with my choice over the internship issue. Delhi is the place but mom wants me to go Mumbai to her friend's law firm. I am totally confused."

"These are the times when I miss you the most. Especially, when I have to take these confusing decisions. Had you agreed, we could have been together," brooded Radhika.

"Look, we have already discussed this issue over and over again, you know why I ...", Aniruddh was interrupted by Radhika.

"Can I ask you something?"

"What is it?" asked Aniruddh.

"Ani, are you sure of what you are doing?"

"Look, Radhika, like I have always been saying, I really don't know if I am going to go anywhere with this. The important thing is that, I really want to do this. I know it's going to be difficult but I am convinced that I won't quit." There was a sense of conviction in Aniruddh that was difficult for Radhika or anyone else to counter.

"Never mind, Ani, I am sure you will succeed with whatever you do," said Radhika, trying to spice up the mood a bit.

"By the way, there's a girl here, she was asking a lot about you," Radhika said, mischievously deliberating upon the word girl.

"Is it? Who? How does she know me?" queried Aniruddh.

"Some, Sheetal Verma. She claims to be your schoolmate," replied Radhika.

"Oh, Sheetal. Yeah, she was my classmate in school. She was the school prefect. What is she doing there?"

"Mass Communication,"

"The girl seems to be pretty impressed with you," added Radhika.

"C'mon, that is impossible. She used to hate our group."

"Yeah, she never liked your circle of friends, but she certainly was a huge fan of yours," clarified Radhika.

"Is it? What else did she reveal about me?" asked Aniruddh with the excitement quite obvious in his voice.

"Aha! Look at you. Hope you aren't blushing now, huh! Stop giggling now, she also said that you were one of the most boring persons to talk to." Said Radhika, taking a dig at Aniruddh.

"C'mon, Radhika, stop being jealous and be a sport, tell me what else did she say in my praise," he was clearly testing the limits of her tolerance.

"Jealous my foot! You can go to hell with your Sheetal Verma, I don't give a damn," and there she was at her best, as the limit was breached.

"Ok, ok….now stop cursing me. Arrey, I was just kidding with you," Aniruddh now tried to pacify her. These were those old tricks and soft altercations that pleasured couples, which might sound obnoxious to the ultra dynamic love encounters of this generation.

"Hey, there is a call waiting, its Murali, I need to take it," said Aniruddh as he saw the phone blinking with Murali's name on the screen. The timing of the call made it all the more important for Aniruddh to attend it.

"Hey, Murali, what is it?"

"Aniruddh, there is an emergency, you should come here outright," said a trembling voice from the other side.

"Now? Murali, it's midnight. What has happened?" asked Aniruddh.

"Just come over here. I can't explain it to you over the phone. You have to be here to prevent the chaos. Just come fast," said Murali, and he snapped the line.

The urgency in his voice made Aniruddh restless. He knew he had to go, but convincing his parents at this hour could lead to another emergency right at the Mishra household itself. As it is, his mother had emotionally loaded him with promises and rituals to avoid trouble.

"Hey, wake up," Aniruddh whispered into her ears.

Deepti was almost going to scream out of fear when her brother covered her mouth with his hands to prevent the noise from reaching his parents.

"Look, I have to go to the university now. There is some emergency, just handle things over here."

"Bhai, are you crazy? Ma will go mad if she finds out, and she would kill me if she knows that I knew about it," said his scared sister.

"Don't worry, I shall be back before sunrise." He convinced her, and tip toed out through the balcony. As he pushed his bike to the end of the street before starting it, he made a call to Deepak and asked him to come out of his house.

"But, what is it? He must have said something at least," queried Deepak as they drove past the empty by lanes of the city. As they approached the main gate of the university, they encountered an unusual gathering outside the gate. Murali knew who it was, the moment he saw the headlights of the bike approaching the gate. He rushed towards the bike.

"Hey, why have so many students gathered out here, what's wrong?" asked Deepak as the crowd swelled by the minute.

"One of our boys, Sudhansu Ray, from the second year, was hit by the conductor and the driver of a private bus. There was an argument on the discounted fare for university students. The Private Bus Owner's Association had promised the said discount. Off late some bus owners have been denying the concession, completely refuting any such promise made. When Sudhansu argued with them, the feud turned into a duel and they hit him," explained an exasperated Murali.

"So, now what, what do these guys want now?" queried Aniruddh.

"These boys want the bus owner's association to apologise and want to teach them a lesson."

"Now!?" said Aniruddh, making the obvious indication at the absurd time selected for the protest.

"The boys plan to block the National Highway and that bastard Dhala is instigating them to burn a few private buses," Murali's tone clearly reflected his balk for Dhala's agenda.

Aniruddh knew Dhala was a true scalawag and could go to any extent for gaining cheap popularity amongst his mates. Almost 200 students had gathered on the road by then. The number was increasing with every passing minute, and so was the restlessness in them.

It is only about time when a group turns into a crowd and a crowd into a mob. A mob doesn't have a face; neither can you associate it with a leader. It is only a conglomeration of a few angry people insinuated by cynical minds that take advantage of the vulnerability around them. The most dangerous and volatile of these mobs is the one formed of a group of students. Being in a mob not only makes them feel stronger and secured but also gives them the illusion of power.

This was certainly turning out to be one of those moments. Not everyone out there was protesting against the alleged manhandling of their colleague. It is pertinent to understand that when a mob gathers, not everyone always stands for the same cause. Some are out there just to vent out their anger on issues quite disparate to the real cause.

"This is the time to be together friends, time to teach those bus owners a lesson. We shall not let a single bus pass by the highway today. We shall burn any bus trying to do so," announced Dhala, even as he kept insinuating the ever-increasing mob.

"This bastard is trying to take advantage of the anger amongst the boys. Ani, we have to stop him before things go out of our control. The boys are mad. They have seen the badly bruised Sudhansu and are filled with vengeance," a concerned Murali said.

Aniruddh always had had an internal abhorrence towards Dhala and his cynical activities. Be it his protest against the university exams or the vandalism in the Vice Chancellor's office over entry timings in the hostel. His activities made him the object of hatred amongst most right-thinking students. Unfortunately though, he had this ability to influence people for his silly theatrics each time he was up to something. This time though, he was playing with fire. Aniruddh knew that the situation made his interference inevitable.

"Look friends, I feel it won't be the correct way to deal with the situation. We should handle the situation with some maturity. Blocking the highway and damaging buses won't solve our problem. It will rather create a negative perception about the students," spoke Aniruddh, attempting to pacify the mob.

"What are you talking? Do you suggest that we sit quietly like cowards and let the matter go by," queried an agitated student.

"By no means am I saying that we forget the issue. Look we are the victims here, one of our friends has been hit, and hence we have the edge in the issue. By resorting to such means, the real issue might get buried and we shall be blamed of mob violence," clarified Aniruddh, speaking at the top of his voice.

"Aha, here comes the messiah of non-violence. Aniruddh babu, gone are those Gandhian days. Today's world respects and recognises power, a coward has got no value and we are not cowards. Friends, are we cowards?" Dhala cried out loud countering Aniruddh. Dhala knew that Aniruddh could actually pacify the crowd and spoil his plans.

"Listen, if you want to chicken out of this, you are most welcome, but we won't quit like you. Friends, lets move out to the highway and block it, collect as many tree trunks and tyres as you can," added Dhala.

Aniruddh feared the worst as the mob started breaking branches of trees in the campus.

"Listen its 2 am. At this odd hour, all we are going to stop is cargo laden interstate trucks. Poor truck drivers have done no harm to us. We have got no message to deliver to these drivers who have been driving for days together. Blocking the road makes no sense now. By the time the buses – our real targets – are out, we will either be in jail or under detention," Aniruddh made another unsuccessful appeal before the students barged out of the gate and blocked the National Highway No.5.

Dhala kept insinuating the mob as the boys started laying blocks on the road. A few of them stopped the approaching vehicles from a distance. Dhala's plan was now getting clear in Aniruddh's mind. He wanted to manufacture a traffic jam by stopping these trucks, so that by sunrise when the normal traffic is out the blockage would have created havoc all around. He knew by the time the police would react, it would have already created a scene and grabbed the desired attention.

Aniruddh's pleas had thinned out in the emotional outburst, as the perfidious Dhala aptly stroked the raw emotions of the students.

NH5 is one of the busiest highway stretches of the country. It runs through three major states. Entering the state of Odisha from the north it stretches all along its length till Chennai, covering 1533kms. The road is often considered the lifeline of the coast. Choke the highway and you can bring the better half of Odisha into its knees. The fact that the highway runs through a number of cities and hamlets makes it vulnerable to the idiosyncrasies of villages alongside it. People know that the highway is the weakest nerve in the government's anatomy and thus it is the easiest way to get the government's attention. India is not alien to such protests and roadblocks. Considered as the most poignant tool of democracy, protests are a part of our life. The golden quadrilateral, supposed to raise the infrastructural benchmark in the country, often falls prey to such gimmicks.

The highways are modern India's protest ground. A hand in case could be the incidents where a passerby is rammed over by a speeding vehicle or a truck. The incident would spark off immediate protests. The most impromptu action would be to block the highway. Any such incident would easily cause a deadlock for seven to eight hours in its peaceful versions.

A violent turnover of things could result in few vehicles being burnt and innocents being harmed.

While these blocks are cause of inconvenience for some, they turn out to be lucrative for others. An hour-long blockade could actually spruce up the business in the nearby village. Little kids would come out with refreshments and eatables and run along the line of vehicles for those stuck helplessly, with honking needlessly being their only way to vent out the frustration. Some villages would rather come out with innovative ways of earning money. They would allow frisky commuters to use the village roads parallel to the highway in order to skirt through the blocked stretch and instead charge a nominal fee for that. This informal 'road-tax' would cost anything from Rs 40/- to Rs 100/-. An hour of blockade could mean an average collection of Rs 5000/- if only 100 vehicles were to pass through. Did someone say Indians lack entrepreneur skills!

Outside the university, the mob had already started impeding the traffic and intimidating the hesitant drivers of dire consequences. The trucks were coming to a screeching halt with their worn out brakes. The early morning hours are a trucker's favorite time of the day. The truckers try and cover as much mileage as possible in these clear hours.

As the black smoke of the burning rubber tyre went up in the air, one trucker suddenly rushed out of the lane overtaking the one ahead of him. He tried breaking out of the makeshift barricade and speed through the blockade. In his attempt he narrowly missed a couple of students trying to stop him. The daring truck escaped leaving behind an infuriated mob and a helpless queue of people completely ignorant of the cause or outcome of the protests.

"Bastard! These guys don't understand decently, we have to teach them a lesson," howled Jayaram furiously.

"Let us teach them a lesson, now," said another student as he rushed to pick an iron rod. He then ran to the first truck and smashed the windshield. The driver and his helper hardly resisted and jumped out of the vehicle.

To everybody's shock, Jayaram punctured a hole into the fuel tank of the truck with the help of an iron rod. He bottled the dripping diesel from the tank and sprinkled it all over the rear. Jayaram then did what Aniruddh and many in the crowd feared. He threw a burning piece of rubber on the truck and the iron wagon went into flame in an instance. Everything happened so fast that nobody got time to react. As the fire engulfed the truck, it threatened the stranded vehicles behind. Aniruddh realised that the situation had gone out of hands as more students flocked in from the hostel.

It was almost 4 in the morning and the city traffic slowly got out on the highway, only to further extend the kilometer long jam. Gradually, the media also joined in and so did a few police personnel from the nearby police station. The police could do nothing more than join the onlookers and be an audience with a modest wooden staff as their weapon.

Aniruddh and Murali stood helpless as the crowd went on a rampage, damaging the nearby bus stop and breaking a few more window shields. The first victim of any protest in India has historically been the poor public property. Damaging public infrastructure in a country that is famous for lack of infrastructure is like hitting your own leg with an axe.

Meanwhile, the local channels were abuzz with the ongoing vandalism and broadcasted the scenes live from the 'ground zero' as they called it. The administration held an emergency meeting as the Home Minister asked for an immediate update on the situation. The blockade had now stretched for more than six kilometers and had caused severe jam at the Acharya Vihar Square.

Rudra Mohan Tripathy, the Home Minister, had to take a call and he ordered the police to clear the blockade immediately. Minutes after the orders were passed, a police jeep approaching from the wrong side halted at a distance of 100 meters from the University gate. Following the jeep was a bus full of police personnel in anti-riot gear and a fire brigade water truck. The anticipation of a police action to thwart the protests fired up the students even more.

"PLEASE COOPERATE WITH THE POLICE." "PLACE YOUR DEMANDS PEACEFULLY." "OPEN THE NATIONAL HIGHWAY." THIS IS A WARNING."

A policeman blared continuously on the megaphone standing on the top of a bus. The administration thought that the students would immediately surrender after seeing the police's strength. What the administration had thought would frighten the students actually agitated them even more as they openly challenged the police.

The riot police formed columns and were ready for the orders when a white ambassador car emerged from the rear and halted ahead of the bus, An officer with a peak cap and a baton in his hand stepped out from the car. It was the city SP, Satyabrata Panda.

Panda was the quintessential no nonsense police officer. His reputation as the tough guy had made him an expert in these situations. Panda rose to fame when he controlled the infamous bootlegging business in Cuttack and brought many a powerful names behind the bar. He has however been under constant criticism for his unconventional and ruthless approach on many occasions. Known to be a close confidante of the minister, Panda was recently posted to the capital city. Many believed it was an attempt to bail him out of a serious human right violation charge against him during his tenure as the SP of a Naxal-affected district. Although, Panda's efficiency and honesty were unquestionable, his means were often subject to serious controversy.

"Look, Dhala, we have sent the message we wanted to. Now lets us stop all this before things go out of our hands," said Murali.

"He he...President babu, what has scared you. Has the sight of the police made you wet your pants?" Dhala rebutted, making no signs of a withdrawal.

"Bastard, you are a slimy guy, you know very well what can happen over here," said Deepak, catching hold of Dhala's collar.

Aniruddh immediately butted in and pulled Deepak back. He knew that a fight between the students could only worsen the situation.

"They have hit our brother and now they threaten us with police force and you want us to run away," screamed Dhala, ensuring that he was audible to those around him. "Moreover, I am not controlling the crowd here. Why do you tell me, they are on their own."

Aniruddh knew it for sure that Dhala would flee off the minute he smelt danger, leaving behind these emotional fools.

"Its too late now," said Murali as he noticed the riot police marching ahead in a column for what seemed like a possible crackdown.

"Panda isn't the one to let it go off easily, he is going to crack down," said Deepak as the column of 12 policemen approached the mob with green helmets on their head and wooden shields in their hand.

As the policemen closed in, someone from the crowd flunged a beer bottle at them. This was the moment Panda was waiting for. He wanted the crowd to do something silly so that he could justify the use of force against them. The bottle did not hit anyone but landed right next to Panda. The police got its cue as they barged in to the crowd. Unfortunately, for Murali, he was standing amongst the front liners still believing that he could convince the police to step back.

Murali fell on the crowd becoming the victim to the first few blows of the police. The sight of their Union President being hit by the police further annoyed the students as they too charged towards the policemen. Things came down to hand-to-hand fights.

"You hit our President, you hit the Student union president," said one boy as he flung another bottle at the police. This one went for Panda's car and dented his bumper. It was 6.30am in the morning and the city was wide awake. Onlookers gathered around the protest site to get a glimpse of the student-police tussle. They saw the police being outnumbered by the students. This was way too much for Panda's reputation.

The Mishra household also woke up to the nerve wrecking visuals of the mayhem outside the university and their missing son. Mrs Mishra was in tears the moment she saw the police barging in the second time towards the students and striking blows on few of them. Mishra babu was silent, but his torpid face reflected every bit of a father that was praying for his son. This time the students would retaliate with something the police had not thought of. Someone from the crowd pulled out a local made revolver and fired a shot in the air. There was a sudden chaos as the police immediately retreated back behind their vehicles. Panda was shocked by this reaction as he was rushed behind to cover and the Personal Security staff surrounded him instantly.

Protests and agitations by students were not completely new to the place, but having been fired upon was something really unusual. Though nobody could trace out the firer, Aniruddh and Murali were completely stunned with the sudden action. There was a moment of stoic impassiveness in the crowd as the students waited for a while to comprehend what had happened.

Panda spoke over the phone for a while and emerged from the rear of his car with his bulletproof vest on. He then passed on some orders and almost instantly a group of men emerged out of the bus with their .303 standard issue rifles. The crowd and the onlookers thought that it was an attempt to create a sense of fear amongst the students, until the armed policemen came to firing positions.

Ten armed policemen came ahead and cocked their vintage .303 rifles as the crowd stood awestruck. May be the students were oblivious of the pre-firing procedures and anticipated it as another of Panda's stunts to frighten them off. They would soon realise how utterly wrong they were about Panda's intentions.

"Fire," ordered Panda as the sound of 10 rifles firing together stunned the autumn morning. There was a deathly silence in the air around, disturbed only by the three policemen still struggling with their cocking handles as their rifles had betrayed them. The crowd took moments to realise that they were being fired upon.

The feeling of being fired upon is one that cannot be described in mere words. The bullet is a seemingly insignificant piece of iron that can be highly underestimated by a novice. The fact that a 9mm round can pierce into the human body and cause fatal consequences cannot be easily perceived. The moment a round is fired upon, the most instant reaction is that of closing one's eyes and holding on to the breathe in an attempt to avoid the pain, if hit. The moment you open your eye and realise that the bullet has missed you, there is a huge sigh of relief. Moments later you find someone in the crowd lying on the ground roiled in his own pool of blood and screaming out in pain. You notice the small hole punched in by the same 9mm round that you had underestimated and pound of flesh oozing out from the place where the bullet has exited the body. That is the moment you remember your gods and thank your stars. Your lips dry and your palms sweat. There is a chilling sensation that runs down your spine. From that moment on, you respect the power of a gun and a 9mm chunk of iron.

There was a strange silence in the atmosphere. The barrels of the guns were still smoking. The crowd froze with disbelief. A young man in his early 20's was lying on the ground daubed in his own blood, yards away from another body lying in a similar state. While one lay completely stoic, the other made uncomfortable moves trying to reach for his neck where the bullet had made a deep wound before making its way out.

CHAPTER 11

It was half past noon, and the air felt warmer than usual. The Capital Hospital was abnormally crowded. Journalists, policemen, political leaders and students thronged the hospital premises and the area leading up to its main gate. The city's largest government health centre was no alien to chaos, but today was an unusual day, with thousands of university kids gathering outside the hospital premises, waiting for news on the status of two fellow students fighting for their lives. The administration was nervous like never before. They knew that the situation was extremely fluid, and that it could turn ugly at any moment. The last time such a thing had happened was during the Mandal Commission agitation, when 14 students lost their lives and three policemen were killed in a violent protest.

"Ashis Samal is the one undergoing the operation," the ASI informed the IG, Law and Order, who had rushed to the hospital.

"And who is the deceased?"

"Sir, he is N Murali, apparently the Student Union President," replied the Sub Inspector, with fear evident on his face."Ashis is the son of Debaraj Samal, a textile owner from Sambalpur, and Murali is the son of N Nageshwar, a farmer from Gajapati district."

Sensing the urgency, the Khurda district collector had rushed immediately to the hospital. The fourth battalion of the Odisha State Armed Police was asked to move to the city with immediate effect. The RAF was requisitioned, and kept on standby.

"Sir, the NH is still blocked, although we have started diverting the traffic from Acharya Vihar and Khadagiri square," briefed another officer in khaki. "It will still take almost four hours to clear the complete jam. The road leading to the university has been cordoned off, but it is almost impossible to stop the students."

The wooden door with red and green lights on top matched the typical Operation Theatre that is seen in movies. This was where one of the students was being operated. Outside the OT, on a wooden bench with folded hands, were Amulya and Deepak. Aniruddh placed his hand on the arm of the bench and was staring outside. There were a series of disturbing thoughts that ran through his mind.

Why did it happen? Had he stopped the mob, two precious lives would have been saved. Is he to be blamed for having pushed the poor Murali into all this? These were the questions that nagged at Aniruddh.

There were many questions that he had no answers for. He knew some of these questions would never find their answers. He also knew that this was no time to ponder for answers. It was time to react. Soon, the city would witness the repercussions of the incident. The entire university would be on the streets, desperate to avenge the death of their Union President.

Aniruddh never wanted all this to happen, but now there was no choice. He had to choose between the devil and the deep sea. He felt miserable, because he was among the few who knew that Murali wanted to prevent all this.

"They shouldn't have fired, it was unprovoked," said a feeble and an unfamiliar old voice approaching from corridor. The man used a walking stick and wore a white dhoti and kurta. His thick black-framed glasses covered most of his face.

"Have their parents been informed?" the man, who seemed in his late 70s, questioned as the young boys continued giving him strange looks.

"What an absolute waste of two young lives. We shall never learn the value of human life. This too shall be forgotten like any other incident in the past," the man said, continuing his monologue even as he took out his specs and occupied the wooden bench placed across the corridor. He spoke with unusually long pauses.

"One is still alive, he is being operated. Please correct yourself before shooting off the hook," Deepak responded, irritably.

"He died the moment you got him here," replied the old man with a strange, stoic face. "The administration has asked the hospital staff to cloak the news till such time they are prepared for the consequences."

The three boys looked at each other, confused and puzzled. They were caught in a moment of emotional vacuum, where they had so much to express and so little to tell.

"Who are you?" queried Amulya, still uncomfortable with the presence of the old man.

"I am Basudev Acharya, an ageing journalist and an active student of politics. These days I spend most of my time studying the 'state of my state' and crying over its grave. I have been in the thick of a lot of important events that shaped the state right from the so-called 'independence'."

"So what brings you here, sir? Is it politics or do you find a sensational story in this?" Aniruddh shot back, with obvious signs of frustration on his face.

The old man bore a smile of composure as he replied. "Like I said, I am not into politics, and I have left my journalism way behind."

"So what brings you here, sir? The real drama is going on downstairs. All the new possibilities and theatrics are being cooked down there. Haven't you seen those desperate faces waiting, eager to hear the news of the death of these guys? Every opportunist asshole is huddled up down there waiting to scavenge over the deaths of two innocent young men," said Aniruddh as tears streamed down his face. "Aren't we experts in making martyrs out of dead men? The fact that one of them actually died while trying to prevent the mayhem will never see daylight. The fact that two families will forever regret having sent their kids away from them in quest of better education … it will all remain confined to the four walls of these two houses."

"So what is your stake in this entire event, sir?" Aniruddh pointedly asked as he wiped the tears off his face.

"Hmm… son, I am too old to look for a stake amidst despair," the old man replied. "I lost all my stakes a long while ago. I have seen through a lot, and my heart is the poor witness, not only to personal miseries but also to the wounds that this state has been subjected to."

The old man stood up, and continued: "I have seen and suffered more than you can ever imagine, my son. Anyway, coming back to what you had mentioned a while ago so passionately. You were right. You were right when you said we make martyrs out of poor, dead people."

The aged stranger paused for a while, and walked to the nearest window.

"Do you see that crowd outside the hospital gate?" he said, gesturing towards the huge gathering of students outside the premises. "For most, it is a dangerous sight. Nothing ignites the youth more than the death of fellow student, especially under such circumstances. And nothing is more powerful than a student group led by an able leader. Those standing out there, they do not seek or expect to gain anything out of this, but answers and justice for their friend.

"The people who have gathered downstairs, with their multiple goals and cynical agendas are vouching for this crowd to do something silly. They are soon going to be used as a tool for a greater and a far murkier political battle," said the old man, looking straight at Aniruddh.

"Sir, we respect your age, but please. We are in no mood for sermons now," said Deepak, shooting an indirect warning to the old man.

"What do you want us to do?" asked Aniruddh, maintaining the intense eye contact. Aniruddh sensed the stranger had more meaning hidden in his words than he had actually conveyed.

"Go out there and be the leader they are looking for," the old man replied, stating his thoughts as bluntly as he could.

"But sir, for your information, none of us supported what happened in the morning," Aniruddh countered. "We were there on Murali's request, to advice the crowd and prevent any mishap. I did not support the events in the morning, and now you ask me to lead a similar crowd to a similar set of events?

"I can't stand on the dead bodies of my friends and claim my leadership, sir. I can't make the death of my friends an opportunity to project my leadership."

"If you won't, somebody else will. Moreover, every protest need not be violent and meet the same consequence," the old man explained. "Thus, it is more important for someone like you, who understands the value of peaceful protests, to lead these young boys and girls rather than someone who uses them to score political gains."

Basudev Acharya walked up to Aniruddh and placed an arm over his shoulder. "Son, history has been kind to people who have respected the importance of time," he continued explaining. "Leaders aren't born out of deliberate selection; leaders are a consequence of circumstances that demand leadership. One who understands his role, takes it up. And one who hesitates, repents throughout.

"Look, whatever has been the cause of the protests has already been eclipsed by the consequence. As of now, the consequence itself has become the reason. If you don't lead them today, chances are they will get deluded by someone with more cynical plans. Life isn't very forgiving, son. To live a life with the guilt of not doing something when you could is far more painful than death itself."

Basudev Acharya sounded more meaningful now. Aniruddh looked at the crowd, and each word uttered by the old man pierced through his heart and knocked on his conscience over and over again. A barrage of questions filled his mind: Won't he be called an opportunist? Isn't he cheating his own scruples? Will the crowd accept him?

"Can I ask you something, sir?" said Aniruddh, looking at the old man who by now had started walking down the hospital stairs.

"Yes."

"Why did you come to me?"

"Hmm…well, I don't know exactly. But maybe history will be grateful to me someday for this gesture of mine. Son, moments like these do not always find itself in need of someone – there are a lot many out there eager to fill the void."

And with that, the old man walked away, leaving a huge dent in Aniruddh's young mind.

CHAPTER 12

———⟨◈⟩———

A young man walked out of the hospital entrance in a blood-stained shirt and moist eyes. It had started to drizzle as Aniruddh walked out of the main gate and stood in front of the thousand-plus crowd. His demeanour expressed much more than words ever could. He wasn't prepared for a speech, but each one standing out there expected him to. Yes, they were desperately waiting to be led.

"There are two dead bodies lying inside the hospital now, wrapped in white sheets and a helpless mother crying next to one of them," started Aniruddh, from the top of the boundary wall. "The doctors have declared them medically dead, their bodies are being taken for post-mortem. Once the post-mortem is over we shall cremate them, and soon the government will fix a price on their lives and announce compensation. The incident will be forgotten and we all will return to our miserable, self-centred lives. At the most, the government will order a toothless judicial enquiry into the incident, and all responsible shall be acquitted. Days will pass and the incident will be registered in the annals of history as an unfortunate event that took two innocent lives."

Aniruddh was fervid as he spoke, with lashes of rain falling on his face. There was a frightening silence that engulfed the gathering each time he took a pause.

"Life doesn't stop with the death of two people. We all, too, shall succumb to the indiscriminate pace of time and circumstances, like we have always done. Actually, we all are so true to our genes. We can talk of justice, beg for justice, plead for justice, but can never fight for justice. How can we betray our inheritance? After all we are the sprouts of a generation that prefers to live with its eyes, ears and mouth shut perennially!"

Aniruddh, like many in the crowd, was slowly getting drenched, not just with the rain, but also with an underlying sense of resurrection.

"But I won't!" he went on. "I can't inherit a legacy that expects me to surrender my dignity, and be incarcerated to an idea that makes me perpetually malleable. I would rather die a coward. I can't live with the guilt of silently mourning the murder of my friends, and forge it on the 13th day. I can't pretend to be dead when there's blood gushing in my veins. I can't turn my back to the sacrifice of my mates."

Listening to him, Deepak was convinced that his friend was at his best.

Aniruddh raged on: "I don't know how many will stand by me on this. But, if required, I shall stand all alone. The bodies shall not be cremated till such time the government acknowledges the sacrifice of our friends, and honours their death by fulfilling our demands. And for the record, Murali was there to stop the mob and not be a part of it. He died the death of a true leader."

The crowd stood still for a moment. And then, they suddenly burst into applause, and shouted slogans in favour of the call made by their new leader.

Aniruddh Mishra was accepted.

The most challenging moments for a leader is when he is accepted by the people – when people surrender their thoughts and actions to the wisdom and leadership of one man, when they troth their conscience to the morality of their leader.

Aniruddh walked back to the hospital with a skittish mind and a confused heart, oblivious to the effect he just had on tensile young minds. His close associates were with him. Vishnu soon joined him at the hospital.

"I have decided that we must sit on protest till our demands are fulfilled," said Aniruddh as he looked at Vishnu.

"Have you decided on the demands yet?" queried Vishnu.

"Yes, we shall demand for justice for Murali and Ashis," said Aniruddh. "We shall demand action against the people responsible for using brute force against a student's agitation."

"The government will suspend Panda and try to douse the matter. The orders came directly from the Home Ministry," butted in Deepak.

"No, we won't settle for Panda. We shall call for Rudra Mohan's head," said Aniruddh, walking closer to the dead bodies.

"Where are the dead bodies being taken?" Aniruddh furiously asked the ward boys, who were pushing the stretchers in the corridor.

"They are being taken for post-mortem," replied a policeman who was escorting the bodies.

"You try and move those bodies an inch and I swear you will be responsible for handling the anger of those thousands waiting outside," Aniruddh warned the policeman.

"What? Now are you trying to be the next '*neta*'? Do you also want to lie on the same stretcher," the snarky police constable replied.

"Kailash, leave the dead bodies," a senior police officer ordered as he walked in, quickly realising what was at stake.

"What do you want?" the officer asked Aniruddh as he walked towards him.

"The bodies won't be cremated until the government fulfills our demands," said Aniruddh.

"What are your demands?"

"Don't worry, sir, you shall get to know them soon."

The Unit-6 ground, located right next to the hospital, was the ideal location for the remonstration.

"Aniruddh, Samal's family is here and they want to get over with the rituals as soon as possible," informed a friend.

"What about Murali's family?" asked Aniruddh.

"I don't think there is anybody here, except for his cousin, Harish."

"Where is Samal's family?"

As he entered the visitor's waiting hall, Aniruddh's energy crumbled at the sight of a grieving mother and sister. But he somehow gathered the courage to walk up to Ashis's father and speak to him. Although his father was visibly calm and had held back his tears, the despondency of a man who had just lost his young son was evident under the façade that he bore. The very thought that he had to light up the mortal remains of a body that he had nurtured and groomed from its inception itself was distressing.

"Bapa re (my dear son), this grief is more than what we can handle. We are in no mental state to enter into anything that could only amplify our agony," said Ashis's father, who wanted to cremate the body as soon as possible and do away with the pain that the sight of a dead son covered in blood brought with it.

"Son, we are poor people. We can do nothing but mourn over the incident as a painful gift of destiny. Please, I request you to allow us to complete the last rites and leave this place as soon as possible," said Mr Samal, his hands folded and eyes wet.

"I know I can never understand and feel the pain that you are going through," replied Aniruddh. "Our losses are nothing in comparison to what you have lost. But believe me, your son died in these very arms of mine.

He closed his eyes on me and I won't let his death go in vain. The bodies will be cremated as and when you want them to be. You have the greatest right over them.

"But please allow us to pay them the respect they deserve. Please let us honour their sacrifice. They stood for a cause and died fighting for it. They can rest in peace only if their death justifies their fight," continued Anirudddh till he convinced the family.

The stage was set for the drama and the script ready. It was action time, as the entire administration sat holding its breath. It was a student agitation after a long time, in the state, and the police was convinced of their abilities in dealing with such a situation.

CHAPTER 13

"This isn't going to be easy, Das babu," said a visibly worried Home Secretary to the DG, Police during the weekly conference. "Look at the number of students that have gathered. It is making me nervous. Panda has shaken a bee-hive that is about to go berserk."

"Don't worry sir, we can handle it," replied the DGP, trying to assure his boss. "I have briefed the force and they know when to hit the knockout punch. We just have to nail the leaders."

"Sir, Panda cannot be blamed for this. He acted upon the orders of the Minister," added the senior most police officer of the state, defending one of his own.

"We all know how it works Mr Das, and you are no amateur in this business. Politics cannot decide the outcome of a law and order situation," the secretary replied, in a tone befitting the seasoned bureaucrat that he was.

The secretary was referring to the widening political rift between the coalition partners that had once come together to form the government. The dream coalition was going through something of a jaundice owing to their differences about seat-sharing in the upcoming elections. The Home Minister, Rudra Mohan Tripathy, was clearly the most influential leader of the second largest party of the state, and commanded huge support in the coastal belt.

"The CM would like this to end as soon as possible," added a man in his mid 40s, sitting next to the DG, Police. He was the Jt Secretary, Home. "You know how jittery he gets when it comes to issues of law and order. In fact, he is not very happy with the way things have been handled."

"You must be prepared. Some heads might have to roll down the hierarchy, and Panda looks the obvious one to me," cautioned the Secretary.

"Huh? But the students made it clear that they wouldn't settle for anything less than the Minister's scalp," said Das cynically.

"I don't think the CM would even think of walking that lane, considering the mutable political equation in the state," the Secretary replied.

"But Panda is one of the best we have. It will leave the department demoralised," said the DG, looking almost as if he was ready to plead for mercy. "The recent Naxal attacks have already pulled them down."

Yes, the bureaucracy is insulated. So it is almost programmed in a way that the police eventually would have to bear the brunt of any political or administrative gaffe.

"When Caesar is being killed, you need to take sides, Das babu. It's either Marc Anthony or Brutus. More than anyone, Panda should have known this. After all, he was the blue-eyed one of the minister," the sultry bureaucrat said, knowing exactly where to pin his words.

-----xx-----

"Sir, sir, what are your comments on the University firing incident, in which two students were killed by the police?"

"Sir, can the government stay numb to this police brutality or was this truly done on the orders of the Home Minister?"

A horde of journalists swarmed the CM as he made his way out of the assembly. Although he avoided the media – his security kept them at bay – he knew this one was going to be there like an Albatross around his neck. He moved ahead with his peculiar, synthetic smile and gallingly boorish demeanour. It was his trademark style. Being rude and disconnected was the secret of his survival – the more inaccessible you are, the more they want to approach you. The more you behave like a king, the more servitude they owe you. Yes, such has been the effect of two hundred years of Imperial rule.

We love to be ruled. Period.

-----x-----

"Do you even check your cell phone? I don't even know why you carry one in your pocket!" screamed a concerned girl, as Aniruddh apologetically listened over the phone.

"I saw your calls, but I couldn't take them. Believe me, things were a bit rough here. Look, do you know there has been an unfortunate incident… "Aniruddh replied, but was cut short by Radhika.

"What do you mean *do* I know? It's all over the news. I even saw you on the television. Couldn't you just say that you were fine!? I was calling every damn person here, like an idiot," she went on, as Aniruddh listened quietly atop a stage at the protest site. The stage had been set up overnight, thanks to Vishnu.

"I am sorry, Radhika, things went out of control in seconds. And before I knew it, I had a friend dying in my arms while the other was struggling for his life."

"I just hope you know what you are getting into, Ani. Are you sure you can handle this? asked Radhika, with the concern in her voice coming through.

"I mean, you are trying to take them head on. This might turn out to be pretty ugly, it might ignite beyond control."

She was miles away from the Unit-6 ground, where Aniruddh and his friends were gearing up for their showdown with the government. But Radhika's concerns were genuine. She knew him well to understand his role in any such event.

'Fighting them is not my concern. It's the 'me' within I am worried about. There are a lot of questions that I am yet to answer myself. The most relevant of them being the haunting dilemma of staging a political orchestra with the dead as instruments….' how Aniruddh wished he could say these words to her.

-----xx-----

"Arey Deepak, what is it? What's the chaos near the gate?" asked an exasperated Aniruddh as a commotion interrupted his conversation with Vishnu.

"The boys are shooing away the workers of the Nationalist Youth Party," Deepak replied. "The *khadi* has come to remorse the act of the *khaki*. They are here to "express their support" for our cause."

The NYP was the youth wing of a National Party that was trying to establish its presence in the state.

"Keep them off, or else our stage will soon be hijacked by these bugs," said Vishnu.

"What time are you speaking?"

"3pm. The crowd would have gathered by then? Has the CM given a reaction yet?" Aniruddh answered with a question.

"No, nothing yet. Make it 5pm. The CM is expected to speak by four, so you will have something to counter and the crowd will be more once the mercury comes down," Vishnu suggested.

It was 10 past five in the evening. The CM had given a rather torpid response to the issue. Aniruddh had spoken for almost ten minutes, and the crowd had begun gaining momentum as the news spread. Around 5000 students had already gathered at the protest site. The two deceased bodies were kept on the stage, medically preserved and stored under glass coffins loaded with flowers. A handful of journalists roamed the site, taking bytes from the crowd.

"...our demands are simple, clear and justified. We are not standing here with a begging bowl in our hands, neither do we intend to make this a political issue. We are only demanding justice. Justice for two innocent young lives that were taken away by sheer brutality and imprudent use of force. Firstly, the man responsible for ordering this use of force has to quit. And it is not the SP. It is the Minister who is primarily responsible. The Home Minister has to quit.

"Secondly, the families must get a respectful compensation for their losses.

"And thirdly, the government must immediately order for student concessions on all public and private transport systems within the state."

Aniruddh concluded amidst huge applause and cheers. The third demand was deliberately placed to extend the boundaries of the protests across the state.

As far as the government was concerned, the second and the third demands were not a problem. It was the resignation of the Home Minister that actually split the political sorority in two distinct halves. While the majority party was furtively pushing for the resignation, the coalition partner was not ready to budge under any circumstance. After all, the Home Minister was the second most powerful political position in the state. Normally, an agitation would have lasted its usual course and had a predictable climax, with the suspension of some administrative pawns. The political clan would easily sneak out, having offered the bureaucracy to take the blame for them.

But this agitation was shaping up in a different flavour. The upcoming assembly elections and the growing rift in the coalition had further opened an already scathing wound. This was a masterstroke, way beyond the political intelligence of a 24-year-old university kid.

"Now that the demands are made, make sure the noise gets heard," said an elderly voice over the phone, as Aniruddh listened carefully. "They will react only when it starts hurting them. Get the media, get the eyeballs and get the sympathy,"

"Do you think they will react?" asked Aniruddh.

"They will, if they know the dangers of nurturing a cancer in the body. You just stick to your stand and keep the stack together."

The agitation had reached its third day and the protests were gaining momentum. Almost all the colleges in the city were closed, and students had turned up in huge numbers. The national media was slowly getting interested in this laidback coastal state. However, the government was yet to react.

Aniruddh realised it was time to increase the decibels.

"The Assembly session is to begin the day after," said Aniruddh. "I guess it is time to move out to the streets. Let's stage a protest rally to the Assembly and then to the CM's residence. I shall make the announcement now."

"Spread the word in other cities and in the media," he added, looking at Deepak and Vishnu.

"Can the word spread around in such a short notice? I mean, we don't have time to gather the crowd and neither do we have the resources to publicise the event," said a concerned Deepak.

"Don't worry, we don't have to. The media will do that for us," replied Vishnu.

"But why would they?" Deepak asked.

"Leave that to me," said Vishnu, and pulled out his cell phone.

"Mandal bhai, namaskar," he greeted someone over the phone.

"All well. I need you to do me a favour."

"Can you send a team immediately over to the SDM's office? I promise you will have something important to cover," Vishnu requested.

"Thank you, Mandal bhai," he said, and snapped the call with a smirk on his face.

Soon after, a group of 15 students led by Deepak and Vishnu gathered outside the SDM's office with banners and chant slogans. The officials inside looked as confused as the passersby. The SDM himself was clueless, and was forced to enquire.

A field crew of one of the leading regional dailies reached the spot and was soon joined by a host of others.

"What is this about?" the SDM enquired.

"They are protesting against the alleged denial of permission by the SDM to the students, for holding a peaceful protest rally against the death of two students the other day," an officer replied.

"But the file never came to me. Why wasn't the request put through to me?"

"They never came up with any such request, sir."

The crowd increased, and so did the media. The SDM was being pulled up by the government for apparently no fault of his, and the proposed rally got all the coverage they needed.

Selling news is like feeding fish – all you need to do is throw one bite in front of a fish.

The worst fears of the administration were fast becoming a reality. Students were on the streets of the capital city on a day when the assembly was in session. The senior officials were overtly nervous, having been advised to maintain restraint at all cost.

-----xx-----

CABINET MEETING: 6.30pm

"Why should I resign? Arey, there has to be some basis for a resignation," the tone indicated all too clearly to the personality that Rudra Mohan Tripathy was. A political warhorse and a six time MLA, he knew the rules of the game in Indian politics – innocent until proven otherwise.

"Rudra babu, the situation is very delicate now," said Narayan Sahu, a senior member and a minister in the government. "The opposition has already started targeting us in various forums. The pressure is just going to increase on the government. You still haven't given an official explanation on the issue."

"Let the opposition say whatever they want," replied the adamant old politician. "I won't react to a few barking dogs on the street."

"These dogs may soon hound you Tripathy babu. They may turn dangerous anytime," warned Narayan.

"Would the CM have resigned if they had asked for it?" questioned Tripathy babu, and that brought the heated debate into a state of deathly silence.

The CM looked up for a moment and just walked off from the meeting, leaving space for astute speculation behind him. Perhaps he could foresee the unforeseen. Perhaps he could see the logical end to this perplexity.

Perhaps he realised that one should not stop a man when he is so rigid on the path of self-destruction.

-----xx-----

The city woke up to a sunny morning. Most of the schools and colleges were shut in anticipation of the chaos on the streets. The rally had received wide publicity, thanks to the media. The roads leading up to the citadels of power and the residences of those who wielded the power were infested by men in *khaki*. The protest site at Unit 6 was already abuzz with a crowd of 6000 young souls. Similar rallies were planned and organised in many other cities of the state. The JNU also did its part by staging a dharna outside Odisha Bhavan in New Delhi.

As the march to the Assembly began, in the lead was a truck loaded with marigold, carrying the dead bodies of the two deceased students. The otherwise dormant city was alien to such political activism since the Mandal riots. Most government officials preferred staying home and cherish the additional holiday they got.

Moreover, the city was a true blood reflection of an indifferent population, amenable to anything forced upon them in the guise of governance and administration. This state, and its people,would forever remain the last symbol of the 'oppressed class', of the British or the Zamindars or the politicians in contemporary India.

The numbers grew exponentially with each passing hour. The hierarchy of the police department began getting nervous as they closed in towards the assembly. The officials decided to hold the protesters a kilometre short of the assembly, and prevent them from getting any closer. The DG even envisaged the idea of a quick evacuation plan of the 'honourable members', if need be. There was a strong undercurrent running amid the otherwise peaceful march. The sheer numbers were intimidating.

"20,000, atleast. And they are still joining," Deepak informed Aniruddh, with a triumphant smile on his face. "People have come from all over the state."

"Any news from the inside?" Aniruddh asked.

"Nothing yet. But the debate is heating up, and the opposition has disrupted proceedings since morning. The CM is in the back foot, for sure," replied Vishnu, before saying:

"I thinks its time."

"Yes. Tell the boys." Aniruddh agreed.

Moments later, a group of young college boys started booing and abusing a group of OSAP personnel standing on the other side of the fence. Initially, the men ignored them, but as the cat-calling and the abusing increased, they became agitated, and warned the boys. In a matter of seconds the altercation turned ugly, as the armed personnel began intimidating the boys.

Now, their worst fears were coming true – a direct conflict between the police and the protesters. The officials in the administration were successful, till then, in avoiding this confrontation because they knew very well that the consequences would be beyond their control. The place soon replicated a battlefield with stones being thrown and sticks being wielded. The situation was getting out of control. The CM was immediately informed and so was the Home Minister.

The media covered the event live and was ruthless with their criticism of the government's handling of the situation. In just under an hour, the pressure on Rudra Mohan became unbearable and soon, the party high command from Delhi had to boot him out on the CM's urgent request. He was depicted as the biggest threat to the coalition's image.

It was half past six in the evening. The CM went on air to release his first statement after the fresh clashes. His initial reluctance to a media brief was kept aside as he was advised by his confidants to come out openly in this issue and express his concerns. This was exactly what Aniruddh had planned for. He wanted the people of the state to know that the issue perturbed the CM. This only reflected his weakness, which he was hiding all along by remaining elusive.

"I strongly condemn the killing of the two innocent young boys in the university firing incident," he said in his Victorian accent that revealed his pedigree.

"I share the grief of the parents of the deceased kids. We can understand their sorrow and we stand by them in this difficult moment. We have decided to honour the parents by contributing a little monetary compensation, which can easily be silhouetted by the huge loss that they had undergone. An amount of Rs 10 lakhs each shall be given as compensation.

"I also take this opportunity to inform the youth of the state that my government has always prioritised the concerns and issues of the youth. Thus, we do acknowledge that their demand for a concession shall be considered, and suitable arrangements will be made within the shortest possible timeframe. The transport department is already on task. I further urge the students to return back to their classrooms and help us maintain peace on the streets. Thank you."

"Sir, what about the Home Minister? What about actions against the erring police officials?"

The CM had left with many unanswered questions. An hour later, TV channels broke the news of Rudra Mohan's resignation, and the transfer of Satyabrata Panda.

"I have submitted my resignation to the CM and the Governor on moral grounds, as long as the enquiry reports acquit me of the charges," said Tripathy in his parting comments.

Tripathy's resignation shook the entire political fraternity of the state. As one section of the government felt victimised, the other was jubilant. Tripathy was the second most powerful man in the state, and his presence was certainly a threat to the CM.

The Unit-6 ground bore a blithesome mood. Mr Samal hugged Gaurav as he lost control over his emotions, and tears rolled down his cheek. The crowd was ecstatic with joy. A sense of victory prevailed in every mind. The victory of the symbolically weak public over the goliath government – it was not often heard of. The very fact that a 24-year-old had taken the government by a storm, and had shaken the political equation of the state was itself a feat worth cherishing for the ever-victimised masses.

CHAPTER 14

———◆———

"Have you started smoking?" Radhika was back from Pune for her holidays after the end of the third semester.

"No, but why do you ask?"

"Your lips have turned black," back came the reply at the end of a long kiss.

"C'mon, they were always like this," Aniruddh tried hard to rub the permanent stains of tar by running his tongue over them. But, then the i-know-it-all look from Radhika made him confess gently.

"Okay, an occasional puff, sometimes," admitted Aniruddh candidly.

Men, however strong, have this self-restraining mentality, where in they love to surrender to someone and women know how to get them on their knees. History is witness to such obvious surrender by strong and influential men all the time. Maybe women are god's natural bridle tied to a man.

"Anyways, what are your plans, you said you wanted to go to Delhi after your course," asked Aniruddh desperately trying to avoid the previous topic.

"Yes, I wanted to practice criminal law and Delhi is the most obvious choice for that, but Mom wants me, back here. She insists, I practice in Odisha, so I am confused," said Radhika as Aniruddh watched her struggle with her entangled strands of partially curled hair.

"What do you say?" bang came the question before Aniruddh could actually recall back her last statement.

"Hmm…well I don't disagree completely with your mother, I think this would be a better place for you. Look, here you know people and so, getting a platform won't be difficult. Every Tom, Dick and Harry with a degree in law and a black suit would be heading to Delhi. I am sure even you would prefer a place with lesser number of competitors to deal with".

"Yeah, you have a point, but anyways…I have got lots of time to decide. You tell me, are you done with your *'netagiri'* or you still loving it," asked Radhika.

"Have you made up your mind on that NGO thing, you had once mentioned."

"Yes, its called Astha. They are dealing with a lot of social issues in the rural areas, but mostly tribal," replied Aniruddh, with rising interest levels.

"They have liked my work and are interested in enrolling me, it is a government aided organisation," he continued.

"How much will they pay you?" came the obvious question.

"Not much, should not be more than Rs 20,000, but I guess that's enough for me, hai na."

"Yes, its actually more than enough for you. So you must give at least half the amount to me. And yes, 'netaji', apart from the orphanage in the outskirts, where else do you plan to take me in the weekend," chuckled Radhika as the sun set behind them atop the Udaygiri caves.

-----x-----

"A 24 year old student has fingered a 60 year old seasoned politician and has managed to get the better of him, not once, but twice," said a fat middle-aged man sitting next to Tripathy.

"Are you trying to humiliate me, in my own house, drinking my wine infront of my supporters," shot back a glum Tripathy.

"Yes, I am. If that is what propels you, then indeed I am humiliating you. Trying to remind you of a revenge that is due for quite some time now," the fat man answered back.

Sarat, do you know why you could never rise high in politics?" questioned Tripathy, giving the ever-so-slimy look.

"This is India," he prefered answering his own question and continued as he pulled the pillow behind him.

"People here are like rich spoilt brats. They fall in love with a figure, they get passionate about him, they worship him, but soon, they get bored of him and then they dispose him of. One, who understands this cycle, survives this carnival, one who fails, alas! fails himself."

Tripathy's words had the wisdom of a career politician, someone who had mastered the art of winning and losing perceptions. He knew when to fight back and when to just sit back and nurse his wounds. He was a political rattle snake that would rather wait patiently for his kill.

"It is not the 24-year-old brain that is behind all this…no…I don't agree to that," said Tripathy shaking his head in disagreement.

"There has to be a mind behind all this."

-----x-----

"They shall throw all their available arsenals on me now," said Aniruddh to an old man sitting across the room in a huge old bungalow in the city's outskirts.

"No, they are wiser than that. These people don't react on impulse. They know that you are too important to be harmed now. They shall wait for their moment and then strike back," replied the old man.

"So, do you think, it is the right time to take the plunge and declare the party," asked an excited Deepak.

"No, certainly not. Remember one thing in politics, you don't create moments, moments create you. You will experience many such moments hereafter. Your act has just given you a space in the big stadium, there is long way to go before you can actually go for a podium finish," the old man continued in his crafty demeanour," You have to understand the people and their problems, you need to understand the nuances of your land and you definitely need to connect with them. This land of ours is like a secluded lake. It looks morbid and forgotten from the outer, but is disturbingly industrious from within.

"You have earned recognition for yourself in the city. Now go to the hinterland, go to the roots. The power might flow from the capital, but it is the villages in India that make or break leaders," the words of wisdom flowed out uninterrupted from the old scribe. "Remember, the rational may support you, but the radical will worship you. Thus, you will need more radicals than you need rational people."

"But sir, why would they accept us, why would they even relate to us? We are complete strangers to them. We bear absolutely no allegiance to them," enquired a curious young mind.

The septuagenarian got up from his armchair and walked to the huge balcony projecting out of his living room. The balcony seemed more like a museum to the archives of the house. He looked towards the river flowing across and said, "when I was a kid, the river that you see, did not run across from here. Only a small tributary sailed past this path. The main river would flow a couple of kilometers ahead, just where you see the mango groves." In the mid-70s, a severe drought hit the state. The monsoon evaded the state for two consecutive years. The riverbed went dry and remained so for a long time. People started settling out there, constructions came up like never before. The ground level rose as a result of the settlement. The river seemed to have dried up until it rained the heavens out in the 80s and the river appeared again. This time, it had chosen a different path, a path free of hindrances and a path yet to be explored. That is how, the river is here, a place which used to be the path for one of its tributaries."

The old man now turned to Aniruddh, and placing his hand over his shoulder said,

"The river will always find its path as people will always find their leader. A leader is not a result of a collective conscious public discourse or decision. He is more of an outcome of the evolving social circumstances and is destined to earn the natural alignment of the masses. The subject, when pushed to a vulnerable situation, will naturally want to be led by someone, this is human nature."

"Go to Kandhamal, the poor tribal land is burning. See for yourself, how easy it is to motivate people to do the most sacrilegious thing in the name of religion even while they hardly make a meal a day."

-----xx-----

CHAPTER 15

Tribal Odisha is a mystery. They remained constantly oblivious to the aspirations and affiliations of the modern society. The social and economic differences became so immeasurable that it almost made their existence a myth. India preferred to keep its tribal hinterland much as a cultural bliss and a medieval gift that perfectly endorsed the idea of 'India- A land that lives in many ages'. Exploited, ignored and illiterate, the neo-societal independent India had not thought of a space for them for the majority of the first four decades of its existence.

The apathy of the government and the misery of the people attracted the benevolent brethren in the Christian Missionaries to a number of such vulnerable belts in the country. The missionaries came as a ray of hope. They got along with them food, education and healthcare. They empowered them to fight injustice and earn their rights. Yes, they also got Jesus along with them. The biggest incantation of this new sect were seemingly empowering in its façade. People were attracted to it because of the equality that it promised to its followers. Exploited for years due to social bigotry and sectarian dogmatism, Christianity was a welcome change for them. The spread of this relatively foreign sect caused major heartburns amongst the self-proclaimed protectors of Hindu religion. Conversions and the spread of Christianity was used as a bait to avenge against the alleged land encroachment issues. The matter was politicised in no time and soon the entire area turned into a boiling pot for an ethnic kerfuffle. It was pretty ironic that a part of the Odisha that remained devoid of the politics of religion for centuries was now engulfed in the worst religious clashes ever in the state. The biggest irony of mankind is that we have done the most heinous of acts in the name of god and religion.

Kandhamal was a typical case of tribal differences given an ethnic colour. The hills weren't used to such communal debauchery. It was clearly a treacherous political game that was planned miles away from the credulous tribal land.

The bus ride to the backcountry was not the most pleasant experience. The dusty countryside looked barren for stretches before abruptly ending in villages. The journey was painstakingly long and arduous. Aniruddh boarded out of the bus along with his ten odd colleagues at the village bus stop.

Hiskutia is a small moribund village with curious looking people and surprisingly silent children. The village seemed as if it has been monitored to silence. There was no usual village lore or the buzz near the pond or the temple or the old banyan tree. It seemed as if the village was mourning its lost credulity. There was no anger, no sorrow, no crying voices nor was there anyone justifying the act. Instead, those faces reflected a sense of guilt. A guilt of having hurt someone known, a guilt of having betrayed a faith, a guilt of having done something horribly wrong.

"Namaskar, Bulu bhai," greeted a short man with his hands folded.

"Arey, Ebraham, kana khabar, How are you my friend," replied back a guy from Aniruddh's group. He introduced Ebraham to the other members of the "Kalinga Yuva Morcha", a volunteer organisation headed by Vishnu and his close associates. The organisation was renamed immediately as an aftermath of the university-firing incident, as it spread all across the state.

Ebraham took them to the village youth club building. Hiskutia was one of the worst hit villages in the riots, with burnt houses and vandalised places of worship all around.

"So Ebraham, how did it all start?"questioned a curious Aniruddh as they sat surrounding him.

"Bhai, it all began with a minor scuffle in one of the neighbouring village over a religious festival and the construction of a gate. The issue flared up and soon it spread like wild fire. People didn't even think twice before slaughtering their very own. It seemed as if they were killing strangers," Ebraham, almost in tears, narrated.

"But, bhai, the real issue has been lurking over for some time now," said another young man sitting next to Ebraham.

"He is Wilson, my cousin. They have evacuated their village because it is facing the brunt of the miscreants and the killings haven't stopped yet," explained Ebraham.

"There have been serious issues over land usage. Minor disputes had cropped up many times in the past. But, this time it just blew out of control. Some miscreants killed a religious seer and that added fuel to the fire.

Women are raped and children are slaughtered while the male population is burnt alive," said an emotional Wilson.

"Has the police acted yet. Have there been any arrests yet?" questioned Deepak.

"There is a local MLA here, who had lost his seat in the previous elections. He is the biggest miscreant. He moves around giving provocative speeches in his area. He belongs to the ruling coalition and hence has the immunity of the police and the administration. The man is influential and enjoys the support of a large number of unemployed youth, whom he lures with money and liquor. His men are responsible for all these killings and heinous acts," explained an evidently angered Wilson.

"Kali Mishra, a trusted aide of Rudra Mohan," educated Vishnu.

"The government won't act against him, he is important to them," remarked Wilson.

"Where is the relief camp?" enquired Aniruddh.

"It's a few kilometres from here, not very far though," replied Ebraham.

"We have to go there tomorrow," said Aniruddh.

"Sure, but what do you have in mind," queried Vishnu.

"Hmm…nothing as yet. Lets visit the camp, talk to the elders in the village and then approach the youth," replied back Aniruddh, still trying to figure out a way to douse the fire.

"We will need some more heads along with us. A large number is always good and Ebraham, they should preferably be form both the communities," added Deepak.

"Don't worry about that, our youth club has roughly a hundred members, 50-60 would definitely join us," assured Ebraham.

"I ll call a few from the capital," added Vishnu.

The 'Kantabadi Relief Camp' in the middle of the beautiful mountains was an execrable adhoc arrangement done by the administration. The camp was a blot on the otherwise picturesque hill country. Pressure from international agencies and from the central government had forced the state government to act. Such camps are appalling depiction of man being fearful of his very own.

Terrified people who had left everything behind in the villages and escaped the brutal exodus had assembled there as a herd, feeling safer. Scared women and silent children gave the camp a dreadful look. Thousands of people lived under makeshift tarpaulin shacks sharing the same plight.

Aniruddh and his volunteers got the permission to do some social work in the camp. They got free medicines and books for the diseased and the children. The young boys and girls worked overnight and built makeshift toilets for the people inside the camp. They fought with the administration for provision of clean drinking water. They even ensured round the clock availability of a government doctor. There were two more such camps where Aniruddh and his volunteers also spent equal amount of time and resources. There were kids who had witnessed mass slaughtering of their family members. The young lot of volunteers worked with other NGOs that provided necessary psychological assistance to revive the kids out of the shock. Meanwhile, Aniruddh and Vishnu led a parallel and effective campaign against the government, forcing it to act.

"There is a lot of pressure to curtail your movements in the camp," said a bespectacled man in his mid-thirties. Pratyush Mohanty was the young District Collector of the area. Over a period of time, Aniruddh had developed a healthy relationship with him. He admired and acknowledged their work and provided the necessary assistance and protection to Aniruddh and his group.

"I know that sir. I knew, sooner or later we would become an eyesore for them," replied back Aniruddh.

"But, you guys keep up your work, leave it to me. I know how to handle them," assured Pratyush.

"Just make sure, that no banners or pamphlets of are distributed here," the officer tried to make himself louder amidst noise of the hooter.

The Home Secretary to the state government had arrived for his visit. This was for the first time; any top bureaucrat had visited the camp. The DC, keeping intact the centuries old sycophantic Victorian traditions of the Indian bureaucracy, aptly greeted him.

"Who are these guys?" questioned the senior bureaucrat as he entered the relief camp pulling up his trousers and clenching his nose, quite evidently trying to avoid the foul smell.

"They are a volunteer group from Bhubaneswar, these young boys and girls have done a really good job here," replied back Mohanty.

"Who gave them the permission?" asked the bureaucrat.

"They have a recommendation from the Chief Minister's Office."

Vishnu had used the good offices of his father and influential uncles to get through with the recommendation letter. The Home Secretary left after his short customary visit. No one from the government visited the camp thereafter for a long time. The state government did not seem to feel the urgency for chalking out a rehabilitation plan for these affected people. The farther you move from the capital the lesser is your relevance.

It was a warm summer afternoon with a trail of white cloud in the otherwise spotless sky. Aniruddh was having a discussion with few elders of the relief camp about their plans of returning back to their villages. Suddenly they heard a motorbike cruising in full speed and making a rather unstable stop right next to the camp office. Ebraham parked the bike in a slapdash manner and ran to Aniruddh.

"Is everything okay?"

Ebraham pulled him to a corner and explained something animatedly and soon Aniruddh hopped on the bike with him.

Apparently, the local police had arrested Deepak along with a few other volunteers. The police alleged that Deepak and his friends were trying to instigate the locals against a particular community and trying to create disturbance in the area. Aniruddh held Ebraham tight as he zipped past the uneven macadam to the Hiskutia police station. Deepak and five other colleagues of theirs were made to sit on a wooden bench under the watch of a bony constable wearing a rather over sized khaki and holding a staff.

"Why have you arrested these volunteers," queried Aniruddh to the constable. The constable pointed at the station in-charge sitting inside

"No, they have not been arrested. Collector saab had asked me to get them here," replied back the in-charge.

"But why would he? He knows, we have the necessary permission," countered Aniruddh.

"Yes, he knows, he just wanted you people to be safe. There were reports that some miscreants will target you guys. I have arranged a mini van for you guys. Leave the place as soon as possible and go back to the city," advised the police officer.

"I don't understand this, if someone wants to hurt us, and you know that, then why don't you arrest them," questioned Aniruddh.

"Huh…the law of the land is different here, you won't understand. Just do as I say, believe me, this is the best I can do to save you. Don't blame me later on, you don't have much time," the concerned officer said.

The danger was imminent. Kali had planned this for quite some time now. The Home Secretary's visit and his abhorrence for Aniruddh and his group and all these events could now be easily linked up.

"Take the van and move out of this place as soon as possible," advised the policeman.

Aniruddh thought it wise to leave the place. But, he was not convinced with the idea of abandoning the place and the people in the middle of this ruckus. With a heavy heart and a silent mind, the young men boarded the mini van. The van was already half filled with a group that seemed like the crew of a media channel.

"Are you also going with us," asked Vishnu to a girl sitting in the first row, who seemed like the head of the group.

"Yes, we have also been warned to leave this place," responded the blue-eyed girl in the front row.

"We are from 'newsline', we were here to cover the aftermath of the riots," added another member of the media contingent.

The van was told to move out as fast as it could by the police constable. They suggested him a certain route by which he could avoid the trouble. The driver looked tensed and scared. It seemed as if he was being asked to move against his wishes. The vehicle drove past a stretch of undulating road for miles. The torturous stretch seemed unending for quite a while before they could finally see the signs of a metal road smudged with the horizon from a distant. As the vehicle zipped along the roller coaster, it came to a sudden stop that forced the wheels to skid by a few yards.

Their worst fears had come true as they were stopped by a group of men, armed with iron rods and *maashals*. The men had blood in their eye and anger in their heart. There was no reason for their anger. It could well have been a manifestation of their ages old hatred for the city and its inhabitants. They looked intimidating and had terrifying intentions. As one member of the media crew dismounted off the mini van and flashed his press identity card, a young man with an iron rod charged at the van and smashed the windshield of the minivan.

The petrified driver jumped out of the van and fled. Perhaps that was the most usual reaction in such situations for a man who plied regularly on these cynically beautiful roads amidst the silence of the hills.

"We are from the press, we have nothing against you," cried out a member of themedia crew.

There was no scope for discussion. The men charged at the van and smashed the window panes in no time. One of them spilled kerosene on the van and lit it up with fire. Thankfully, Aniruddh and the media crew had moved out of the bus by then. The rowdy mob wasn't ready to hear anybody as they started hitting the men in the group. The girls shouted for help and pleaded them to stop, but the group enjoyed the kick they got by venting out their anger. The unarmed volunteer friends of Aniruddh and the media crew were getting beaten up without even knowing their fault till one of them was courteous enough to stop the beatings and tell them:

"This land is not suitable for your political activism, you are oblivious of the realities here. This is a battle to preserve our identity. A battle against the demonic act of conversions and religious manipulation. We are fighting on behalf of our god and we swear on his name, anyone trying to come in between shall not be spared."

The men left them bleeding as they heard the siren of a police jeep approaching them.

Most of them had sustained bruises and minor fractures. The girls were left unharmed. They were admitted in the district hospital, a good 80 kms away from the site of the incident.

The in-charge, Hiskutia PS put them in a goods lorry and shifted them to the hospital. He was waiting near the ward to record their statements, when Aniruddh noticed him and signalled him to come close.

"I had warned you, didn't I?" the policeman said, vindicating himself as he sat next to Aniruddh's bed.

"What did you barter us for?" Aniruddh asked him looking straight in his eye.

There was an awkward silence for more than a couple of minutes as the two were locked in aggressive stare. The policeman was the one to blink first as he said, "you will never understand what is it to lead the life of a government servant in this part of the world. Yes I did tradeoff, but not for money. You will never understand that."

"Babu, you know what we policeman really are. We are like the shepherd's dog. We have been put on duty to guard his sheep from straying and from the wild dogs. The wild dogs know that we are powerless. The shepherd knows that we are only as powerful as he wants us to be. He can't let us be any more powerful, for he fears that someday we might turn up against him. The sheep think that we are there to protect them. In truth, we are only one amongst them, but for the fact that we can bark."

There was nothing that Aniruddh could counter the man with. After all, the policeman, fighting for his own survival, was justified in his act. The men who hit them had their own belief that they were servile to. Neither was wrong. He stared at the photo of a deity hung on the hospital wall and tried to reason out with himself.

"Hi, how are you doing now?" asked the blue-eyed girl, as she came and sat next to Aniruddh on the bench placed outside the ward.

"I am fine, hope the other girls and your crew members are okay," enquired Aniruddh.

"Yeah, the girls are fine, although a few team members have been injured. They have also broken the camera and few other equipments," the girl replied back.

"I wonder, what a female journalist, the like of yours, is doing here in the tribal mad lands," asked Aniruddh.

"I thought these days journalists don't have to travel that much, the real news just barges into your studios," added Aniruddh, lighting up a cigarette.

"The real stories still make you travel a lot, what comes to the studios is more of drama. Anyways, I am a stringer, so the travel is mandatory. My name is Ritika," back came the astute reply.

"Dramatics is what keeps the channels going, isn't it," poked Aniruddh.

"Hmmm…so who are you, and what were you doing in the tribal land," she asked, taking the cigarette from him and pulling in a fag.

"We are members of a volunteer organisation called 'Kalinga Yuva Morcha' and we are here to help the tribal in the relief camp with basic necessities and rehabilitate them," answered a passionate Aniruddh.

He went on for the next ten minutes as Ritika watched him share his ideas and concerns to her.

"These are poor, simple people for whom virtue still stands for vanity. They are being misled and misguided by wicked minds," he added.

Ritika looked at him with a smudge of a smile on her face as she prepared to leave.

"What do you plan to do next?"

"Don't know. May be I ll get well and get back to the relief camp," stated Aniruddh.

"Wish you all the best. Take care and stay safe. I think you should get well soon, who knows what lands up next," Ritika said before the Newsline crew headed back to Delhi on the same day.

-----xx-----

CHAPTER 16

------◆◆------

Enquiry reports and sources clearly indicated the involvement of Rudra Mohan in the attack on the group through Kali's men. Aniruddh knew he had to fight a larger battle and getting involved with Rudra Mohan would only waste his time. Instead of condemning the attack, the Chief Minister's office released an advisory against travelling to the 'disturbed areas'.

Exactly a week had passed by and Aniruddh was still figuring out his plan of action when Vishnu gave him a call.

"Did you see the news?" yelled Vishnu over the phone.

"No, why?"

"Switch on the damn television set and jump to channel 214," he yelled yet again. Before he could say anything Aniruddh snapped the phone and ran to the TV room.

Channel 214 was Newsline. The channel was repeatedly running a video that looked like some sought of a brawl captured live by someone. The voice that played in the narrative sounded similar to one Aniruddh had heard quite recently.

"These young men, who called themselves volunteers of Kalinga Yuva Morcha, were out there, helping the people in the relief camps, running schools inside the camp, providing clean water to the victims, when they were brutally attacked by a local radical group that enjoys the patronage of the ruling coalition. The ex-MLA Shri Kali Mishra is said to be have a major role in obstructing any relief work in the area. Sources even claim that the government has no plans of rehabilitating the victims before the elections as they want the community votes to be low in number," Ritika Ghosh was relentless, sharing her experiences in the tribal land and a group of young volunteers whom she met.

Soon all major news channels played up the Kandhamal story to its brim. Aniruddh Mishra's little chit-chat with a leading journalist just gave him the right impetus he needed to be back on his feet.

The image of a badly bruised young man, with a bandage over his forehead, talking of revolutionary ideas and concerns for the tribal made headlines in all the leading dailies the next day.

"Yes, but I remember you mentioning that the camera was also broken by the hoodlums," queried Aniruddh surprisingly over the phone.

"Yes, but my video journalist somehow managed to capture some in her handy cam," replied back Ritika.

"Look, now the matter is heating up and I think you must make the maximum out of this coverage," added Ritika.

The KYM announced a press conference the very next day. The entire media including the national news channels were present for the presser. Aniruddh was already a known figure amongst the politically inclined youth of the city, and everyone wanted to hear what he had to say.

"Come hard on the government. Go for the CM and target his silence. Highlight the fact that he hasn't visited the riot hit area even once after the horrific incident. Rake up the resettlement issue. Tell everything the government did not want to be talked about or heard of," advised Basudev babu to his young apprentice.

"Remember, your only aim should be to force the CM to give a statement."

In a jam-packed youth clubhouse lobby, the presser went on for almost an hour. The entire government was hooked on to television sets fearing the deadly consequences of the revelations that the young man was about to make.

"What is going to be your next move, Aniruddh?" asked a journalist.

"We are going back to Kandhamal, let me see who stops us this time," Aniruddh said.

He was a natural orator. His confidence and comfort while facing the cameras and while taking the questions was impeccable. The news was an instant hit. It gave the much-needed thrust to their movement.

This time around the KYM gathered a much larger crowd than their last visit. A huge cavalcade marched off for Kandhamal with Aniruddh and Vishnu leading the campaign. They were stopped at a number of places en route. People wanted to have a look at the face behind the voice that stood for them. Aniruddh got a hero's welcome in the Hiskutia block. The same police officer, who had bartered them off to Kali's men was now making all efforts to ensure his safety.

Ebraham had organised a road show followed by a meeting with the heads of eight affected villages of the district. The meeting was to be held in the only senior secondary school of the block. The school had remained deserted for the last four months after the rioters burnt the old thatched classrooms. Expectedly, the worst victims of riots were the children.

"The conspirator is not amongst you. He has got nothing to lose out of this mess. He hasn't lost his dear ones, and his children haven't been orphaned. His villages and places of worship haven't been desecrated. He is still sitting in the comforts of his room, miles away from all you people, looking at you and laughing at you," an angry Aniruddh said.

"Dadu," continued Aniruddh, addressing the eldest amongst them. "He is able to do all this because he knows, he can easily break you apart. He knows that your voices are easily silenced. The government doesn't listen to you, the people you elect and send to the capital betray you in the very first month. You people here, over a period, have become like the old banyan tree of the village. Nobody cares for it anymore, but they all want to bask under the shade you provide. Your existence justifies their perennial chant for 'upliftment of the tribal', 'concern for the tribal'. Nobody out there counts anything more than your numbers. You people are just numbers for them, which matter every five years. You shall fight amongst yourselves, kill each other, and lead your miserable lives.

"I am going out there to fight for your cause, to ensure that the government punishes the guilty and initiates your rehabilitation. The choice is in your hands, come out and join me like a united community, or remain divided and go back to your same miserable lives," Aniruddh banged the door of the classroom and left the school, asking them to come with their maximum strength to the protest site.

Sometimes you have to tell people how miserable they have been to flare the revolutionary instincts in them. Great movements have begun only when people are made to realise their tenebrific existence.

Aniruddh had hit the right chords. The tribal land had woken up to the call of a leader who wasn't one amongst them, but who stood for them. He had already won their loyalty by standing beside them during their hours of darkness. Now he had won their hearts and controlled their mind too. The tribal land had a new hero.

-----x-----

CM's Residence, Emergency Meeting

"The kandhamal issue has picked up momentum once again, sir," briefed the Chief Secretary.

"But, we have already paid the compensations and I believe the situation is pretty much under control now," replied back the CM, reflecting his lack of knowledge about issues far from the capital.

"Their demands are different this time," informed the new Home Minister.

"They want the culprits to be punished and rehab to start early,"

"But I was told arrests have been made as per FIRs and investigation is going on as per legal procedures."

"They want the real people behind this….."

"But, we cannot put people behind the bars, just on public demand. They have to be proven guilty," the Chief Secretary was cut short by the CM.

"More than 10 FIRs have Shri Kali Mishra's name on various charges," clarified the Home Secretary.

"Why is the opposition after Kali Mishra, what are they gaining out of it?" queried the CM.

"It's not the opposition, sir. A number of their leaders also have FIRs on their names. They are quiet as ever."

"Its KYM and Aniruddh Mishra, the young man who led the protests in the University firing incident," informed Surendra Barik, the Home Minister.

There was a smile of frustration on the CM's face as he looked at his Cabinet colleague and said, "Don't tell me, we are going to bow down to this young kid, once again."

"Sir, he has galvanised the entire district behind his movement. The tribal are listening to him like he is one of their own," added the DG, police.

"And, what the hell were you doing all this while,"

Sir, we were keeping a close watch on this…."

"You keep doing that, I guess anything beyond that is not within your capabilities," the CM's frustration was clearly visible.

"Look, you people do whatever you have to, I am not going to bow down to this thing."

Soon after that, the official representatives were asked to leave as the CM sat along with other party members to discuss the political fallout of the developments in Kandhamal.

"We are paying a heavy price for this coalition. I don't think we can sustain the forbearing damage this is doing to us. It's time to take a call on that now," the CM for the first time hinted upon breaking the alliance.

The ruling party was clearly not getting any benefits out of the coalition. They had the numbers and they knew that the independent candidates would certainly stand by them.

The CM announced the surceasement of the coalition. This gave him the leverage to order an independent inquiry into the riots and punish the guilty. Kali Mishra was taken into custody on account of the FIRs filed against him. The Supreme Court took cognizance of the matter and ordered a Special Investigation Team to probe into the riots.

The people of Kandhamal considered it their victory. Aniruddh Mishra was upgraded from a mass leader to a messiah. The government subsequently ordered a rapid rehabilitation for the affected people.

"Sir, a visit to Kandhamal is due for a long time."

"Yes, you must plan it soon," said the CM, as Dillip Konhar the MLA from the region proposed it to him.

"Did you meet the young guy?" queried the CM.

"Sir, I have met him once, but he is a high headed arrogant. He enjoys a huge public support there, and so is flying high now," replied back the sullied MLA.

"And you claim to be the representative of the people from that area!

"I shall meet him personally during my visit to your area. Please organise for that," the CM told.

-----x-----

"Although he shall be meeting you personally, most of the real talking will be done by Adarsh Narayan Das. He is the political advisor to the CM and an extremely cunning man," Basudev babu told Aniruddh over the phone.

"How do I deal with him?" asked Aniruddh.

"Just remain focussed with your immediate task in hand. He is no more the CM and you are no more a kid. Now, you both are on the same platform," Basu babu said, knowing exactly why and by whom was the CM advised to give in to the demands of Aniruddh and the tribal population.

Adarsh Narayan was clever enough to judge the advantages of the growing popularity of Aniruddh Mishra as a potential mass leader of the tribal land and wanted to take him in the party.

The entire district was decked up for the CM's visit. There were posters put at all the major connecting roads in the district. The otherwise neglected region ironically felt pampered for the first time.

The CM's chopper was scheduled to land in the playground of the senior secondary school. The ground was cleaned and was being watered continuously since the last two days to prevent a ground wash from the chopper. A formidable barricade built of bamboo was erected all around the place where the chopper was designated to land. Innocent faces stared at the sky looking for possible signs of the helicopter. Most of them had actually gathered to witness the flying marvel rather than see their Chief Minister.

At half past 11am, almost two hours after the announced schedule came the Chief Minister's helicopter. It landed at the centre of the ground perfectly aligning itself to the H–mark and throwing a storm of dust at the onlookers. The dust blinded the audience as they looked startlingly towards the machine. Amidst layers of settling dust, emerged a tall man in white kurta and pyjama. A few smartly dressed bodyguards flanked him as he marched towards the people who were waiting eagerly with bouquets in their hand. For the people of the village, the attraction was still the dragon fly machine. The man in white clothes was as inaccessible to them as he ever was. He drove away in the car waiting for him.

"Your work in the tribal land has been praiseworthy, Mr Mishra," said the CM, the Oxford accent clearly reflecting out in his baritone.

"Thank you sir, but I am afraid though, I can't say the same thing about the administration here," replied Aniruddh. There was an inconvenient silence in the entire room. Nobody in the audience had expected such a reply to the CM. Adarsh Narayan could no longer let his CM remain exposed to this burning young haystack as he quickly jumped into the conversation.

"Yes, we realise the obvious lapse on the part of the administration in handling the situation. The CM, as you must have heard, has already asked for a detailed investigation on the subject. An investigation committee had been…"

"We have heard all that in the news, sir. Hope the report sees the light of the day," spoke Aniruddh, cutting Adarsh Narayan short and clearly expressing his displeasure over the abrupt interference.

He already made him feel like a man of lower stature. Adarsh Narayan realised the wiser thing to do was to contain interactions with this wrecking ball at the media event.

The next day was a hunting day for the major regional newspapers, as they went on length describing the showdown at Kandhamal. Aniruddh Mishra was the underdog who won hearts of the people. The people of the tribal land got their demands fulfilled.

Government announced an additional allocation of Rs 250 Crore for development of riot hit areas and building of infrastructure. Panchayat committees were formed to resolve pending issues and douse religious hatred. Aniruddh's popularity spread far and wide as more and more people heard about him and his team.

-----xx-----

CHAPTER 17

The KYM was gaining prominence in various parts of the state now. They travelled across the length and breadth of the state, and though funding was a challenge for them, having people like Vishnu Mishra on board helped a lot. They witnessed destitution and disparity wherever they went. The existing malice in the political framework had completely eroded the government machineries, like a cancer in the human body. People, it seemed, had accepted this system as *fait accompli*. The government never delivered as the people never asked. Pseudo-populist schemes and imprudent subsidies got their votes for them. A freebie intoxicated people, a dead opposition, and an incognizant bureaucracy delineated the condition of the state. While every other part of the country was changing either for good or bad, this region remained more or less insulated.

It was a pleasant winter morning in January 2008. Naxalism had raised its hood yet again in these parts, and the arrogance of the central government in admitting the fault lines, and their claims that the 'situation is very much in control' fuelled the fire. The more they were ignored, the more dastardly their acts of violence became. For the intellectuals in Delhi, they were a topic of debate. For the neo-socialists, they were the answer. India comfortably ignored the dead bodies in the red land until they became too many to ignore.

A total of 18 people from a village in Malkangiri district were brutally hacked to death, in public, by the Naxals. The dead included three women and four teenagers. They were brandished as informers of the police and people who defied the rules of the "liberalised zone". The Superintendent of Police, a rookie officer who had just passed out of the training academy, was giving his byte to the media that had assembled to cover the massacre.

"Go there and meet some people," advised Basudev babu.

"We hardly have any base there," a concerned Vishnu replied. "The people are hostile to any outside support. I don't think it is wise to get entangled in it now."

"I have a reliable source out there. He enjoys his share of popularity and respect in the 'liberalised zone'. He will help you guys," assured the old man, taking a big sip of the bourbon whisky kept in front of him.

"Do we have to do everything that he says?" asked Vishnu, as the two drove back from the old man's home in his Maruti 800. "It feels as if we are losing out our freedom to him, and becoming his stooge."

"What makes you think so? He is certainly more experienced than any of us. Moreover, he has always advised us well, Vishnu bhai. Hasn't he?"

The discussion ended abruptly as Aniruddh changed the topic.

-----x-----

There was an uncomfortable silence at the dinner table as his mother served dal, and slapped two chappatis onto his plate. Usually, she asked before serving. Mothers have a typical way of confronting their grown up children when they are unhappy about something – The normal discourse would suddenly turn out to be a self-empathising parody, and the child would be addressed in third person.

"I am the most ill-fated mother on Earth. I come to know about the plans and activities of my son either from the television, or from neighbours," Mrs Mishra yelled at her husband as she served the mixed vegetables boiled curry(shantula).

"I was about to tell you," Aniruddh tried explaining, but was cut short.

"No, no, please tell him not to bother himself. How dare we ask the great Mr Aniruddh about his plans," she said, almost banging the steel glasses of water on the table.

"Arey. Ma, don't worry, we will be safe," he tried to pacify her.

"Reports say 18 people have been slaughtered in one night, and you are trying to tell me you will be safe there," she shot back, looking straight at him this time, venting her anger, worry and frustration simultaneously.

"Is it so necessary to go?" asked Mr Mishra, speaking for the first time that evening.

"Yes, baba," Aniruddh replied, as his exasperated mother hit her own forehead.

"Look, beta, we have never interfered with your plans and activities since your college days. But that doesn't take away our share of worries that we have for you as our son. Just remember one thing, we make enemies as fast as we make friends. So just be careful with your moves."

The family dinner continued without a word being spoken after that.

-----x-----

"He will meet you at the post office in Chouraha." said the man sent by Basu babu, as they drove off. "Give him my name and he will take you to the village."

The hills of the south folded endlessly to form imperial green valleys. The texture of the earth and the smell of the wild flowers were amazingly fresh, and it was the perfect day to drive along the countryside. The beauty of the land, however, was marred by a tinge of betrayal that seemed to linger on the stoic faces of the people along the road. Their eyes reflected the fear and helplessness. They exhibited a state of emotional dormancy, where no amount of misery bothered them anymore. It was said that nobody from the families of the people who were hacked cried that day. They were too emotionally dead.

The deathly silence of the village offended the serene winter morning. A couple of media personnel from the vernacular press were seen hovering around trying to capture a moment of this, and take it to the doorsteps of the India that would still be hung-over its victory against Pakistan in a game of cricket.

There were a couple of khaki-clad men, looking very much like the police, who were trying to question a few villagers on the incident. The women of the families that had their men killed sat next to each other and looked endlessly towards the forest. There wasn't a drop of tear in any of those eyes, or an expression in any of their faces.

Their arrival created no curiosity among the villagers. They were too used to sympathy tourism after such incidents.

"Where can we find Majhi babu?"

Majhi babu was the link that Basudev had referred them to.

"There he is," said the policemen, pointing at a frail man in a blue-chequered lungi and a shirt.

"Basu babuhas sent you guys?" asked the old man, lowering his wooden-framed reading glasses.

"Yes," Vishnu replied.

"Hmm...Good. Come with me," said the old man and guided them through a tapered alley to his home. The roof was covered with mud tiles, and the courtyard had a fresh layer of cow dung paste. The man shouted directions in fluent Bengali, ordering water and tea for the visitors.

"There are more number of Bengalis here than the locals. They sent the Bangladeshi refugees hereafter the '71 war," the old man explained, looking straight at Aniruddh. "The refugees are hardworking people, and are smarter than the local tribes. There is a lot of animosity within the two clans, but they know neither can survive without the other. It is typical India, you see."

"And what about the Naxals?" asked Aniruddh.

"What about them? They are also the outcome of the same democracy that you and I are part of," the old man replied, rather snobbishly.

"But their ideologies are conflicting," Vishnu rebutted.

"There is no ideology any more, there is only money," he said, "It is a lucrative business now."

Majhi babu handed them the steel glasses of tea, served by his Bangla house aid, and said: "You will know more when you meet him tonight."

"Meet who?"

"Hasn't Basu babu told you anything? He wants you to meet his link in the PWG," said the old man, looking at the confused faces.

"Link in PWG? You mean, the People's War Group?" Vishnu asked.

The next few minutes were dominated by an unusual silence, as none of them knew exactly how to react. There were two little kids with marasmic bellies savouring a diet of curd and rice at one corner of the courtyard, as people called out religious chants on the street and carried the dead bodies for cremation.

-----x-----

The black blindfolds made it difficult for them to orient their positions, as they were being driven along a jagged patch for over an hour in a van. There were two other people dressed in combat fatigues that accompanied them along with the driver of the van. They carried automatic rifles with them, and their faces were covered with red masks.

The van came to a screeching halt after moving nonstop for two hours. The armed men moved out along with their guests.

"Rati, please remove the straps," ordered a man in an abnormally polite tone.

As the blindfolds were removed, the duo realised they were in a tent, deep inside the Dandakaranya forest, sitting right across the most wanted man in the region.

"I have very high regard for Basudev sir," said the man in fluent English."He was my guide for my Phd. I couldn't say no to him."

He sounded far more polished and educated than his appearance suggested.

"Anyway, I am Comrade Raghavji. I am the Zonal Commander of the PWG here," said the man responsible for the death of 18 innocent lives.

Vishnu introduced himself and his friend.

"Ahh… a lot is being said and heard about you in the recent days," remarked the Naxal leader.

"So, tell me, what makes you interested in this godforsaken land of ours? The mainstream was never interested in us. We have always been a topic of discussion for the left of centre."

"The brutal killings in the village. …" Aniruddh began, but was cut short.

"What about the killings? They were informers. The cadre had to take revenge for the death of six of our comrades in a police encounter last week," came the straight-faced reply to a question that was never asked.

"Fear is the oxygen that you survive on, I understand that."

"Do you think, the people here lived without fear before us? Fear is their destiny," said the rebel. "They don't understand this fight that we are fighting for them. Revolution demands blood."

"Do you believe this can absolve them of their miseries?" asked Aniruddh.

"We have given them the courage to speak out. The administration is at least concerned about them now. The government can no longer just neglect them."

"Your means are highly questionable, and they are certainly antithetical to our democracy," expressed Aniruddh, with a mix of fear and frustration in his tone, but he didn't dare raise his voice. He was sitting in front of one of the most wanted men in the region, with gun-wielding Naxals all around them.

The rebel burst into sarcastic laughter, and said, "You baffle me brother. I heard a lot of that bullshit while I was studying in JNU. Democracy is the luxury that the elite few like you enjoy and talk about in your cushy lives. Democracy is not meant for these hungry, uncivilised jungle-dwellers. These people were deliberately isolated from the democratic processes of this country, till the time they realised they are heard only when they make some noise. That is exactly what we are helping them to do.

"We both are fighting the same system, Aniruddh. You are fighting from within, and I am fighting from the outside," said the young leader, staring straight into his eye.

The discussion continued for the next hour till the leader left to attend an important wireless call. The duo was then escorted out from the venue, blindfolded once again.

As the van zipped past the jungle tracks, the smell of unknown wild flowers and stale leaves added to the mystery of the forest. They had met a group of people with conflicting ideas and questionable ideologies. Money was certainly a driving factor. But was it the only factor?

-----x-----

"How was your meeting with Raghav?" asked Basu babu, with a tinge of excitement in his voice.

"It was a good experience, the person seems to be impressive in the first go," Vishnu replied.

"What about you, Aniruddh?" the old man pestered him again.

"Indeed he is impressive. But I also saw a spot of guilt in his eye. I don't know why I believe he is not as strong a man as he pretends to be."

"You find the most wanted man in the whole of eastern India, a bit soft?" snapped Basu babu, clearly annoyed with Aniruddh's response.

-----x-----

Meanwhile, the multi-crore mining scam had just surfaced, and political squabbles peaked. Big names from industry and politics were involved in the scam, and the equations kept changing with each passing day. For the first time ever, the CM's honest image was questioned. This gave rise to minor oppositions from within the ruling party itself. These names were carefully noted and monitored by Basu babu.

The KYM also initiated a fight against the government to book the actual culprits, and not the weak links. Vishnu was the party's face and earned a lot of media coverage for his merciless attacks on the government.

The industries took the direct brunt of the cancellation of mining leases. Transporters abandoned their trucks along the highways to avoid the maintenance and running costs. Although, the mining barons survived the shut down, the ancillary and dependent units could not.

"They have arrested Dhiren Pattnaik today," Deepak informed Aniruddh.

Dhiren was Radhika's father. He and Radhika's mother were divorced, but the man had a perfect relationship with his daughter.

Aniruddh was visibly disturbed on hearing the news. He knew how much Radhika loved her father. Before he could articulate his thoughts, his cell phone had her number flashing on its screen.

"They have arrested him," she said, not a sign of remorse in her tone.

"Listen, it is just an investigation …" he began, but she cut him short.

"Look, this doesn't affect anything. If he is guilty, he deserves it. As for me, I am his daughter, and I will certainly be hurt today," she said, trying to separate the issues.

KYM had initiated a major campaign against Dhiren and a few other mining barons. Sometimes, one has to marginalise certain relations to help build other ones that are more important in that timeframe. Radhika was a girl who understood life and its practicalities. She had to strike a balance, between the man she had to live her life with hereafter, and the man she thought was important till date.

CHAPTER 18

———⟨≫⟩———

Amidst all this, one young man was gradually booking his place in the contemptuous world of politics and its nuances. He earned as many enemies as admirers. The youth worshipped him as his stature grew with each passing day.

He wasn't rising alone though. There was another man, by his side, who was becoming equally popular. Vishnu Pradhan had support and the blessings as the rugged, rural voice who had his roots in the coastal lands. Aniruddh was believed to be more of a city dweller.

However, some recent developments had made them more popular than a few leading politicians in the state. They were revered among the youth. The underprivileged considered them as their messiah because of their anti-establishment stand and clean image.

"I think it's time for you to make the announcement," said Basu babu, taking a sip of the bitter gourd juice kept in front of him. The old man was diabetic, and believed strongly in this therapy.

"The elections are approaching, and you have just about a year and half to strengthen your organisation and make it fit enough for electoral politics."

"But a year and half will be too short a time to establish a party and make it fit enough for a fight," said Vishnu, his concerns coming through.

"You already have a party. You just have to declare it political."

"A lot of other things are involved, sir. You know it better than us," Deepak butted in. "Organisation at the grassroots level, party cadre, funding … we have nothing with us, as of now. I don't think we can be ready, at least not till the next elections."

"Look, you have an anti-incumbency factor that is very much existing. But due to an almost defunct opposition, the advantages are not being exploited. You can be the ideal substitute to the present government," the old man insisted.

"People desperately want a new leader. The present political environment is incapable of giving them one. You must fill the void."

"What do you think, Aniruddh?" Basu babu then asked the only man he was actually trying to convince.

"We don't have a strong grassroots cadre."

"You may not realise it yet, but there must be thousands of people out there who would be already idolising you. You just have to reach out to them, and galvanise their support. In a country like ours, you really don't need much to be a mass leader. You just need to strike the right chords at the right time. Give them what they want. Tell them what they want to hear. Acknowledge their miseries and remind them of it wherever you go."

The old man was craftily gearing them up for their new innings.

"Money? Where is the money going to come from?" The election expenditures cross all limits now. You know that better than all of us," countered Aniruddh.

"I have spoken to some people. They are ready to fund you for the next elections," asserted Basu babu.

"Who are these people and why would they want to help us?"

"Some industrialists and a few NRIs interested in investing here."

"Then we will remain indebted to them forever."

"The government is never indebted to anyone. You don't have to toe their line. If you don't give into their demands, they will try and look for somebody else and you will find someone else who is ready to fund you. The cycle continues.

"This is the right time, my son. If you delay it, you might never get a chance like this ever again," said the old man, trying his best to convince the group one last time before they left.

-----x-----

Two days after the discussion, the KYM called for a press conference. Journalists of all major national dailies and primetime news channels were invited. The stage was shared by Aniruddh, Vishnu and Deepak – the three most prominent faces of the KYM.

They announced their decision to go political.

"We are tired of this system, where the government is oblivious of the problems on ground. We have decided to take our fight to the assembly now. The state of the state can only improve by a complete change in this stagnating government machinery," announced Vishnu, as Aniruddh nodded in agreement sitting beside him.

"Our party will be called as the Kalinga Sangarsh Morcha. Aniruddh Mishra was unanimously elected as our president in the convening meeting of our party."

"Do you intend to contest the upcoming Assembly elections?"

"Yes, we will contest in all 147 assembly constituencies in the upcoming elections," replied Deepak.

"But do you have that kind of an organisation to back you up?" asked a journalist.

"Do you think you have a support base in the ground?" needled another.

"I think we have enough support to defeat the incumbent government of the state," Aniruddh replied with glaring confidence

The certitude in the only line that he spoke during the entire presser made him an instant hit in the media.

-----x-----

"This young guy looks very promising," remarked Adarsh Narayan.

"He might be a threat," replied the CM.

"Naah! I won't rate him that high."

"Mark my words, this guy can turn the tables."

Although the established parties were not threatened, they were certainly a bit uncomfortable. The dormant state politics hadn't seen much competition in quite some time.

"The party constitution should bestow more powers upon the convener and the executive council. This will help maintain inner party discipline," suggested a man in his late thirties who went by the name of Dr Bichitrananda Sahoo, a successful doctor in the coastal belt and an eminent public figure. He was one of the few new members of the KSM.

"But the inner party democracy should be strong enough to prevent any sort of dictatorial instincts," countered Aniruddh.

"Yes, most of the work can be done by love. But to harm someone, you need power. You may not like it, but you will have to harm some people at times," said Basu babu, not mincing any words.

The party was now working at full swing. The top leaders spread themselves all over the state to motivate people to join them. Funds started flowing in slowly, but it met only the basic requirements. The membership drive was gaining a lot of prominence, as people were interested in this new political venture.

Things were going smooth till the end of the year, but the party received its first political blow on December 31, 2008.

The top leaders of the party had all arrived at the office–a small space taken on rent in the heart of the city. The leaders were cuddled up in the conference room, as no outsider was allowed to enter. Aniruddh was seated in the centre while the others surrounded him in a round table. The television was on, and a lady addressed the press.

A lady from the Angul constituency had alleged a top party leader of sexual harassment and rape. She claimed she was repeatedly harassed and sexually abused by a top leader of the KSM, in the pretext of giving her a party ticket. The leader she named was Vishnu Pradhan.

The situation was grim in the party office. The newly formed party had no baggage to carry around before this incident. They clearly did not know how to handle the situation.

"An immediate denial statement," recommended Deepak.

"Did you ever meet this lady?"

"Yes, I did. But there were a lot of people in the room at Angul when I met her. She is lying," said an agitated Vishnu.

"I will kill this bitch. How can someone stoop to such a level for publicity?" said a senior party member, banging his fists on the table.

"Cool down. Anything rash you do will only go against you."

"She has the sympathy of the public now, don't forget that," advised Deepak.

"Tell the press you have nothing to do with it. Tell them you are ready for a medical examination or a DNA test to prove your innocence," said Dr Sahoo.

"Arey, I am prepared for any test," Vishnu snapped back, hurling out abuses.

The lady filed an FIR against Vishnu Pradhan. He was arrested on various charges under the IPC and CrPC, and later released on bail. Although he wasn't proven guilty, the woman was successful in gaining sympathy and demonising him. The media, as usual, had already pronounced him guilty, and pressure was building on Aniruddh to suspend him from the primary membership of the party.

Aniruddh was in a dilemma. He was stranded between conscience and his friendship.

"The day you expel him, you accept him guilty. The political community is going to tear you apart if you do that," said Basu babu, who knew Vishnu was an important link in the KSM. "Just wait for a few days, the matter will die down. Do you think people in this country have the time and luxury to stick to one issue?"

"The media?"

"The media is just waiting for another issue, never take them too seriously."

Vishnu continued as a member of the executive council of the party. Predictably the media forgot the issue after a while. It was later found out that the conspiracy was hatched internally, though the perpetrator was never caught.

-----x-----

KSM's popularity was growing day by day. The young energetic leaders of the party worked overtime to spread their work, and the 'vision document' for the state.

But they were trying to sell a dream to people who hardly had the luxury of a sleep. They were trying to awaken the aspirations of a population that was much happy leading a marginalised and meagerly contented life. They were trying to tell a state where 60% of the population was living below poverty line, that even they could be a part of developed India.

Reaching out to the people is a difficult thing, and convincing them to believe you is still more difficult. Intention doesn't gets you vote, perception does. The people were not only poor; they had reached a state of political dormancy. The government of the day perfectly understood the character of its people, and was more than efficient in keeping them addicted to its freebie culture. In short, the people had nothing but were still surprisingly happy with the government, and had nothing to complain against.

"It is going to be difficult without the funds," said Dr Sahoo. The top leaders of the party had assembled at Basu babu's house to discuss issues relating to the shortage of funds.

"The steel company we were in talks with has backed out," said Deepak, the party treasurer.

"Yeah, they struck a deal with the government. Adarsh Narayan is a pimp. He knows his clients well," remarked Vishnu.

"There is another company that has shown interest. They have Chromium interest in the state. It's a huge aluminum company called

Metalate Corporation," said Basu babu, handing over a few documents to Aniruddh.

"Metalate is a huge company. They have a lot of off shore investments as well. Why are they showing interest in us?"

"The Chinese steel plant debacle made the investors very nervous. They have lost faith in the present government. We provide them a viable alternative," replied Basu babu.

"Hmm...but even their support won't be of much help," said Deepak. "The ruling party candidates spend as much as Rs 3-6 crores per constituency. This excludes the advertisements, the publicity and the management of print and electronic media. We are no competition to them."

Deepak was right. The ruling party spent an insane amount of money in their constituencies, and the new party was just not financially equipped to give them a fight.

"I have a small suggestion that can help you out of this crisis," said a young man, sitting silently in a corner of the room, drawing the attention of all the others. He looked like any other guy just out of college.

"You have a plan?" Basu babu looked at him with his eyebrows raised, before adding, "He is Bhanu, my tenant's son."

"Also, dadu has adopted my father," said the young man to clear the confusion.

"He has just graduated from law school and is about to join some firm. Don't go by his looks. He is a genius and will soon become a devil in black coat," Basu babu added with a smile.

"You were saying something," Aniruddh reminded.

"Yes, I have a plan for you that can help you out of the financial problems," said the nerdy-looking young man.

"Go ahead, mister wise man," said Basu babu, removing his reading glasses with a giggle.

"First, you have to break your party. Form factions and split into two or may be three groups."

"What!" shock was the most expected reaction.

"Yes, you heard me right. Break your party, and your top leaders must join the mainstream parties," the young man continued. "You are potent figures in the political circle now. No party would think twice before giving you a ticket. You contest from the respective parties from your constituencies, thus enhancing your possibility to win. And it also solves the issue of funding."

The young man didn't sound too convincing, but everyone gave him a patient hearing.

"What about the party? What about our core principles?" asked Vishnu.

"The winner has the luxury of principles. You need to win. Winnability might not be the moral factor, but it is certainly the single most important factor in electoral politics."

"Then we might end up contesting against each other in the elections."

"No, I never said that you have to fight each other. You just need to contest from different party tickets from separate assembly constituencies," the young man continued explaining.

He had already attracted the attention of all the other members in the room, although no one was able to comprehend his plan as yet.

"Then?" asked Aniruudh. The young man went over to the white board and explained.

"There are a total 147 seats in the Assembly. The ruling party has a majority with 85 seats. It is just 10 seats over the magic figure. The second largest party has 36, and the third has a paltry 18 seats. The remaining is a group of fringe one-man parties and independent candidates."

"That is the breakdown, but we already know that," Deepak butted in.

"All you need to do is field 40 candidates from various party tickets, and 20 independent candidates," Bhanu explained. "You have to win a maximum of 18 seats, to be safe 20 seats to form the next government."

He sounded and looked confident, but it did not match up to the response he received.

"Do you really have a plan or you are trying to vile away our time, dude?" snapped Vishnu, his patience crossing the limit.

"Hold on Vishnu bhai. Continue, Bhanu," said Aniruddh, expecting a remarkable climax.

No one blinked an eyelid as the young man went on for the next hour. Nobody spoke a word for the first 15 minutes after Bhanu had spoken. It took some time for the whole idea to sink in. The seemingly impossible now felt achievable.

"It won't be as easy as you make it sound," said Deepak, the first to speak.

"No, it won't be easy. But it is possible."

"Won't it be unethical?" asked Aniruddh, and Bhanu had no answer.

"Sometimes, unethical means are the only way to do an ethical thing," Basu babu chipped in. "The present government cannot be changed by any other means. Had there been one, it would have already seen the light of the day."

Basu babu seemed convinced with the plan.

"We are not cheating or doing anything illegal. It's just a game and we are using the rules to our advantage in a better way. That's it," added Deepak.

"Won't be as easy as it sounds. Will need a lot of arm twisting," added Vishnu, who was equally impressed with the idea but had his own doubts.

"Plus, we have to stay together till the end, come what may. Everything depends on how strong we remain through all this. The plan will only work if all the players stick together through good and bad," said Aniruddh, as he got up to walk out to the balcony.

Basu babu's riverside bungalow had a perfect view of the river and the bridge over it that connected the twin cities. Thousands of vehicles passed over the bridge with red lights blinking at the back. The bridge connected the two biggest cities of the state.

Basu babu walked to the balcony with small, careful steps, leaning on his walking stick.

"You have to fight to win the war. You have nothing to lose. People won't judge you from the means, they will judge you from the outcome of the battle," he said, leaving Aniruddh to his thoughts.

-----x-----

CHAPTER 19

"In a major political development in the coastal state of Odisha, the youth leaders of the recently formed KSM have called it splits," reported a national news channel during primetime. "The otherwise politically dormant state has suddenly been pretty active in recent days courtesy their activism and involvement of the youth."

The decision was taken and they were all ready to play their parts. Aniruddh, along with three members, joined the ruling Kalinga Janta Dal amid much fanfare, and a welcome bouquet from the CM himself. Deepak and four other members joined the Democratic Congress Party, while Vishnu stuck with KSM. After a week, Dr Bichitrananda was told to announce him joining the Lokhit Morcha. The political sorority believed that intra-party differences led to the split.

The war room was set up at the KSM's office – the first floor of a humble building in a low profile area – and it was the perfect location. Bhanu was requested to stay put and plan the whole thing till the elections. A couple of other volunteers joined in, and the room looked more like a corporate workstation than the office of a political wing.

The media tore apart the KSM, and its leaders were termed opportunists and immature kids in politics. The political annihilation of the KSM was almost complete in the intellectual circles of the state. During all this, the members got their share of free publicity – the more you stay in the news, the more popular you become.

Just 10 months were left for the assembly elections, and the lobbying for party tickets were at its peak. Adarsh Narayan had promised Aniruddh his choice seat, but had not yet guaranteed the others. A total of seven people had joined the Kalinga Janata Dal from the KSM, and each got a party ticket to contest from. This created huge differences and bad blood within the ruling party ranks – a development that meant all was going according to plan.

Aniruddh got a ticket from the capital's north seat. It was a ruling party bastion, and the sitting MLA was convinced with the promise of a Rajya Sabha seat and a larger role in the party. The other members of KSM mostly got their preferred seats as was promised to them by Adarsh Narayan.

"Look, nine out of the 20 seats that we are fighting for from various parties are a sure shot victory. The remaining 11 are where we need to put in our efforts, along with the independent candidates," explained Bhanu, taking a sip of hot tea from an inch-long plastic cup.

"Which are the difficult ones?" asked Vishnu.

They all made it a point to meet after a month, post midnight in the erstwhile KSM office that was modified to a high-tech, election-monitoring cell. It was an important strategy meeting. Every inch of space was filled in the hall, and all the important stakeholders of the party executive committee were present.

"Rourkela, Ajeet Lakra, our man, has got a ticket from KJD. It is going to be tough, Lokhit Morcha has a strong cadre there. Plus, they get the support of the labour union of the steel plant.

"Polsara is a traditional KJD stronghold, but the sitting MLA is old and doesn't move out and he has no kids. So there is a small void there. The vote share distribution will do the trick for us. Kamal Barik is our independent candidate from Polsara. He is a trader, and will split the trader votes which have been Lokhit's traditional stronghold," explained Bhanu, going through the permutations of each of the 11 constituencies and their solutions.

"These constituencies are important because we have to uproot the established parties. There is a certain pattern of the electorate here. We have to understand that and use it to our benefit. Some go blindly with the party, whereas to others, the person matters. We have done our ticket lobbying in accordance to our 'winnabiliity' index based on the survey," the intricate details of the groundwork were being revealed now.

"Almost all the ruling party candidates are personally weak, and lacked a clear public mandate. They have been winning because they belong to the ruling party. So it does not matter who contests. As long as the party is same, people will go for the sign here. We have put our relatively doubtful candidates from the KJD ticket here, after a series of lobbying and bargains with Adarsh Narayan."

Bhanu did most of the talking.

"In some constituencies, the victory till date could be attributed to a slight flaw in the election system, where the man who gets the maximum votes is declared the winner and there is no minimum number of voters that dictates the validity of an election. So you can find a man winning a seat with 22% of the votes, because the overall voting percentage would not have exceeded 36%. Imagine if we could somehow increase that to at least 45 or 50 %? The whole dynamics of the seat would change. This is the unexplored vote share that is yet to be tapped. In most of these places we need to literally pull out the voters and make them vote for us.

"Take for instance the Janka constituency. The total number of registered voters are 2,75,000. The winning candidate got only 31% of the vote share. The second candidate got a close 28. The rest were inconsequential as far as the podium was concerned, but their vote shares were crucial enough in preventing the runner's up from giving a heart attack to Prafulla Rout, the winning DCP candidate. Only 1,15,000 people voted in that election. Rout won the elections with 31% of vote share. This means, Rout is an elected representative in the assembly, with only 35,650 people voting for him and his runner up gets 32,000. The other inconsequential candidates managed anything between 3-7%. Had the turnout been more, Rout could have lost. We have to tap on this large chunk of registered voters and make sure that they get their ass out to vote."

Bhanu kept staring at his computer screen as he briefed the team, turning to it as questions cropped up.

"What about the independents?" queried Dr Bichitra

"Not all of them are fighting to win, so we need to concentrate on those who have to win," said Vishnu. "The rest will manage to eat up the expected vote share, like Rout's opponents did."

"Funds?" another asked.

"We divert the various party funds that we all get from the parties we are contesting," Vishnu answered again in a tone that clearly indicated his understanding of the plot.

Aniruddh's silence, however, still attracted mixed feelings about his concurrence with the plan.

-----x-----

It was the first working committee meeting of the KJD post the ticket distributions and the joining of new members. The party office at the plush Forest Park location was flooded with workers and leaders. A horde of small time politicians loitered around the campus in an attempt to cosy up to the senior leadership of the party – Politics must be the most inspiring of all professions. Everyone has a chance to move up the hierarchy in his space and capability.

The CM himself was to be present for the meeting along with senior members and parliamentarians of the KJD. Security was beefed up all along the approach road to the party office. White kurta-clad big names stepped out of their swanky SUVs. The larger the leader, the longer was his cavalcade. One could guess the political weight of a man by the number of vehicles that followed him, some of which were surprisingly empty.

The Chief Minister arrived with Adarsh Narayan Mohanty, his political advisor. The suave ex-bureaucrat was believed to be the brains behind the man, and his proximity to the CM and his interference in party affairs often drew flak from senior party workers. The CM, however, took all-important decisions only with his concurrence. He covered up for the CM's lack of knowledge on the state. He was a grassroots man, who served almost his entire career in the state. He knew the state and its people inside out.

As expected, Mohanty dominated the meeting. He laid out the party's strategy for the upcoming elections, and the political environment in the state. The list of candidates had already been announced and there were major representations. There was a huge undercurrent of dissatisfaction, which he cunningly underplayed.

"We have been able to internally resolve issues and differences over the ticket distribution. This is an unique achievement for the party," he declared.

Members banged the table – a symbol of applause, often symbolic to the anger and frustration hid within. He went ahead with the announcement of probable names for the Lok Sabha elections before concluding the meeting. Only a few other very senior party members spoke during the whole meeting.

"Arey, Mohanty babu did not announce his name in the probable list for Lok Sabha," a sitting MLA was heard saying after the CM had left with his aide.

"Huh!? Mohanty babu may lose his deposit if he does so. Let him do what he is best at. Place his ass over a cool pack of ice, place a pack of ice over his head, keep sugar on his mouth and a rod in his hand." At that, the other senior members tried covering their smiles.Shri Narayan Sahu, one of the most popular rural leaders of the state, made the crude remark.

The power centre in the KJD was gradually shifting and the internal rift within the party was burgeoning in the political edifice.

Meanwhile, Bhanu and his team were handling social media quite efficiently. Individual campaigning and potential vote banks were targeted, while they opened a signature campaign for increasing the voting percentage. They were simultaneously engaged in mobilising the youth by making it 'cool to vote'.

The scene was getting dirty as the elections came closer. Some independent candidates fielded covertly by the KSM were physically abused or kidnapped, just to be released after two or three days. Each time such an incident would occur, Bhanu and his team would start an aggressive troll on social media. The regional media would then be forced to follow them, and soon the issue would get primetime footage.

During the couple of months preceding the elections, the country seemed all geared up with banners and posters of irrelevant leaders eating up city spaces. The state was gearing up for another expected dominance by the ruling party. There was an unusual political lull that lasted weeks together before it suddenly disappeared, and the state was in the middle of a scintillating political drama.

It was ten past midnight and Aniruddh was chatting with Radhika over Skype – the couple had seen relationship span the days of letter writing to queue at the local PCO booth to the days of mobile phones. Skype was a boon for long distant couples. The busy campaigning schedule allowed only a limited time for chat.

"Hold on. Stay online, I am getting a call," Aniruddh cut Radhika short during her animated narrative.

"Who is it calling you at this hour?"

"Akash!" he replied with his eyebrows raised.

"Hey, Akash. Is everything fine?"

"Bhaina, I have to meet you. There is something urgent that I have to tell you."

Akash Baral was another member of KSM who had joined the ruling party, and had a ticket for the upcoming elections.

"What is it?" Aniruddh asked, snapping Skype session with Radhika.

"There is a huge political development that is about to take place either tomorrow or day after."

"Political development?"

"Yes, in the KJD. Bhaina, Adarsh babu has opened his cards."

"He is splitting the KJD and has the support of 25 MLAs with him. The DCP has promised him principle-based support from outside and he is on a spree. The man is trying to buy, threaten or convince the rest. He called in for me. He wants to meet you," said Akash, almost gasping for breath.

"I can't meet him before I meet the other members of the group. Take some time from him. I shall get back to you," said Aniruddh, ending the call and almost subconsciously running his hand over his head, thinking over this implausible new development.

The whole thing had suddenly shaken up the rather soporific political narrative of the state. Though the news was still not made public, the political sorority was well informed about the trusted aide's 'Valkyrie' stunt. The problem for many was not the news of the split but the fact that they now had to display their loyalties in public. This was the most awkward political position one could find himself in.

"The man has just made our job simpler, we must go with him," said Deepak, visibly elated over the news as the entire story was narrated to the gang at Basu babu's place.

"He has punched him at the right time. The KJD will fall apart like a pack of cards now," remarked Dr Bichitra.

"No, Adarsh babu has chosen the most inappropriate time to do such a thing," said Basudev Acharya, speaking for the first time.

"The CM is still in power and enjoys a healthy majority as well as popularity. Betraying him before the elections would only make him look like an ambitious beguiler. He might have thrown the king out of the throne, but, in a democracy, people enjoy the most when they do it themselves. Not when a cunning counterpart does it. Adarsh Narayan has dug his own ditch. The entire anti-incumbency will now get converted to sympathy. The CM only gains more."

"What should we be doing?" queried Akash.

"Defection is as good as betrayal. It is time to stick to him in this hour of need. Be the Mark Anthony to this Caesar, when the honorable Brutus harms him. The goodwill that you gain will be needed by you in future," said Basu babu, who loved giving examples from Shakespeare. His wise words made a lot of sense to all those who understood it.

The political atmosphere in the state was boiling with each passing hour. The CM cut short his visit to US and took the first flight back home. The negotiations were at full flow and the facilitators had a field day. Money was offered as generously as anyone could imagine. Personal favours were pulled and promises were made with every single deal that was sealed. However unstable the underbelly was, the façade still looked threateningly impassive as the CM's arrival loomed.

An emergency meeting was called in at the KJD office. Adarsh Narayan and his supporters sensed the forthcoming danger. Although the word was still not out in the open, every single politician in the state worth his salt was aware of the grand plot that was being hatched. The CM arrived at the party headquarters, chaired the meeting, and immediately suspended Adarsh Narayan from all the important posts as well as from primary membership of the party. The other 12 MLAs, all of whom supported Adarsh, were also suspended from the party.

Adarsh Narayan's *coup d'état* had failed. He immediately called a press conference to justify his stand and prove his innocence. He blamed his counterparts of being jealous of him, and of having planned this treacherous game to discredit him.

"One day, the truth shall be known and that day, I am sure I shall walk out clean," said the man who till the night before was considered the second most powerful man in the state. He was now only a name that was followed by the media for a week before being left in the oblivion. Things are dynamic in the world of politics. Identities change fast and ideologies change even faster.

A number of alliances and coalitions were announced in the succeeding days of delicate political equations. The dormant state had suddenly erupted into activity.

The election code of conduct would soon be put in place, and so, the season of schemes was at its peak. The public was showered with alluring schemes and loan waivers. It was getting difficult to please the Indian electorate though.

"Earlier, people would ask for subsidies and lower prices. Now they just want everything free," said a disgusted Bichitrananda. The KSM members had very low net worth, and hence were not able to keep up with the growing financial competition in the campaigning trail.

-----x-----

"You look ten years older in that white kurta. Why can't you go for some other colour? Brown suits you." The Skype call with Radhika was a routine Aniruddh wouldn't miss even during busy campaigning days.

"Hehe!" he chuckled. "I can't go for campaigning wearing a brown kurta. Moreover, white is best to beat the heat," he added, in the rather delightful way in which he explained things to his love.

"So have you decided on your internship yet?"

"Nah! Mama wants me to come to the state high court. I want to go to Delhi. So we are in the middle of this dilemma. I have no reason to go there," she said, adding the last line after a deliberate pause and with a tad more emphasis.

"No reason to come here?" Aniruddh asked, picking up on the emphasis.

"Aur kya? Whenever I come there, we can't even meet properly. It's either your place or my place, and that too in the evenings. No scope of going anywhere in public. No restaurants, no parks, no coffee shops. It's much better when you come down to Pune."

She could relate to the experience of hanging out with a public figure. It could be a little too tasking at times to be a known figure in this country. A public figure with a girlfriend would make up for juicy headlines, but a political figure with a girlfriend was almost akin to blasphemy.

The humid month of July soon heralded the monsoons and it brought much-needed relief to the coastal state. The rains also brought an end to the hectic campaigning season ahead of the elections. The country was all set to organise, witness and be part of the largest democratic process in the world.

The campaigning ended two days before the voting dates, as the warriors and the foot soldiers retired back to their camps and waited.

Elections are the biggest festival in India. It is celebrated throughout the country, cutting across regional and religious divide. It hijacks all civilised discussions from boardroom to bedroom. The media takes the event to higher levels of histrionics as news channel device innovative means to engage people in discussions. The melodramatic anchors and the chivy reporters on the ground turn this democratic process into a theatrical experience. Every single victory is scrutinised, every defeat analysed as political pundits and psephologists dissect every aspect to irritating details.

But, alas, to the 46% illiterate Indian population that consists of 70% of the voters, it is all about caste or class, or worse still, a bottle of liquor.

"Five people have been seriously injured in Jagatpur district, the KJD and DCP members had a duel," said Vishnu as they all sat glued to the television screen on the day of the election at the KSM 'election cell'. The room was filled with erstwhile members and all the important stakeholders. It was their war room, and it sure gave the feeling of the D-day.

"Naxals have destroyed three polling booths and burnt the EVMs in Malkangiri. They had called for a boycott," came another update. There were a few boys and girls sitting glued to their systems, updating statistical databases and preparing graphs. There was a huge map of the state affixed in the centre wall that was regularly marked in red and white colours by another young man. Red and white was the colour of KSM.

The first two phases of voting were relatively peaceful. As the day of the third and the final phase of voting approached, the tension in the air was evitable. KJD had done their internal surveys and were expecting a landslide victory yet again. The DCP was almost certain of a disastrous result owing to the anti-incumbency at the centre. The Swayam Sevak Party expected to outperform the others at the centre and hoped to make inroads in the state once again.

"Thirteen out of 21 polling stations in Angul have seen violent duel between KJD and DCP supporters. Three people have been seriously injured in the clashes and ten others have been admitted in the hospital," read the news anchor.

"I hope the injuries are not too serious," said a tensed Aniruddh.

"Only one had serious injuries on his ribs. The rest are just fine. The government doctors were paid to forge the medical reports and put them in ICU," replied Deepak.

"Salipur and Patkura assembly seats have also seen high tension and likely reports of booth capturing and tampering of EVMs have been reported," a volunteer announced.

"Complains lodged?" asked Aniruddh.

"Yes."

"Re-elections?"

"Almost certain," replied Bhanu, looking terrible with untrimmed stubble.

"So, it is going as per plan."

"Yes, until now. So, we have got the final count to 144," confirmed another volunteer glued to his system.

The television primetime was filled with post poll predictions and analysis.

"So, that's it. The game on the ground is over, and now its time for the games behind the screen. Let's get our act together," said Vishnu, as they all hugged each other and left the KSM office.

-----xx-----

CHAPTER 20

Three Toyota Innovas were neatly parked outside the vintage Victorian bungalow. The brass name tab read Shri Basudev Acharya. Apart from the regular visitors, Basu babu's drawing room was host to two very unusual guests that evening – Shri Narayan Sahu and Shri Gopinath Barik, the senior KJD leaders.

Sahu was the tall leader of the southern districts. He was an MLA for 25 years, and had won his previous election by a record margin. You got an idea of his clout in the south from the fact that the politically naïve CM, in his first election, was given Sahu's seat as it was considered to be a 'zero risk' constituency. Sahu had the image of a disciplined party soldier, a behind-the-screen man.

Barik was more of the vibrant and upcoming kind. He was one of the youngest members of the Rajya Sabha. A typical product of Oxford, he lacked the skills to be popular at the grassroots and had lost the last Lok Sabha elections miserably. However, money gained him a Rajya Sabha seat and many considered him the face of the KJD in Delhi. He was young, educated, rich and popular. Many considered him as the heir apparent to the bachelor CM.

Basu babu had chosen the right pawns.

"Skepticism has grown exponentially post the Adarsh Narayan incident. People are being chucked out for minor misconduct," said a worried Narayan Sahu. "The popularity of the CM has made him even more dictatorial. Please don't consider my visit to you as an affirmation to the deal. Basu bhai, it is my respect for you that brings me here."

"Moreover, your prepositions aren't clear enough as well," added Gopinath.

"We can open our cards only after some clarification from you, Narayan babu," replied Vishnu.

"Basu babu, don't mind, but I think your plans look too ambitious and premature for me to commit to," said Gopinath with a smirk on his face.

Basudev looked at Gopinath and smiled back, in the manner of a father smiling back at his child's irrational questions.

"Your father was a wonderful human being. You remind me of him. He would have been a truly proud father today," said Basu babu, showing Gopinath a photo of him standing next to his father, Shri Devdas Barik, one of the most respected industrialists of his time.

"Anyways, son, how is Akanksya? She married a businessman in Patna, if I am not wrong?" asked Basu babu. The question wasn't a comfortable one.

"She's doing fine," he replied quickly, expecting the old man to change the topic.

Gopinath Barik had two sisters – Akanksya and Anusuya. Only a few were privy to the fact that they were Gopinath's stepsisters. His mother was Devdas Barik's second wife. Gopinath was born to her from her first husband who is believed to have left her for greener pastures. Devdas Barik gave Gopinath the status of his eldest son and heir.

The older sister, Akanskya, was studying in JNU when she fell for a student union leader and bore a child with him. But the man joined the Naxal movement, and left Akanksya with the promise to get back. The poor girl was left to fend for herself as Devadas Barik disowned her. Nothing was heard of her for a long time, before she was found in an inebriated state in the streets of south Mumbai. She had apparently aborted her child, was under the influence of drugs and penniless. The Barik family was believed to have paid huge amount to various media houses for keeping the matter quiet.

"A fine lady she is, indeed. May god bless her," said Basu babu, and the message was delivered as intended – Gopinath Barik was silent for the rest of the discussion.

"Narayan, I know your clout in the party and amongst the workers. Your work and your stature have never been acknowledged. The man for whom you vouch your loyalty sadly feels intimidated by you."

"But, Basu bhai, it is difficult to convince the others. Plus, the anti-defection law will make it difficult to pull through," said Narayan babu, hyperventilating – the first signs of a man being convinced by a plan, even if it looked dangerous. "A lot of money will be required for pulling the stack together. These are days of high stakes, Basu bhai, and you know it well."

"If we can't pull them together, then we will have to herd them to a corner. You start the process. Nobody knows the herd better than you, my brother," said Basu babu, putting an arm over Narayan's shoulder.

"What about the anti-defection law?" asked Gopinath, speaking after a long time.

"We are getting a 2/3rd out, that would solve the problem of anti-defection," said Aniruddh, speaking for the first time.

"Are you serious? You mean, you plan to break the ruling party and get 2/3rd to join you?"

"Apparently," answered Vishnu.

"How?"

"Don't worry Gopinath bhai that is our look out. You just do your bit."

-----x-----

Just four days were left for the counting, and there was an unusual stolidity in the political atmosphere of the state. The undercurrents were felt in the KJD camp, but none dared to speak out in the open. An air of suspicion and fear gripped the entire political fraternity. The fall out would make or break a few. People had chosen sides; they were just waiting for the right time to declare their options.

It was five in the evening, and the third day before the counting. The media was abuzz with the rumours of a press conference by a few senior leaders of KJD. The official message was sent an hour before the presser. The Soochana Bhavan was packed with media personnel and party workers of the KJD. At a quarter to six, Shri Narayan Sahu arrived along with Gopinath Barik, Aniruddh Mishra and two other leaders of the KJD, followed by Vishnu Pradhan.

The media went beserk, seeing all of them in one frame. The political pundits were shaken to the core when they saw a leader of the stature of Shri Narayan Sahu bending down to greet the greenhorns.

"The state has been craving to see a change in leadership. It was our responsibility to call for a revolutionary change in the state. We had this input from our interaction with the people, how fed up they were with the present government and the leadership. It's time for change and we are proud to be a part of it," stated Narayana Sahu, refusing to field questions as he handed the microphone over to Barik.

Barik was a shade bit smarter with words. He knew how to handle the media. His offshore education helped him confuse them with words.

"This new political initiative, with our young and dynamic leaders here, fetching a development plan for the state, will take this great land of ours to its glorious past," called out Gopinath, looking at Aniruddh.

"The Progressive Odisha Alliance will work solely for the development of the state, and shall strive to make it one of the developed states of this country," said Vishnu, making his presence felt.

"Who is the leader of this alliance?" asked a journalist.

"We have our first convening meeting tomorrow. All important decisions and appointments shall be finalised then," replied Barik.

Isn't this a larger plot to destabilise the incumbent CM and the government? Why this announcement just two days before the counting? What were your differences with the CM? This is the third time, the leaders of KSM have made a shift, aren't they becoming a political joke?

The salvo of questions was mostly left unanswered.

"Do you aim to form the next government? How many MLAs have supported you?"

"The results will make things clearer. Please wait till the counting day," replied Vishnu as they left the stage after the ceremonial joining and raising of hands.

The presser started and got over amidst so much chaos that it took some time for the TV reporters to get their acts together and go on air. Most of them kept reassuring themselves of what they had witnessed. The most loyal faces of the KJD had now ditched the party. The questions just wouldn't stop. The silence of Aniruddh, however, left a lot of questions unanswered.

Why did they do it? What was the lure? Who is the man behind this great game? What now?

The political dynamics in the state suddenly became unusually vibrant. The political sorority was now divided into small factions. Each faction had its own importance, and each leader his own price. The market was open for trading. The highest bidder would get his numbers.

"How did you pull Debasis Pattnaik to the stack? He is considered to be like a brother to the CM?" asked Deepak.

"He wanted some progress in the mining ban, almost all his money is stuck. The CM had promised him, but hasn't fulfilled it yet. He says promises won't keep us alive," clarified Vishnu, as they headed to Narayan Sahu's place for a crucial meeting.

The KJD had already approached the courts and had initiated a legal discourse to that effect, charging the defectors with the provisions of the Tenth Schedule of the anti-defection law.

It was now mandatory for the defectors to get atleast 2/3rd of the total strength of KJD by their side to protect their candidature and make the plan work.

These were days of heightened political activity. Narayan Sahu and his group had just made the game a shade more interesting.

The KJD office was bustling with party workers and members. Sloganeering against the defectors had been continuous for over 48 hours. Names were being called and effigies were burnt. The CM did not come out of his house. He left the media high and dry for the whole duration of the drama.

"We have managed 34, we need 30 more to reach the 2/3rd figure," said Narayan babu.

"Debasis has promised the mining lobby will get us four more," assured Vishnu.

"I had a word with Ashok Majhi, the tribal leaders are still not opening their cards," said Dr Bichitra.

"What about Adarsh Babu?"

"His 12 are in, although he has his list of demands and positions that he expects," replied Deepak to the query raised by Basudev babu, who sat through the meeting in his wheel chair.

"We are cutting this very close; we are dealing with so many demands and negotiations. I just hope we are not pushed into a tight spot," said Aniruddh, looking worried.

"I have confirmed news, the CM is contemplating a decision. The announcement is likely anytime. Then he will rush to the governor for dismissal, on grounds of Tenth Schedule of the anti-defamation law," said Gopinath.

"Great, well that is exactly what we want. Create confusion in the ranks. How many is he going to dismiss? We shall keep him guessing till the end. The more he reacts the more confusion he creates," replied Basu babu.

"By the way, we are yet to complete the paperwork on the new alliance. Aniruddh and other leaders have to sign on the declaration and oath paper. The decision on the CM candidate also needs to be finalised," reminded Gopinath.

The others, however, looked surprised as Aniruddh was almost accepted as the uncrowned leader.

"Yeah, we have to do that soon, Gopi babu. The new members will be asking for that," replied Deepak.

"Tomorrow is a very important day for all of us, Narayan babu. We have to stay together through all this and pull in our maximum strength to see to it that our beloved state is freed from the shackles of this tyranny," cried out Basudev, as the young members huddled around him.

It was the all-important day of counting. The entire country was glued to their televisions, India was about to give a historical mandate. The coastal state, too, was abnormally active in the political battlefield after the fresh developments.

"How bad is it?" asked the CM, having anticipated the fissure in the party owing to the ousting of senior leaders.

"I won't say it is bad, but yes, it is going to hurt us," replied the man with the CM, on his balcony, sipping the morning tea. Security had been tightened around the CM's residence to prevent any unforeseen event.

"What about the Lok Sabha?" enquired the CM.

"We are sweeping it."

"Good, atleast we have something to bargain for, if we fall short of numbers in the state."

"Yes, but that depends upon the numbers they get at the centre."

"They might not need us at all."

The conversation went on for a few more agonising moments before the runner barged in with the cordless landline phone.

"Party office. Parida babu," he said as he handed over the phone to the CM.

Parida was the interim general secretary, appointed in the wake of the current turbulence.

"Sir, 30 others including three sitting members of the Parliament have been approached by them. They might hit $2/3^{rd}$ with that number. This immunizes them from the anti-defection law," informed Jagat Parida.

The CM hung the phone after a brief moment of silence. It was probably the most intimidating moment in his 16-year political career. A 27-year-old amateur was about to snatch his power away from right under his nose.

Everything now depended on the results.

-----x-----

It was ten in the morning, and the humid city weather gave way to clouds of speculations. The KJD was obviously leading as per the initial trends in the counting. The irony was that the party, which got the mandate from the people, was fighting for its own identity and existence.

The members of the newly formed alliance were huddled up at the KYM election cell. There was an obvious elephant in the room. People had put their entire political careers at stake. If this didn't work, they would be ostracised in the political circle.

"Bichtira babu, Deepak and Vishnu bhai are leading from their respective constituencies. Narayan babu is ahead with 25,000 votes," came the initial inputs.

"Bubu Mishra is trailing in Baripada, and Srikanth Ransingh in Cuttack, Choudhwar. We come down by two, they were safe seats," said Deepak.

Trends kept coming at a faster rate as the day progressed. The tension grew with each new trend.

"All 16 candidates from the opposition that have owed allegiance are winning."

"Check the status on independents?" ordered a visibly nervous Barik.

"Six have already won, seven are leading and the rest have lost, as per plan, of course," Bhanu yelled back.

"What is up with Adarsh Narayan's gang?"

"Eight out of the twelve are winning; we are comfortable with that, considering the fact that we had counted just the six."

"Results withheld in two Maoist infested constituencies – Sundergarh and Nabarangpur – plus the Athamalik constituency due to poll day violence," announced someone from Bhanu's team.

"Great. That brings down the total count. We did not expect a win in either of those seats."

The atmosphere remained pensive till the last result was announced. Never before in the history were the victorious candidates so unsure of their futures. The political calculus of the state looked more confusing than an unsolved calculus equation.

The final anticipatory figures, as put up by the media houses, gave the state an absolute hung assembly, with a huge number of them liable for suspension on account of defection.

The KJD managed a total of 58 seats. The Odisha Progressive Alliance got 46 seats and 13 out of 20 independent candidates fielded by the KSM won their seats. The DCP won 18 seats, the SSP won ten seats, and the remaining two seats were won by the Communist Union.

The OPA was still short by 15 seats, even when the independent winners were accounted for.

"Yadav ji had promised to fall back. They will definitely need us," said a frail man at the Pabitra Niwas, the CM's residence.

It was 11 in the morning and the Lok Sabha results trickled in faster than ever before. The CMs's face became more destitute with each passing lead of the SSP.

The Swayam Sevak Party had already won the 144 odd seats and was leading in another 115 more. It was to be a historic mandate, if the leads continued to remain the same.

"I don't think so, they will need even the traditional support they always needed. We were still a distant option for them," remarked the CM, disdainfully getting up from his cane lounge chair and walking to his balcony.

The victory by the SSP at the centre could not have been more absolute. They had won a whopping 315 Lok Sabha seats, leaving the others way behind. They had an absolute majority. They needed no external support.

Closer home, the KJD and the OPA were fighting a crucial battle of numbers. The parties clogged their winning candidates in herds at far away resorts and forest guesthouses to prevent them from defecting or getting hijacked. The future of the unicameral assembly of the coastal state lurked in darkness for the next three days as KJD filed for suspension of defecting members.

Four days after the results, the leader of OPA, Shri Narayan Sahu, called for a press conference and declared that their party had the numbers and would stake claim to form the next government. On being asked about the details, he expressed his compulsion, on account of discreetness and security of the legislatures.

The next day, Shri Narayan Sahu and Vishnu Pradhan marched up to the Raj Bhavan and handed the letter of support from 89 MLAs to the governor. They also had the support of the SSP that had formed the government in Delhi. The developments were sudden and surprising, while the KJD were still contemplating its course of action. The governor invited them to form the government and prove their majority in the house.

Aniruddh Mishra was declared the unanimous choice for the post of leader of the party and the Chief Minister.

Back at the house of Shri Basudev Acharya, marathon meetings and negotiations were still on. All stakeholders were summoned up in a sequential manner as Basu babu personally sat through the negotiations. This was the first occasion he came out and openly declared his political role.

"Mathur Sahib, you are a very old friend. Your contribution to this revolutionary political arrangement in the state will always be credited. The way you have got us the support of those MLAs is indeed remarkable," the old man told Mithilesh Mathur.

Mathur was the chairman of Metalate Corp. His interests in the chromium rich hills of the state drew him close to Basu babu, who suitably fuelled his ambitions of setting up the largest chromium mining unit next to the mineral rich tribal lands. The case had been lingering for quite some time, with void assurances from the state government.

A frustrated Mathur was on the verge of pulling out of the project when he met Basudev, and the new arrangement was sealed. He did not do much. He just bought the members who would otherwise have never joined the OPA.

"But, sir, Aniruddh's reservations about the land is making me increasingly nervous. He even gave a statement during the campaigns, openly dismissing the idea of mining the mineral rich Chandbhanga hills," said Mathur, his concerns evident.

"Don't worry, Mathur sahib. I shall convince him, just give me some time."

The important visitors that night included the infamous Adarsh Narayan. His role was instrumental in getting the errant KJD members fall in line. Those who had expressed reservations in joining the OPA had to be reminded of their consent letters sent to Adarsh Narayan during his failed coup, which he had so carefully preserved for any future occurrences. They became the most powerful medium of bargaining with those errant MLAs, who demanded an awful amount of money.

Every possible trick in political science was put into play. A careful mix of subversion, coercion, cohesion, compulsion and compromise were instrumental in demolishing one of the strongest political bastions of independent India.

The dormant state, no more lay dormant.

The new political base, however, was established on a negative platform that had an uncertain future.

-----xx-----

CHAPTER 21

—————◆—————

"Do you feel the masses will accept us?" asked a visibly worried Aniruddh to his political guru. The old man comforted him, sipping on his daily dose of slushy Darjeeling green tea. The Kuakhai river flowed next to his bungalow, tranquil as ever, unperturbed by the political storm around it.

"It will be difficult for you. You are not the product of a standard political protocol. Our alliance is the result of a hasty mixture of heterogeneous political arrangement. You will be highly susceptible as a Chief Minister," remarked the veteran journalist.

"More than anything, you have to manage the perception of the media. At present, the media is projecting you as the villain. Once the media is won over, half of your battle is won.

"In politics, the scrutiny is merciless. Good or bad, public scrutiny will continue to remain. The opposition clearly has the sympathy of the people as you are viewed as vile. You have to manage the public, the media and the perception all at the same time. But believe me, it isn't too difficult in a country like ours," the old man explained.

"The coalition is also going to give you some sleepless nights. You need to prepare yourself for the worst at any point of time. The sooner you get the public by your side, the better it is for you. To rule over the people, you have to conquer the fourth estate first."

Aniruddh heard him like an obedient disciple. All his youth he wanted to serve his people, but when the time came, he was surrounded by a strange diffidence that made him unsure of his abilities. But destiny had grand plans for this young man.

-----X-----

She hugged him tight and looked happy. There was a certain glow in her eye. The 'Samant House' had three SUVs parked outside. They had the most sought after person in the state visiting them.

"Thanks for flying down at such short notice," said Aniruddh, holding her hand.

"How could I miss it? I had to be present for the biggest moment of your life," said Radhika, planting a kiss on his chin. "But I think the media is being mean. It seems as if you are being shown as the villain. The people wanted a change and you have given them the alternative."

"Don't worry, the people will accept us in some time," said Aniruddh, although he sounded as if he was reassuring himself more than anyone else.

He suddenly sprung on to the bed and sat next to her. "Hey, if you don't have an objection to it, can we get married?"

The sudden proffering from the emotionally introvert Aniruddh left her astounded. She kept staring at him for a while as the statement sunk in.

"What happened?" Look, there is no hurry. You can take your time," said Aniruddh, realising his proposal was way too abrupt. "Look, I know, there is a lot of uncertainty in my life right now. But, I guess, it isn't going to change much. Maybe, I love this. Maybe, I have to …" but he was cut short.

"No, no. I was never worried about that. I always knew what I was heading for when I fell in love with you. I was only appalled by the way you proposed. I never thought you could do that … ever."

She loved him the way she always did. She knew him more than anyone else.

There were reservations in the Samant family about their relationship, but Radhika's mother, Mrinalini, could never be forward about her opposition. She knew the things at stake. She was a media magnate, and clearly understood the value of a son-in-law as the Chief Minister of the state.

The 27-year-old was the object of hatred all around, but he was soon going to be the youngest Chief Minister of independent India.

The engagement was a low-key affair, and the marriage was scheduled for the following month.

As for Aniruddh, he had played a masterstroke that many could hardly interpret. In a knot, he tied up the support of the largest media house of the state.

Radhika's mother owned the Chakyu group that had under it six vernacular newspapers and three local channels. The media was won over, or conquered, rather.

-----x-----

The festival 'Raja', gave the state their new CM – the youngest ever to hold that position. The rise of the street protestor through the portals of power was heralded as a phenomenal political event. A 27-year-old jeans-clad graduate hijacked the reigns of the state from the political heavyweights right under their noses.

Never ever was an elected CM of a state sworn in under such public skepticism and political incertitude. While at the centre there was the parliament with an absolute majority, the state assembly hung dangerously at the mercy of a few defectors.

The portfolio distribution went off smoothly. All the major stakeholders were given their share for the unprecedented loyalty they had shown. Shri Narayan Sahu was the Deputy CM, and held the important portfolio of Home. Aniruddh kept Finance and Urban Development with himself. Vishnu Pradhan got Industries, and Dibakar Das, an ex-KJD MLA now from the Adarsh Narayan faction, got the prized portfolio of mining.

A majority of the council of ministers was in their late thirties or early forties. The media termed it as the 'Jeans Army Invasion' of the state assembly – at least a third of the members were seen in jeans, t-shirts or short-kurtas.

Amid a hostile political atmosphere and a cynical media appreciation, the Chief Minister held his first press conference. The media community was thirsty for blood and was confident of drawing first blood at this conference. The Dy. CM and Deepak Rout, who had been elected as the new party president, accompanied Aniruddh.

"Sir, the KJD leadership has accused you of making a mockery of electoral democracy, horse trading and taking a back door entry by cheating the mandate of the people?"

"The KJD can say whatever it wishes to. We are answerable to the people of the state, not to the KJD leadership," replied Deepak.

"What makes you think that this merger of conveniences could give the state a lasting government?" the question came from a senior journalist of a reputed media house, and was directed straight at the CM.

Aniruddh knew that sooner or later, he would be asked these questions. The CM took the microphone, and looked every bit the confident young leader he was.

"At the outset, I would like to wish all my brothers and sisters on the occasion of *'Raja'*. May the festival bring joy and prosperity into our lives," starting out with a message of joy did exactly what it was devised for – it reflected his humane side, as opposed to the impression of him being a cold slayer.

"Look, I can never deny the fact that the circumstances in which we came to power are viewed under serious skepticism and is a matter of concern in certain circles. The reservation among the people of the state with respect to our government is understandable."

Acknowledgement is the greatest factor of trust, and Aniruddh knew how to win over the trust of his people.

"We needed change, and the people of this great land deserved an alternative. An alternative that could foster hope and belief in millions of people. An alternative that could get the state out of its maladies. An alternative of hope and a feeling that would reignite the 'Kalinga Gaurav' amongst the people."

He sounded much better than what many had expected.

"We have deliberated for days together trying to chalk a thorough a roadmap for the overall development of the state. Our government shall focus on inclusive growth and opportunity for all. The aspects of infrastructure development, health care and education shall be given utmost importance. I firmly believe that instead of asking for special status and demanding extra funds from the centre, our resource potential is capable enough of making us one of the richer states of the country. We are not ailing with anything other than what I would refer to as 'aspirational austerity'. We have been forced to enjoy our indigence and successive governments in the past have benefited their coffers by creating this image of a pauper out of its own people."

The man on the stage, speaking out on the microphone, facing hundreds of cameramen and media people, was not sounding anything like the Aniruddh Mishra the people had known earlier. Maturity in speech is the most important virtue of a leader. People love to hear their leader speak well and speak sense.

As Aniruddh went ahead with his presser, a nervous state was now slowly gaining its nerve back. The one hour in which he spoke was revered as the best hour of political discourse in the state for the last two decades. The issues that were touched by him were directly linked to the people. Thus, someone who was an object of hatred suddenly became the new ray of hope. The clarity in thought and the honesty in his intentions were clearly reflected in the young CM's face. The media also played its part.

-----x-----

The job in hand wasn't easy. The previous government had left behind a legacy of deficit and overdraft. Public services and government facilities were at its nadir. Development was restricted to a few urban pockets, while much of the state still remained impoverished due to lack of opportunities and avenues.

"Investor faith is at an all time low, sir. The delay in the $12 billion Metaxing Steel Plant has made the investors skeptical about the state," briefed the Finance Secretary in one of the hundred sessions that the CM attended in his first week in office.

"How far have we gone with the issue in the Metaxing project?" asked Aniruddh.

"Sir, procedurally we are done. Politically, we haven't begun yet. The opposing forces have a better reach and influence over the people. Land acquisition isn't the issue. The people are being constantly misled and provoked by local leaders. Some issues are relevant, while most others are baseless and employed only as delay mechanisms," explained Rajesh Pujari, the chief secretary.

Mr Pujari was a highly reputed and capable officer. His no-nonsense attitude put him at loggerheads with most governments in the past. Radhika's grandfather, and the founder of Chakyu media group, recommended him to the CM.

"Can we interact with the people, try and understand the issues, and maybe talk to them directly?" queried the CM.

"Sure, sir, but we have to be cautious about the security issues. It is a hostile mob you shall be talking to. Things can flare up at any time. I need to take the local administrative opinion before advising you in favour of such a step," replied the secretary.

"I need the officials of the company as well, if possible," Aniruddh added before leaving the conference hall for his office.

Aniruddh enjoyed an elaborate security arrangement by virtue of being the CM of a Naxal-hit state with a history of violence. Though he was averse to it, Aniruddh had to comply with a minimum set up that included four armed men around him and two armed vehicles full of police commandoes for prophylactic security.

Initially, his OSD had a tough time managing his cordon, as the CM would dismount his vehicle at any place to meet people. He would break the cordon at public gatherings and cause a nightmare for his security entail. However, he was gradually made aware of the limitations and the precautions he needed to adhere to.

He was not only new to this position of power and authority; he was also a husband now. His busy schedule rendered it impossible for them to lead the life of a normal couple. As the CM's better half, Radhika enjoyed her share of limelight as well. She was invited as guest to many social events. Her calendar was equally packed. The only time they could sit together as a family was at breakfast.

"Deepti had called up, her semester is getting over next week," said Radhika.

Aniruddh's younger sibling was completing her engineering in computer science in Bangalore.

"Oh yes, maa had mentioned it, skipped my mind completely. How did her papers go?" queried Aniruddh.

"She is a bright girl, she will do well. She has been selected by the recruiters from Infosys," replied Radhika.

"Is she interested in working now? I always thought she wanted to pursue management? What has changed her mind?" asked Aniruddh, clearly indicating his reservations about her taking a job.

"She is wise enough to take her own decisions, you can't think for her, obviously?"

"Yeah, but she is still very young. I think I can talk her out of it," claimed Aniruddh.

"Yeah, you can talk anybody out of anything," came the sarcastic reply.

"Debu uncle had called up yesterday. He wants me to start practicing in his law firm," Radhika continued.

"Do you want to?"

"Yeah, I think I shouldn't lose touch."

"Sure, then go ahead," he said nonchalantly, still glaring at the newspaper.

-----xx-----

CHAPTER 22

———◆◆———

The day of the CM usually began with a morning brief from his PS on the schedule of the day, followed by a daily meet with the Chief Secretary.

It was a day of a crucial meet with the Superintendents of Police of all the districts. The CM wanted an in depth feedback on the issues of naxalism and the means to deal with it. Aniruddh had his own plans, which he wanted to divulge at the end of the meet.

The session continued with a series of presentations and mandated briefs scripted and chiseled to its bureaucratic best, devoid of the truth as always. The CM heard everyone patiently till his turn came at the end.

"What I could learn from the elaborate briefs is that, although everyone identifies the problem, but none is willing enough to recommend anything concrete," the CM started with an unappealing grin on his face.

"Well, I certainly feel the urgency of raising a competent force to fight the menace from its epicentre. We need to give real impetus to the two-pronged approach that you have been talking about,"

"We have planned to raise a Special Task Force to deal with all Naxal related exigencies which the regular police or the administration is inadequately trained to handle. This force will look at the dual aspects of security and development in the affected districts. Each district headquarter will have representatives of the Task force, that will monitor progress and implement government policies in these areas. The law-enforcing unit of the Task Force will have specially trained personnel from the police force. They shall be adequately trained and equipped to fight the menace," Aniruddh outpoured his thoughts, even as the senior police officers were surprised by the preparedness of the young CM. The amount of research done by him astounded them as he revealed further details of the action plan.

The DGP's concerns over budget and additional burden to the force were adequately addressed by the CM and his team. His announcement of an additional fund of Rs 500 crores for the raising of the Special Team reflected the sincerity in his endeavour.

The CM followed up his speech by a series of guidelines and codes for the police force. His advice to the senior officials on the conduct of the beat policemen was the most relevant and plausible. He seemed tough and critical, but the police did find a leader in him, who they believed would certainly stand by them.

The people of the state witnessed positive changes in governance that was hitherto missing. The administration started functioning with greater efficiency than ever before. The new government introduced schemes that empowered the farmers and insulated them from risks. Value addition and skill development were given priority rather than populist schemes and freebies.

"We need to work harder to uplift the 'state of our state'. The farmers and the working class need to come out of their insecurities and draw their strength from the government and I promise the desired support from government," the CM would announce in every speech of his.

Farmers across the state were encouraged to register themselves and were given free insurance for their harvest. They were now not averse to experimenting and taking risks.

Sick industries were immediately disinvested and creating numerous industrial corridors with fast track approval systems encouraged private partnership. A Special Industrial Tribunal was set up to resolve legal issues at a faster rate.

Town Planning was the CM's priority sector. Aniruddh appointed senior engineers and retired administrators as special advisors to ensure planned expansion of major cities and formation of new township.

The first two years of the government were highly successful. Things rolled out and files moved faster than ever before. The state was slowly gaining momentum for the first time in the last two decades. The young CM, who had begun his political career under huge skepticism and incertitude, was now one of the most loved figures in the state.

Aniruddh was also the most powerful leader of the coalition. He would eventually ratify all major decisions before they were passed. He behaved like an ombudsman over every ministry. This would discipline the cabinet, but at times, was a major cause of dissent amongst the other cabinet members.

"He is interfering far more than what could be called constructive. There is no space to work. All the files cannot be routed through the CM's office. His decisions are imperative and nobody dares to counter him," cribbed Vishnu to the old Basudev. It was a common saying in the political circles that Aniruddh could defy his father, but not Basudev.

"I understand your concern, Vishnu. I will speak to him when he visits me."

The more popular he became, the more authority he wielded. The more authority he wielded the more he grew in stature.

Aniruddh would soon face the first challenge of his political career. The young CM was obsessed with bringing reforms in the functioning of various religious institutes in the state. Most of them were managed abysmally by corrupt, incompetent but influential people.

The state's biggest assets were its religious sites. However, the management and the lobby of the temple administrators made it virtually impregnable for the government to interfere and clean the filth within. The rich and the powerful administrators continued with their orthodox and greedy means of managing these institutes.

Aniruddh wanted to bring in a complete revamp in the administrative structure of these temple committees.

"This could be politically suicidal at this stage. There might be widespread protest and civil unrest in various parts," remarked Deepak in a meeting.

"Look Aniruddh, religion is a sensitive issue in this country. If you dare to flare it up, be prepared for the wrath as well. People here do not like the government to finger around with their faith," advised Shri Narayan Sahu.

"Moreover, the government should stay away from such sensitive issues relating to religious faith and beliefs," added another.

"I understand these concerns, but I still believe that as the elected representatives of the state, it is our responsibility to provide a clean and hassle free environment for the people in these temples. The temple administration and the stakeholders have made a mockery of these holy shrines," the CM argued.

"How do you plan to deal with the lobby? They will go berserk, the people might delineate. After all, we love to be bullied by our gods and their keepers," said Dr Bichitrananda.

"The move might resonate mixed feelings, but it will certainly be beneficial for everybody in the long run. Isn't it the responsibility of the government to take some strong decisions keeping the larger interest in mind?"

Aniruddh argued vehemently in favour of the Temple Administrative Reforms Bill that he wanted to introduce and make a law. Under provisions of this bill, all religious institutes in the state would come under one regulatory body. This body would look after the administration, finance and security of the institutes. The body would be governed by a set of rules amicable to the religious sentiments of the people.

The existing temple administration would definitely look at it as an attempt by the government to take over control of these bodies. This surely was going to open a can of worms.

The Lord Jagannath Temple Board was the most powerful religious body in the state. Like any other religious institute, this too wasn't devoid of political influences. The Chairman of the board Shri Daitari Panda was a highly influential temple seer. Sabyasachi Mahapatra, a three time MLA from the city who had recently been defeated, was the secretary. The man was a wolf disguised as a dog. He was both greedy and dangerous at the same time. It wasn't easy even for the CM of the state to counter him on religious issues.

The cabinet could not reach a consensus on the issue and hence the agenda was postponed till the by-elections. It was for the first time that Aniruddh had faced such an open balkiness in his own circle.

"How many do you have by your side," queried the old man.

"None."

"Then why are you pushing it now, give it some more time. Let the draft be prepared, let there be a consensus. You can't go at it alone," Basu babu advised him.

"Look, first you need to get the people by your side. The politicians will fall in line with the sentiments of the people."

"What about the trust, the present committee. What about Daitari Panda?"

"He he!!," the old man smirked as he took a sip of the Bourbon whiskey.

"The oxygen of religion is faith, the faith of the followers. Daitari fuels the faith of the people. The public won't mind an alternative to him. Somebody who they think is one of their own.

"Find out the source of his power and strike him. You have to level the ground before you sow the seeds. Daitari is your biggest challenge, not your cabinet colleagues," Aniruddh, as ever, listened to Basudev like a disciple.

-----x-----

"Why was clearance given to the fertilizer plant without my knowledge?" Aniruddh frowned at the cabinet meeting.

He was mentioning about a proposed fertilizer plant that was to come up in the coastal belt. The project had hit controversy after the National Green Tribunal had objected to the site being too close to the coastal belt and poised threat to the marine wildlife. The Marine Conservation Force had also raised questions on the toxic waste disposal system of the proposed fertilizer plant.

The matter was now dealt by the Ministry of Industries and Commerce. Vishnu Pradhan was the minister in charge.

"The project had been stalled without any valid reason. The Green Tribunal is unnecessarily putting spokes. It is sending wrong signals to prospective investors in the state," clarified the minister.

"We have given a go ahead to many such projects despite observations from the tribunal. But, we must respect their verdict whenever the concerns are genuine," countered Aniruddh.

"The ministry has taken all concerns into account before sending the file to the CM's desk."

"Look, we have already been criticised for flouting environmental norms on numerous occasions. These issues reflect poorly on the maturity of the state government. I request all concerned to maintain due diligence before clearing any file," the CM insisted.

"But the file is still on your desk, awaiting clearance."

"Yes, then may be, the media announcement should have waited as well."

Vishnu remained silent for the better part of the meeting. There was certain unease in the room thereafter. Relations are infectious in the world of politics. It was not only Vishnu who was snubbed that day. His entire faction felt so.

-----x-----

"Look Mr Mathur, that issue is a ticking bomb. Nobody would put his political career at stake by approving that project at this moment," said a young man sitting across the mahogany table in one of the city's five star hotels. He was involved in an intense conversation with the Chairman of the Metalate Corp.

The company was desperate to mine Chromium in the state. Apparently, they were hunting for the Madhegiri hills in the southern district of the state. The site had become controversial after serious agitations from the local tribe, objecting to the 'desecration' of their religious abode in the form of the hill.

"Do you really believe that a political career can be at stake for the sake of a hill," said the crafty old businessman.

"See, the CM's stand on the whole issue has been pretty negative, right from the beginning. Nobody will dare take a stand against him in the present circumstances. His position is very strong now," said the other man, massaging his bare foot. The man sitting across the table was wearing a fine linen kurta and a loose pyjama. His partially grey hair from the sides made him look older than his actual age. He had put on power glasses with an expensive, sleek black frame.

"His stand matters as long as he matters."

"What do you mean, Mathur?"

"I mean, individuals have very little value in politics. What matters is the position and the strength one can wield," said the businessman as he bent closer to explain his plan in detail.

"It won't be easy."

"I know that. We already have the people in mind."

"He wanted me to convey you, that we need some more time," repeated the other man in the room.

"Look, it's already been a year now, nothing has moved. Huge amount of money is going down the drains with each passing day. The bosses aren't ready to wait any more," the businessmen sounded agitated, as he gulped the remaining whiskey in the glass at one go.

-----xx-----

CHAPTER 23

---◆---

"How does an officer of your calibre and efficiency satisfy himself professionally as the IG, Fire services?" he questioned, looking straight at the police officer.

"May be you should ask your CM," replied back senior IPS officer Satyabrata Panda. The officer albeit had risen up in ranks, did carry the baggage from his past. He was placed in an irrelevant appointment by the present government, courtesy his role in the university-firing incident.

"Satya, believe me, you deserve much more than this."

"Look, I am sure, you haven't come this far to express your sympathies to a helpless and irrelevant police officer. May be you should come to the point."

"Okay, then, there is someone in the government, who wants you back in the forefront," said the kurta clad bespectacled man.

"They want you to be back in the field. IG, Southern Range post is going to be vacant soon. If you are interested...," the man was cut short by Panda.

"What is the quid pro quo," he was seasoned enough to understand the deal.

"Nothing much, I promise. It would be strictly under the ambits of your professional capacity. Don't forget, considering your non-empanelment, the state is now your only hope," he added.

-----x-----

"BREAKING NEWS" blared a TV news anchor as Aniruddh stared stoically at one of the news channels. There were newspapers scattered all around his breakfast table as he went through the news that had caused quite a stir early in the morning.

"A leading newspaper claims to have gained access to a copy of the draft version of the controversial Religious Institutes Administrative Reforms Bill. It is believed that the Bill was placed in the previous cabinet meeting, but could not get a nod because of stiff internal rift within the government. The Bill is considered to be the CM's priority and was tabled personally by him. The controversial bill, proposes complete government control and regulation over the temples in the state. This could be subject to a lot of opposition from the existing Temple Administration," reported the channel.

Various channels broke the news amidst heightened political activity all through the day. While the opposition targeted the CM for the controversial bill, the Temple Administration vouched to fight against it with all its strength.

"The present government wants to play with religious sentiments of the people. This will not be tolerated. There will be a mass uprising. We shall galvanise the whole state if required," cried out Sabyasachi Mahapatra, the Secretary of the Managing Committee.

The CM made his way through a flock of media personnel swarming outside his office for a reaction. He put up a smile and rushed inside the building while his security helped him wade through the media.

Aniruddh summoned his personal staff along with the Chief Secretary and a few senior officials of the CM office.

"It is quite obvious that the documents have sneaked out of this office and I want to know who is responsible for this," the CM questioned, maintaining his composure.

"Sir, we maintain a very strict protocol for classified documents. It is very unusual for it to have sneaked out of the CM office," his Principal Secretary countered him.

"It was a draft bill and I was still working on the finer points. Nobody else in the cabinet or otherwise had a copy of the same, how can it happen? The source has to be within the office...unless...," Aniruddh thought for a while and stopped abruptly.

"Anyways, please be careful. Pujari babu, please arrange for a press conference. I must clarify the issues before it gets worse," said Aniruddh looking at the CS.

"Daitari has already reacted to this. Sabyasachi Mahapatra threatens to lead an agitation," said Deepak as he barged into the CM's office and sat on the cane sofa set kept ahead of the main desk of the CM.

"Hmm… things have heated up," said Aniruddh still glancing at the television.

"Who do you thing has done this? Who would be benefitted out of it?" queried Deepak.

"Now, what?" he added, without even bothering for answers to his previous questions.

"Ummm…nothing. I have called for a presser, lets see who pulls out his card."

"Anyways, did 'you' approve this?" queried Deepak, laying emphasis on the accusative pronoun and pulling out the government gazette notification appointing Satyabrata Panda as the IG, Southern Range.

"Yes, I signed on it. The file had come from the Home Ministry and I didn't consider it important to ask Narayan babu."

"But, why would Shri Narayan Sahu do such a thing. Isn't he aware of the…."

"Sir, Daitari panda has threatened to stop all rituals in the temple, if you do not clarify on the bill," howled out a reporter standing next to the door in the jam-packed conference hall at the secretariat.

The CM answered back with a smirk on his face.

"I have already clarified my stand and I do not think there is any other clarification required on the subject."

"Sir, do you think that the other temple committees will support the bill?"

"If the Temple committees support transparency, then they will certainly appreciate our bill when it is complete."

"Sir, the bill contains crucial aspects of administrative control and proposes to cut down the number of sevayats?"

"You see, I am still not aware as to what concocted version of the bill has reached the media. The bill, in its comprehensive form, will also ensure the protection of the sevayat community and look after their well-being. There is a lot of economic and social disparity even amongst the various sevayat sects. We aim to empower all by means of social and economic opportunities. Their services need recognition and it can be channeled in a more professional manner," the CM said replying back to the queries in the presser.

-----x-----

"It is important for you to keep your folks united now. The CM has already played his card. He wants to divide your people. Daitari has to keep up the resistance and the agitation in his own way," Mathur connived with Sabyasachi at a holiday resort outside Puri.

"The expenses are rising."

"Don't worry, all that shall be taken care of. You have to ensure that the issue is kept burning and that the other committees are with you in this."

Meanwhile, Sabyasachi instigated Daitari to call for a "mahasamelan" of all temple committees to express their displeasure. Protests broke out all over the state as fringe elements took centre stage. The agitations polarised the general public and created an atmosphere of uncertainty. It led to the ruling party splitting as the CM's faction supported the bill whereas the in-house opposition cried foul.

-----x-----

"Sir, the reports of a deal is confirmed. The money has been transferred to a 'benami' account held by him. Recently, he has also invested huge amount of money in real estate. We can twist his tale anytime now," the Director SIB briefed the CM on Sabyasachi Mahapatra.

"No no, nothing as yet, just keep a discreet watch on him," directed Aniruddh.

"Sir, there is another report that I wanted to bring to your notice," said the senior IB officer, adding staidness to his tone.

"Collation of specific Intelligence reports hint at a possible attempt at your life by the naxals during your visit to Malkangiri in the next month. They are reportedly unhappy at the raising of the new Anti-Naxal Task Force. Therefore, it is recommended that the CM postpones his Malkangiri visit."

"Any details on the specific group and its leadership?"

"People's War Group, Southern Odisha unit. They mostly operate on either side of the Odisha-Andhra border. Potential IED threat to the CM's convoy or some suicidal tactic might be used."

"Sir, there has been an unusual surge in the naxal activities especially in that belt over the last three months," added the IB officer.

"Any specific reasons?"

"Not unusual whenever there is a change in the command structure of the police there. The IG, southern range has just taken over and since then there has been a number of police-naxal encounters."

"Mr Satyabrata Panda took over as the IG in the month of April," the name rang a certain bell in the CM's mind. Random thoughts crossed all over his mind.

"Sir, I would once again recommend you to cancel the Malkangiri visit or postpone it for some time."

"Thank you Mr Mallick, I shall think over it and let you know," the officer got an indication and prepared to leave

"Mallick babu," Aniruddh signalled him to take his seat back.

"What is the general pulse on the Temple Reforms Bill? What do you think is the public perception?" the CM asked his trusted intelligence aide.

"Sir, the Pandas (priests) are obviously dissatisfied with the move. There is a sense of insecurity."

"And what about the people?"

"Sir, honestly, the people are not bothered. They just need a hassle free 'darshan' and better services. But, yes, it is not very difficult to instigate people in the name of god."

"How are your sources in the Temple committee?" queried the CM.

"Sir, I do have contacts, but they aren't credible enough. Give me some more time."

The senior intelligencer left the CM's office leaving behind a host of unanswered questions.

-----x-----

The CM is badly cornered with the Temple Reforms Bill," said the bespectacled man in a posh hotel room in the capital city.

"Daitari's theatrics have added on to the spectre," remarked Mathur.

"How many have we got with us now?" questioned another man sitting across the room.

"Nine are with us, plus the Swayam Sevak Party has promised to help."

"Look, Metalate is ready to spend more, if required. The big bosses are getting desperate with this project. It should not fail this time," cautioned Mathur.

"The plan didn't fail the last time either," countered the dhoti-clad man.

"Yes, but the plan was hijacked by Aniruddh and he defies listening to anybody now."

"You must understand the importance of moments in politics. Everyone has his moment and we must flow with him then, lest we all sink. When the moment fades, change your flow. That is politics for you. Two years back it was his moment, not anymore though," explained the old man tapping shoulder of the bespectacled young man sitting next to him.

"I am not doing politics, sir. I am doing business. Moments for me, are the once that earn something," countered Mathur.

"Can you do business without politics, Mathur sahib?" poked the other man as he looked over his reading glasses at him, indicating his annoyance over Mathur's remarks.

"Anyways, here's what we plan to do."

"There will be an assassination. Panda is made responsible for the inquiry. We also have a CM's close aide with us. He links evidences to our bait. We just have to sell the investigation report in the media. The word on the plausible rift is already out in the open. The SSP pulls out the plug and withdraws support. We hold our stack together and form the next government with KJD. We just need a martyr out of the whole thing to retain the support of the public," the old man revealed the devious plan and looked at the others in the room for a nod of agreement.

-----x-----

"The possible rift between Vishnu and you is getting unwelcome media coverage," Basu babu told Aniruddh as candidly as possible.

"But there is no such thing as a rift. We have our differences over certain issues," Aniruddh tried to clarify. The CM had gone seeking his mentor's advice on the leaked bill.

"Do you feel intimidated by him?"

"Hmm...not exactly, but at times he remains in the opposing fences and is difficult to convince."

"You are surrounded by too many people who are not naturally inclined towards you. You must learn to differentiate between those who are subservient and those who are merely obsequious," the old man explained the overture in his crafty way.

"And in what category do I put Vishnu in?"

"Umm...he is like an 'irredenta', you are generally confused about his controls."

"So?"

"So, let him be. Don't push him too much."

"But, you never warned me before," Aniruddh said.

"You never felt intimidated before," answered the old man.

-----x-----

Aniruddh was sifting through files in the office along with his Secretary when the PA informed of a visitor on the intercom.

"Send him in."

Ranjan Mallick, the state head of IB entered the office with a bunch of files clutched under his armpit. The other hand was engaged in holding the two cell phones he carried.

"Ahh! Mr Mallick, come in, have a seat," said the CM as his secretary made his way out, following standard protocol maintained during the visit of the Dir, SIB.

"Yeah, what have we got?"

"Sir, the assassination reports are confirmed. They are going to make a bid at your life," Mallick spoke with the usual stolidity in his voice.

"Sir, reports have confirmed movement of at least three to four top naxal commanders within the state. Plus, there has been an increase in the influx from the bordering state of Andhra Pradesh.

"And it is believed that the local police has been asked to maintain some loose holes for them to sneak in," Mallick said the last line after a considerable pause.

"Why so?"

"Sir, they claim to have got orders from the top. Apparently, the movements can be traced back to the time since Panda has taken over the charge of the Southern Range."

"Sir, someone internally is trying to harm you. Panda is being used as a medium," he added.

"Hmm…any idea on the mind behind it?"

"Not yet sir, but we are working on it."

The SIB chief left the CM pondering over the happenings of the past few days.

Why would Narayan Sahu want him to die?

Is it Gopinath Barik or it is a game hatched by Vishnu himself in connivance with Narayan Sahu, who got Satyabrata Panda posted as the IG.

"We are not going to Malkangiri. Postpone the visit and take a fresh schedule of events," the CM directed his PA.

"Why sir, any other important engagement that has come up," queried the PA, Debasis Maharana. Only a very senior OAS officer would have the guts to question back the CM in this manner.

"No, no, nothing important. The Dir, SIB warns of some security concerns and had recommended to postpone, citing threat to my life during the Malkangiri visit," the CM confided with a smile.

"Surprising sir, we still hadn't declared it even in our draft programme. Surprising how the naxals have access to such information," Maharana raised a valid point.

"Yeah, you never know, I might have divulged it in some public gathering or meeting. These things spread fast, you know that Debu babu."

Aniruddh tried hard, but failed to recollect. He thought he must have told someone, but it often happens that we never really remember something when we desperately try to jolt our memories.

Aniruddh felt as if he was slowly being trapped in a larger political conspiracy. People who would not only want his political legacy to end, but also wanted to see him dead. He sensed the aura of betrayal affecting his work and his peace of mind.

Politics is a world that is empowered by the same temporisers that uphold it. It is the art of sleeping with one's enemy, yet waking up alive. He realised, he could no longer remain supine to the conspiring cabal around him.

-----xx-----

CHAPTER 24

"Hi! How have you been?" Aniruddh asked over the phone.

"Aha! I'm doing great. Not everyone gets an early morning call from the youngest and the most vibrant Chief Minister of India," jested Ritika Ghosh, an old friend of Aniruddh's who was a senior reporter with the BBC now. Aniruddh knew her from the riot relief camp days, when, as volunteers, they both had escaped a deadly attack on them.

"So, you haven't completely forgotten me, right?" Ritika went on.

"Your remarks are totally warranted," Aniruddh replied.

"But you know me too well, so I won't take the pain of explaining my absence from your call history."

"Anyway, mister Chief Minister, you don't owe me an explanation. But you do owe me a treat! Congratulations on your marriage!"

"Oh, thank you dear. It's been some time now."

"Yeah. So what's up?"

"I need a favour from you, Ritika…" said Aniruddh, fairly straightforward.

"Favour? From me?"

"Yes."

"Hmm…Shoot"

"I want you to run a small story for me. The story is credible, and I vouch for it."

"But why would a Chief Minister want *this* as a favour? You could just call up any news channel in India and ask them to run it for you," Ritika reasoned.

"Yeah, but I want to exclude myself personally from it for some political reasons. Plus, I want it to have some impact in the western media. It has to be given a socio-environmental angle."

Hmm, sounds interesting. But I need the source and I will need to do a credibility check. Also, I will need permission from my editor to put it on air."

Aniruddh explained the entire story to her over the next 15 minutes.

"Look, there are some big names involved. The repercussions might be catastrophic. The editor will want me to use a credible source," said a concerned Ritika.

"Okay, I shall give you a source, but make sure he is protected. Please do not forget the redactions before getting it on air."

"Don't worry about that," she assured.

"I have done my research. Your bosses would be more than happy to fix these names."

"Okay, send your guy to London by this weekend."

-----x-----

"It isn't so difficult to reach you after all. I thought it would take much more of an effort," Aniruddh told someone over a secured line.

"It was easier, because it was you. Anybody else would have found it virtually impossible."

"How are you?"

"I am fine."

"Heard you had brain fever. Have you recovered?" Aniruddh asked.

"Quite an impressive network, I must say. I thought we were long forgotten in these wild forests."

"I do keep a tab on my friends every now and then."

"'Friends' is a word that can actually put you in trouble CM sahib."

"Hahaha!"

"So, have you tasked your men to track me and hunt me down? Do you plan to increase the bounty on me?"

"No no, Raghavji, I have no such plan. If I can reach you over the phone, I can reach you in person as well. I have no such plans. But you surely are plotting my death, planning to blow me up..."

"Hehe! CM sahib, don't worry, you are far behind in the list. There are many above you. But just because you said 'friend', I must confess, there is no such plan being hatched in this region. I can't speak for others though. A number of factions have sprouted recently. There has been a sudden rise in the funding pattern. Seems your state is attracting some real investors," Raghavji said with a laugh.

"You seemed to have pledged to eliminate us," the Naxal leader continued.

"I have to act. I can't let extremism affect normal lives."

"Normal lives are not even bothered."

"Raghavji, I always have had a lot of admiration for you. You know that very well. I still consider you as much a nationalist as myself."

Aniruddh tried to bring him to the talking tables.

"Nationalist is the wrong word. The idea of India as a nation failed a long time ago. The people we represent are live examples of this failure."

"Then represent them at the right forum."

"Who says that yours is the right forum?"

"At least the law of the land recognises this forum. These people need you, but you are doing no good to them by your means. Come to the mainstream. Represent them from where you are heard. Look, the bitter truth is, nobody in Delhi gives a damn about the plight of the people in these jungles," said Aniruddh, asserting himself.

"Yes, you are right, nobody gives a damn. Hence, the explosions and the IED blast. So that the noise reaches people in Delhi..."

"It's like any other noise Raghavji, people don't value it. It is just another irritant to the make-believe, feel-good world they have been living."

"Anyway, you have finally decided to come and visit our forest. Wish I could personally welcome you and take you around this beautiful land."

The call is snapped.

-----x-----

The BBC broke the news in its weekend edition on Asia. Ritika personally flew down to do a piece on the plight of the Kongrai tribes, and their fight against Metalate. She particularly highlighted the corporation's attempt to back channel the settlement with the tribes.

But the real deal was the link between the Metalate Corp. and the California based investment firm Hemmingway Brothers Inc. This was the news Aniruddh wanted the western world to take note of. As the two corporate giants faced severe criticism in the media, stock prices plummeted and led to a temporary moment of panic humanitarian groups and NGOs in the west ripped Hemmingway Bros Inc. apart.

Displacement of the tribal population and environment concerns over the proposed chromium mining made the west go weak in the knees. It was considered gauche to be insensible to such issues. Out here, in our part of the world, nobody gave a damn. The west could afford such idealistic luxuries and flaunt their social fecundity. Not us.

Metalate was just the façade. The real money came through Hemmingway. Within weeks of the BBC exposure, Hemmingway Brothers Inc. pulled out of the project and snapped the venture. Metalate could not sustain a non-productive investment for such a long duration. The money stopped flowing in.

-----x-----

"Sir, what is your opinion on the Temple Reforms bill?" A senior journalist asked Vishnu.

"Some aspects of the bill are debatable and needs due correction," replied Vishnu, who was touring his constituency that was dominated by the upper class Hindu Brahmins.

"So do you have concerns over the bill?"

"Yes, I believe some clauses are open to debate and can be reconsidered. In any case the bill is yet to be tabled before the cabinet."

"So here we have a senior cabinet colleague of the CM, expressing concerns over what is largely believed to be the CM's pet project," the raucous reporter concluded, facing the camera.

That was followed by a series of remarks and counter remarks that continued for some time. The media often is the most overrated institution of democracy. At times, it is a mere tool for manipulation that behaves predictably. It isn't difficult for a seasoned politician to turn the media into his stool pigeon.

For Vishnu, it was an ideal situation where he was being pitched at the same platform as Aniruddh. For Aniruddh, it was the medium to highlight his lonely fight for transparency in religious institutions.

"Daitari isn't bowing out as expected," a concerned Deepak told the CM in a private meeting.

"In fact, he has stacked up almost 20 of the major temple committees with him. Sabyasachi Mahapatra has threatened closure of all temples if the bill is not stopped," Narayan Sahu added.

"We have to create a fissure. Their agitation is gaining momentum," remarked Nanda Kishore Tripathi, the legislative member from Puri.

"Daitari Panda is an institution. He represents the very citadel of religious authority and power that they fear losing. Our target is not Panda, our target is the position he holds, the authority he wields," stated Aniruddh.

"If we remove him, he becomes a martyr. If we place someone above him, it becomes quite obvious," said Deepak.

"Hmm. I have something in mind. Let's see," Aniruddh stopped at that.

His insecurity was rising by day. He felt equally intimidated by his closest associates as well, including Deepak.

Metalate Corp hired Radhika's law firm. As they sued the state government for breach of agreement, Aniruddh was widely criticised within the party. He put up a brave face in the public and called it a purely professional commitment that his wife had to oblige. Behind closed doors though, the tension had built up.

"Did you consider quitting? I mean, I can put in a word to the other firms," said Aniruddh.

"It shall reflect very poorly on me, to quit the firm for such a reason. I shall be deemed unprofessional," she said, and the discussion ended there.

The insecurity in his mind compelled him to keep a watch on her.

"Call records only, no follow-up required," he ordered.

"There is a storm brewing up rapidly within the party. I am sure it is someone from within," Aniruddh later opened up to Basudev.

"And you think it is Vishnu?"

"I fear... I think it is him. What do you think? Can he do such a thing?" he asked.

"You see, human behaviour is not templated. He wants to do something, but that doesn't mean he is capable of doing it," Basu babu said in his typical, crafty manner. "You have to act, sooner or later."

"Yes, I have to," Aniruddh agreed.

"Anyway, when have you planned for the Malkangiri trip?"

"Next week."

-----x-----

"I have wanted to meet you for quite some time now, sir."

They exchanged the usual pleasantries as Aniruddh was escorted inside the modest palace of the Gajapati Maharaj of Puri. The palace, unlike many others in the country, is situated right in the middle of the busy market street opposite the Jagannath temple. The meeting, therefore, had to be organised at midnight, in strict adherence to the CM's directions of complete secrecy.

"It is indeed an honour to have you here Mr Chief Minister," said the King, polite as ever. He greeted him and offered Aniruddh a seat next to an old brahmin.

Kingship was banned in the 1970s, but the monarch of Puri continued to enjoy a few privileges, like many others in the country. And though he was not as opulent as the kings in the north, he was a highly respected and educated personality. He was an apolitical figure, held in the greatest reverence in religious as well as political circles.

In India, you are respected if you are famous. You are revered, if you are famous and wealthy, and you are worshipped, if you are famous, wealthy and apolitical at the same time. The King's USP was his non-affiliation to any political party. He was already the ceremonial chairman of the temple committee, but had a very limited de facto role.

"The Royal family has restricted its interference to rituals and ceremonial references only," said Aniruddh, having already disclosed the reasons for his visit over the phone. "Your highness, the temple is the heritage your ancestors have preserved from the medieval days. You are the *'adhyasevak'* as well as the guardian of this heritage. Your interference is solicited only to clean this shrine off its malfeasance by the caretakers," added Aniruddh, emphasising his point.

"But, why me?"

"Sir, even I don't have an answer to that. Maybe, the lord himself has directed me to do so. I may have come with an agenda, but the nobility in my thought is unquestionable. I cannot force you into this, but it will certainly be the greatest service to the lord. Maybe this is your *'rajdharma'* in this age."

Aniruddh left the palace after discussing the modalities of the new administrative arrangement for the temple committee, bestowing additional administrative powers with the Gajapati Maharaj.

-----x-----

"I have decided to go ahead with the Malkangiri visit," Aniruddh informed his staff, overriding his previous decision as he called for the SIB chief.

Mallick rushed to the CM's residence early next morning – the meeting is unscheduled, like all his previous meetings with Aniruddh.

"Sir, you have to cater for additional security though. The chances are…,"

"Don't worry about that," Aniruddh cut him short. "You just plan for the mission that I have tasked you for. The surrender of a senior leader of his calibre is certainly going to make headlines. Ensure there is adequate media presence when he speaks out."

Mallick departed briskly to tend to his tasks. Aniruddh then picked up his phone and dialed a number. A familiar voice responded.

"I have given him the necessary details. Make sure that things are kept sharp at your end as well."

"Everything is set. I hope things will turn out as per our promises to each other."

"Do what you have to, and I shall reciprocate aptly."

-----x-----

Sabyasachi Mahapatra was getting desperate with each passing day about the seizure of funds. It was becoming increasingly difficult for him to hold everyone together. He called in for the move; Aniruddh had been waiting for quite some time now.

"Mahapatra is planning to declare a shutdown of the temples. He has asked the other committees to follow suit after Puri. What do I do now?" asked an old voice.

"Just go ahead with what he says. I don't want to jeopardise your safety. I shall take care of him," Aniruddh said assuring him.

"Get me the Dir, ED and the Income Tax commissioner," said the CM, breaking protocol by giving direct orders to these people. But at this juncture, he couldn't trust anyone.

"Get working on the *'Benami'* accounts of Shri Sabyasachi Mahapatra, and the kickbacks he received recently from a reputed industrial house. Track all his transactions in the last one year. All actions to be discreet, and please, maintain complete confidentiality till further instructions from me. Also, track the investors and money involved in his hotels in and around Puri."

A group of media personnel cornered the CM at the inauguration of a public library hall.

"Sir, what is the government doing to end the logjam with the temple committees? The committee has threatened a lock down of the temples," asked a scribe.

"Yes, it is indeed sad that the place of god is dragged into such petty controversies," he replied. "The bill hasn't been tabled and the stakeholders are getting jittery about their power. The committees have been hijacked by a few powerful and selfish individuals."

"Will the government contemplate the use of force?"

"I don't think that should be required," he said as he rushed to his car.

As expected, Sabyasachi reacted to Aniruddh's statement and called for the shut down of the temples with immediate effect. The move shook up the whole state. There were diverging views on the issue – some stood with the CM, while others vehemently criticised him for interfering in religious matters.

-----x-----

A black Scorpio got off the metal road and zoomed past the fire lane in the thick forest. The headlights of the vehicle pierced through the arcadian darkness of the forest on a moonless night. Suddenly, two men with L1A1 self-loading rifles slung on their shoulders emerged out of the bushes and signalled the vehicle to stop. These were mostly, weapons snatched away from the local police force.

One of them pulled out the co-driver and blindfolded him, while the other did the same to the driver, all the while warning him against making any movement. The co-driver was then taken through the bushes into the forest. They walked for an hour before stopping next to a flowing stream. The blindfold was removed, and the man came face-to-face with a tall and lanky Naxal in combat fatigues and a red bandana. An AK was slung casually down from his shoulder, and his face was mostly covered with a red chequered towel. He was N Rajangouda, the most wanted Naxal leader of Andhra Pradesh.

Within moments, the deathly silence of the forest was shattered by the sounds of gunfire.

The next morning, Aniruddh woke up to the ringtone of his personal mobile phone.

The chief secretary's voice greeted him at the other end, saying, "Sir, there is some disturbing news from Malkangiri...".

"What is it?"

"Sir, the Dir, SIB, has been shot dead in the Malkangiri Forest Division, near the Satiguda Dam. The body of a top Naxal leader from Andhra was also found next to him. The STF confirms the death of four other Naxals in the near vicinity," said the CS, nearly breathless.

The news quaked the entire state. The media hounded Aniruddh the moment he entered the secretariat for an emergency meeting.

"Sir, the Dir, STF is here."

"Sir, we had not expected the Dir, SIB at the spot. There was absolutely no prior information of any such meeting," clarified the STF chief.

"Nobody in the IB was aware of the visit either," the DGP added.

As the day progressed, further details emerged from Malkangiri. The media was getting impatient, and a few had already started off to the south.

"Sir, we must give a clarification before the media builds up its own story," advised the chief secretary.

"Yes, call for a press conference at 3pm. I shall do it myself."

"Sir, shouldn't we wait, at least, for the initial enquiry report?" asked the DGP.

"The enquiry will be confidential, and a classified report shall be submitted," the CM said.

The media room was packed to capacity. They were awaiting the arrival of a senior member of the administration to give a statement, but were surprised to see the CM himself.

"Shri Ranjan Mallick was an efficient and courageous officer. Last night, the officer attained martyrdom during an operation with the Naxals in the Malkangiri Forest Division. It is indeed a great loss to the state and the intelligence community. The operations were coordinated at the highest level and had my approval. The state has lost a brave and competent officer in the line of duty. I pay my deepest condolences to the family of Shri Mallick."

The Chief Minister's statement buried all other versions and potential controversies that had been doing the rounds. He awarded a compensation of Rs 50 lakhs for his family.

Soon, the media lost its interest in the story.

"I hope the cleanup is being done properly?" he queried over the phone.

"Yes, don't worry."

"I had to order an enquiry. The team will reach the spot any moment now. They should not come back with anything cogent."

"What next?"

"Just sit tight and wait till I give a go ahead. Someone will reach you soon."

-----x-----

"It's been a week now. The temples are still shut. People have started criticising the government's silence and inaction," Deepak reminded Aniruddh.

The chief secretary walked in to his office along with the Dir, ED.

"Sir, there is enough evidence to twist his tale now. He can be arrested immediately on grounds of economic offences," the CS suggested.

"No, don't arrest him. It will make him a martyr. He will immediately play the victim card. Cut a deal with him. Send all the evidences to Sabyasachi and give him a clear deal. Once we have him by his neck, we can twist it anytime we want. My immediate concern is the normalcy of the situation," said Aniruddh, sounding confident of his decision even as the others looked confused.

"Sir, there is still no solution to the agitations in Puri. How long will the stalemate continue? Is it because none of you are ready to keep your egos aside?" asked a television journalist in an interview with the CM.

"What ego? There is no place for ego, especially when it is a matter of god," replied Aniruddh. "The Lord is not the property of an individual or a temple committee. Millions of devotees have been barred from the daily '*darshan*'. It is not a good sign. I am open to discussion. In fact, I have planned a visit to the holy city. I shall go myself to seek the Lord's blessings. If they want, they can stop me. I am ready to discuss, but only after the temple gates are open for me and the public."

Aniruddh played the discussion card and won moral ground even as his ED guys roughed it out with Sabyasachi at his residence.

"You don't have much of an option. There is enough evidence to fix you for a long time. Plus, the reputation you hold will also be gone forever. It is your call now."

"What guarantee do I have?" asked a cowed Sabyasachi. The otherwise flamboyant rebel was shown all the evidence that linked him with '*Benami*' transactions and disproportionate wealth.

"The CM himself is eager to hear the outcome of this meeting," said the ED guy, looking over his reading lenses.

Sabyasachi succumbed to the pressure. The CM's visit to Puri was heralded as a huge success as the temple gates opened up after ten days of shutdown. Rituals began in the shrine once again as millions flocked to the holy city.

"We are grateful to CM sahib for addressing our concern and talking to us," remarked a visibly depressed Sabyasachi, trying hard to fake a smile.

Daitari Panda made the surprise announcement of the king being nominated as the administrative head. The king appeared with the CM and Panda and the media and the intellectuals applauded the CM's move of nominating a respected and apolitical figure. There couldn't have been a better person than the king himself for the administration of the temple.

Aniruddh had played a masterstroke. Even seasoned politicians could not have contemplated this move.

-----xx-----

CHAPTER 25

❖

"This young man comes out with interesting surprises with each passing day," said a dhoti-clad old man to the bespectacled young visitor to his place.

"But what happened to Sabyasachi Mahapatra? How did he give up so easily?"

"He was tracked way back. Aniruddh was just waiting for the right time to bargain," the old man replied.

Remind them of their sins when they are at the peak of their moral reputation.

"I guess it's time to pull out the aces."

"Are you sure?"

"Yes, it's time. Tell the SSP leadership to be ready for the pull out, and the opposition should not falter this time."

"Good morning, sir. You had asked for me?"

"Yes, Mr. Panda, Good job done. Now, for the next phase of action, you have to wait till my orders," the CM instructed his IG.

Satyabrata Panda was the one who had revealed the plans of the Dir, IB and his corrupted loyalty to Aniruddh. Panda could be professionally imprudent, but politically, he was sapient. He clearly knew the path of getting back into the CM's good books. He had also hinted to Aniruddh about the people who had approached him along with Mathur.

"Sir, things are all set for your visit. There is absolutely no cause for worry," Panda assured him.

-----x-----

"That bastard has switched sides," said an agonised young man to the older one in the room.

"Never mind, Panda was never a safe bet anyway."

"We cannot waste any more time. The numbers are with us, and we must strike now," said the man, and picked up the landline to call someone.

"I think you should do it now, Rudra. This is the right time to take your revenge. He is moving alone for a function."

Rudra Mohan Tripathi was the man whose political career was wiped out by Aniruddh's agitations. He had been waiting patiently for his revenge.

The CM's much-hyped visit to the Naxal affected areas got the added attention post the death of the SIB director. Aniruddh was riding high after his moral victory in the temple agitations. His stature had increased by manifolds, and the public perception of him was extremely positive.

It was ten in the morning. The leading chopper caused for a gale of dust from the moribund earth beneath. The otherwise preoccupied population looked up, daring the scorching sun just enough to get a glance of this tender ray that approached them. They had heard a lot about him, and his work in the state.

Democracy is good, not because it offers you a choice, but because it keeps your faith alive by giving you fresh options every season.

"The choice between peace and violence is not difficult as long as you understand the value of peace and the evils of violence. Years ago, I had the same anger and frustration inside me. But I chose to change the system by being in it. This is the only system that can empower you to fight for your rights. Today, I have come here to give you what you deserve. I welcome my brothers and sisters to shed the path of violence, and join us in changing the system. It is your land. You rule here."

Aniruddh's speech flared up the sentiments of the local people and they responded positively. These were people with meagre demands and minor problems. They were 'aspirationally austere'– they were the population of a 'dormant state'.

"Sir, the pilots are worried about the weather. They are advising against the return journey by air," said the OSD.

"Sir, we can arrange for your night stay at the Kalimela Circuit House," offered the collector.

"No, no, I have to go back today itself. We have got enough time. We can pull it off by road."

The scheduled road trip was an administrative and security nightmare in this Naxal heartland, but he decided to go against all advice and headed back for the capital city.

A series of quick meetings and formalities preceded his departure for the arduous journey ahead.

The IG personally escorted him in his car, on the CM's request.

"Raghavji is ready to surrender," Aniruddh informed Satyabrata.

"Sir, it is surprising, but great news indeed."

"Yes. You have to stage the surrender, but keep it under wraps till I give further orders."

"Any demands?" queried the senior police officer.

"Yes, he wants certain charges dropped and given some immunity," replied Aniruddh.

"We can discuss that later. The surrender is more or less his compulsion now. He is sick, and needs round-the-clock medical cover."

"Sir, it is believed that he was funded pretty well by an NGO named 'Chetana' which got its money from ALICO, the mining giants, to keep the Metalate Corp officials out of their proposed site. Now, with the recent development, the funds must have stopped," Panda revealed.

His mobile phone suddenly buzzed, but the call snapped instantly. They had been travelling for almost an hour inside the dense forests. The OSD's car and three other vehicles were moving on either side of the CM's vehicle.

The IG dismounted and peeled off after the district boundaries. The CM's convoy moved on, even as the phone rang again. Aniruddh received the call and heard a rather affright voice. He immediately asked his driver to stop the car, and signaled the others to halt the convoy.

Aniruddh stepped out of the car, and searched for better network. Within seconds, the call snapped again, but not before conveying the dreadful message. Aniruddh nearly collapsed, and needed the support of a hanging branch. His staff and the OSD rushed towards him.

"Sir, is everything okay?"

Men are strong enough to conceal their emotions only if they are prepared for it. Aniruddh looked shockingly at them and broke the news, staring endlessly at the dark sky in the middle of the unforgiving Naxal territory.

"Vishnu Pradhan has been shot dead in his constituency," he said.

-----x-----

The incident shook up the entire political community in the state. The shooting of the second most powerful man in the state cabinet was indeed a shocking event. The murder created ripples, as the political class resorted to a skanky blame game. Agitations increased on the streets of the capital and in Vishnu's constituency. The CM's cavalcade was stoned during his funeral.

"Pradhan bhai had made more rivals within his party than what he had in the outside world. So, a fair investigation must be carried out and the case should be handed over to the CBI," a stray DCP MLA remarked in the media, creating quite a stir as fingers indirectly pointed at Aniruddh.

It doesn't take much time for a speculation to become a statement in this age of hyperactive media. A statement is then made a sensation. The pressure built up on Aniruddh as more fingers pointed at him. His silence only made matters worse.

A week had passed by after Vishnu's murder. Amid heightened political activity in the state, the Swayam Sevak Party threatened to withdraw support to the POP on grounds of law and order failure in the state under the incumbent government.

The SSP declared that a faction of the ruling alliance were also ready to pull out of the government, and demanded fresh elections. A press conference was announced, but the POP members did not show up, citing reasons of safety and confidentiality.

"Sir, the reports are confirmed. It's him. The Jharkhand STF has caught hold of a man who claimed to be a contract killer. He was caught with a bag full of currency notes at the Kharagpur railway station on a Kolkata bound train," the DGP updated the CM on Vishnu Pradhan's murder.

"Our team is on its way to get his custody for investigation."

-----x-----

"With each passing day, I feel more and more vulnerable," Aniruddh admitted to Basudev.

"Don't worry, these instances in politics will only make you stronger."

"Vishnu bhai's death is beyond my understanding. Would someone kill him just to indict me?" he asked, seeking the old man's opinion.

"Hmm…so, who all are with the SSP trying to break the government?"

"No idea, they haven't come up with any names yet," replied Aniruddh.

"You have to remain careful now. Get hold of your stack and keep a watch."

"Who do you think is behind all this?" Aniruddh asked his mentor, looking straight at his eyes.

"Who benefits the maximum from your downfall? Someone who feels insecure because of you or has been harmed by you. The position that you hold attracts foes as easily as it makes friends."

"Do you ever feel intimidated by anything in your life? If so, what do you do then?"Aniruddh asked again.

"I am too old to be intimidated by anything now," he replied with a laugh. "Maybe I have seen through my best and worst years."

The old man, taking support of his crutches, got up from the sofa.

"You never discuss your past with me. Your life, your family, kids."

Aniruddh got up as well, and stood beside him out on the balcony. Both stared at the flowing river across the street.

"Huh!?You know everything. There is no family. Lived a happy life as a bachelor all along," replied the old man, shrugging off the query, making it sound irrelevant.

"Who is Kanchan Barik?"

The mention of that name resulted in a sudden display of weakness in the otherwise sturdy old man. He rushed inside, and collapsed on the sofa. Basudev Acharya looked frazzled. He impatiently abraded the fabric on the sofa and gazed at Aniruddh, shocked.

There was a moment of awkward silence in the room for a few minutes as Aniruddh walked in. It was obvious that he was trying hard to hold his tears. He felt as though someone had plucked his heart right out of his chest.

"You should have told me once. You could have just ordered me."

Aniruddh followed up and sat on the ground next to the old man's feet.

"This grand conspiracy, the cabal group, this apostasy, all this was to prop up your only son, Gopinath Barik. He is the son you had with your estranged wife, Kanchan. You left her to move out of the country for greener pastures.

"You tracked me from the university agitation, and groomed me to this position. You changed the person in me," he scowled at Basudev Acharya, his eyes blood-shot.

"But, why Vishnu? It could have been just me. Why kill him?"

Basudev Acharya looked straight at the wall facing the sofa, and lay dead still as truth unfolded rind by rind.

"Answer me, why Vishnu?" frowned Aniruddh.

"Because he was your natural heir. I had to finish both of you for the sake of my son. The son I had left way back. It was my redemption as a father. The father that I could never be," replied the old man, hapless and frail.

"We thought of you as no less than our own father. We kept you on a pedestal. Much higher than that..."

"Huh? A man owes the greatest allegiance to his blood," replied the old man.

"You owe allegiance only to your greed and ambitions. You cannot owe anything to anyone. The pawns you used and disposed off, the men you sacrificed to see your plans come through will seek answers," cursed Aniruddh.

"So, what are you waiting for? Call your men, drag me out and kill me!"

Basudev seemed senile as he pulled Aniruddh closer, begging him to kill him.

"No, I can't kill you now. Had I been the old Aniruddh, maybe I would have. You have changed me. Over a period of time, I have grown up to become more and more merciless. You shall pay the reparations for killing the man in me."

He held the old man, made him sit back on the sofa, and whispered calmly into his ears.

"You shall live to see your son suffer. You shall live to suffer," said Aniruddh, as stoic and cold as the winter sky.

"Keep him under house arrest till further orders. Snap the telephone lines and make sure he meets or speaks to no one," Aniruddh directed the police staff accompanying him, and left Basudev's bungalow.

After a long silent stare at each other, Deepak asked.

"Are you sure about it? I still can't believe it, Aniruddh."

"Even I could not. When Panda came up to me with the details, I thought he was trying to exact vengeance. I have been tracking him since then. All conversations, all his meetings, his financial transactions, everything."

"We were mere stooges in his grand plan. But I still haven't figured the Metalate Corp angle" said Deepak.

"He never wanted the Metalate thing to work from the beginning. His NGO, Chetana, had already received huge funds from ALICO to keep Metalate Crop at bay. He used Mathur and his money, the same money was used in funding Raghavji to threaten the employees of Metalate," Aniruddh explained.

"He needed money to buy the KJD MLA's after the election. He used Mathur, promised him help and my approval for the project. When Mathur became too hot to handle, he traded him off and revealed Metalate

Corporation's Hemmingway connection and smartly allowed the news to reach me."

"What about the Temple Reforms bill?"

"The Reforms bill was certainly a point of contention between Vishnu and I. He knew it and took apt advantage to flare up the tensions. Sabyasachi was his pawn," CM continued.

"And Daitari?"

"Daitari Panda is a noble man. He revealed Sabyasachi's interest to me. In fact, he was present when I had the important meeting with His Highness."

"Oh, God!! I am going blank," said an exasperated Deepak, slapping his right palm on his forehead while grinning helplessly.

"When did you get your first intuitions?"

"You remember my Malkangiri visit plans?"

"Yes."

"I distinctively remember having kept it a complete secret. Nobody else knew about the plan except for Basu babu. And I also remember of having requested him to keep it discreet,"

"So?"

"The whole travel plan was leaked weeks before my visit, and Raghavji knew about it. There was no other way the plans could have been divulged. Even my personal staff was not aware of them."

"What was the Dir, SIB's link with him?"

"That bastard was his pawn to keep me ill-informed. He, along with Basu babu, had planned to mislead me till the end, about the dangers to my life. All this time, they were plotting to kill Vishnu and implicate me. Ranjan would have presented the evidential records against me.

"Panda's posting as IG, South came in as a blessing in disguise for us. He was the one who revealed the plans after arresting the Naxal leader N Rajangouda."

"He was arrested? Didn't he die in the same incident as Ranjan?" asked Deepak, still in complete shock.

"The encounter was staged to eliminate Ranjan. He had to be punished."

Deepak noted the stolidity in Aniruddh's face, even as he described an approved plan to terminate his own SIB chief.

Huh? All this will take some time to sink in..."

"Exactly, but we don't have much time with us. Gopinath Barik has already played his cards. The SSP has promised him external support. They might win if there is a No-Confidence motion in the house."

"Why can't we arrest him for the murder of Vishnu?"

"We can and we will, but that may not save the government. The damage will be done by the time he is arrested and proven guilty. Moreover, the arrested criminal has not yet confessed to his crime."

"What now?"

"I don't know what I am doing. You just keep a track on the movements of Gopinath," said Aniruddh, and then called for his vehicle. He directed his PSO to travel with him in his personal car, and left behind the rest of his convoy.

Next day, the newspapers opened up to the story of the apprehension of a senior Naxal leader at Basudev Acharya's bungalow.

"While, significant documents on red terrorism and left wing extremism have been recovered from the possession of Shri Acharya, the ex-scribe is considered to be the master mind of Naxal activities in the state. The apprehended Naxal leader named Raghavji by the cadre has confessed to his links with Shri Acharya, while the octogenarian has remained absolutely silent since his arrest," a report in the media stated.

"In other news, the CBI has summoned senior POP leader and Member of Parliament Shri Gopinath Barik in connection with the Vishnu Pradhan murder case. It is believed that the state police has got substantial proof against Shri Barik, incriminating him as an accomplice in planning the murder of his party colleague," read the news anchor.

"You seem to be growing younger with age," said Aniruddh.

"Haha! I think the wine is doing the trick," the man replied, taking another sip. He got up to welcome his uninvited guest at his farmhouse in a picturesque location on the outskirts of the city.

There aren't many who savour wine after lunch in this part of the world.

"You have travelled 45kms to meet your staunch opponent without an appointment," remarked the ex-Chief Minister.

"Yes," replied Aniruddh.

"What made you so sure that I will agree for a meeting?" the senior KJD leader asked.

"I generally am very unsure of the steps that I take…"

That forced the ex-CM to burst into laughter.

"So, what have you come here with?"

"A bottle of fine Californian wine for you," replied Aniruddh.

He burst into another spell of laughter, and clarified his question.

"No, I meant, what brings you here?"

"The political turmoil in the state is what brings me here."

"Hmmm….But the turmoil is a result of your misadventure. Why should I help you now?"

"You are not destined to end up with a glass of wine in the outskirts of this city. The current polarised situation in the country demands a leader of your stature and experience. There is no one since 2014 who can stand up to this challenge. I want you to be our leader for a bigger role in the national scenario," said Aniruddh, revealing his trump card.

"How can I restore my faith in you, after all that has happened in the past?" came the reply after a pause that weighed the merits in Aniruddh's proposal.

"You can either sulk about the past or make merry of my present plight. We both understand our requirements and limitations. So, let's keep this discussion as short as possible and speak our minds. People out there have already made their plans," said Aniruddh, showing he had indeed learnt the art of negotiation.

They stared at the endless patch of green farmland ending only at the horizon. Maybe they could relate to each other's apathy and loneliness at the top.

Power is not a very easy thing to possess and handle. While the pursuit of power can make us maniacal, it can become emotionally abrasive when we have it at times, we don't need it. Sometimes, it is important to be powerless and buoyant.

A grand alliance was formed in the state, with the ex-CM and KJD leader as its convener and Aniruddh continuing as the Chief Minister of the *'dormant state'*.

-----xxx-----

ABOUT THE AUTHOR

Dibya Satpathy belongs to the Eastern Coastal state of Odisha. He is a graduate of the prestigious National Defence Academy and is presently serving with the Indian Armed Forces. Passion for writing drives this soldier close to the pen as he scripts his first novel. His love for his state is eminent from the backdrop of the story that portrays the passive undercurrent of the contemporary times of his native place. The author currently lives in Lucknow with his wife Minoo.

Printed in the United States
By Bookmasters